CONTINENTAL CHRISTIE

ALSO BY AGATHA CHRISTIE

Mysteries
The Man in the Brown Suit
The Secret of Chimneys
The Seven Dials Mystery
The Mysterious Mr Quin
The Sittaford Mystery
The Hound of Death
The Listerdale Mystery
Why Didn't They Ask Evans?
Parker Pyne Investigates
Murder Is Easy
And Then There Were None
Towards Zero
Death Comes as the End
Sparkling Cyanide
Crooked House
They Came to Baghdad
Destination Unknown
Spider's Web *
The Unexpected Guest *
Ordeal by Innocence
The Pale Horse
Endless Night
Passenger To Frankfurt
Problem at Pollensa Bay
While the Light Lasts

Poirot
The Mysterious Affair at Styles
The Murder on the Links
Poirot Investigates
The Murder of Roger Ackroyd
The Big Four
The Mystery of the Blue Train
Black Coffee *
Peril at End House
Lord Edgware Dies
Murder on the Orient Express
Three Act Tragedy
Death in the Clouds
The ABC Murders
Murder in Mesopotamia
Cards on the Table
Murder in the Mews
Dumb Witness
Death on the Nile
Appointment with Death
Hercule Poirot's Christmas
Sad Cypress
One, Two, Buckle My Shoe
Evil Under the Sun
Five Little Pigs
The Hollow
The Labours of Hercules
Taken at the Flood
Mrs McGinty's Dead
After the Funeral
Hickory Dickory Dock
Dead Man's Folly
Cat Among the Pigeons
The Adventure of the Christmas Pudding
The Clocks
Third Girl
Hallowe'en Party
Elephants Can Remember
Poirot's Early Cases
Curtain: Poirot's Last Case

Marple
The Murder at the Vicarage
The Thirteen Problems
The Body in the Library
The Moving Finger
A Murder Is Announced
They Do It with Mirrors
A Pocket Full of Rye
4.50 from Paddington
The Mirror Crack'd from Side to Side
A Caribbean Mystery
At Bertram's Hotel
Nemesis
Sleeping Murder
Miss Marple's Final Cases

Tommy & Tuppence
The Secret Adversary
Partners in Crime
N or M?
By the Pricking of My Thumbs
Postern of Fate

Published as Mary Westmacott
Giant's Bread
Unfinished Portrait
Absent in the Spring
The Rose and the Yew Tree
A Daughter's a Daughter
The Burden

Memoirs
An Autobiography
Come, Tell Me How You Live
The Grand Tour

Play and Stories
Akhnaton
Little Grey Cells
Murder, She Said
The Floating Admiral †
Star Over Bethlehem
Hercule Poirot and the Greenshore Folly

* novelized by Charles Osborne   † contributor

AGATHA CHRISTIE

CONTINENTAL CHRISTIE

TWELVE EUROPEAN MYSTERIES

HarperCollins*Publishers*

HarperCollins*Publishers* Ltd
1 London Bridge Street
London SE1 9GF

www.harpercollins.co.uk

HarperCollins*Publishers*
Macken House, 39/40 Mayor Street Upper
Dublin 1, D01 C9W8, Ireland

First published by HarperCollins*Publishers* 2026
1

Continental Christie © 2026 Agatha Christie Limited.
All rights reserved

AGATHA CHRISTIE, POIROT, MARPLE, TOMMY AND TUPPENCE, the
Agatha Christie Signature and the AC Monogram Logo are registered trademarks
of Agatha Christie Limited in the UK and elsewhere. All rights reserved.
www.agathachristie.co.uk

A catalogue record for this book is available from the British Library

ISBN 978-0-00-873808-2

Set in Bembo Std by HarperCollins*Publishers* India

Printed and bound in the UK using 100%
Renewable Electricity at CPI Group (UK) Ltd

All rights reserved. No part of this publication may be reproduced,
stored in a retrieval system, or transmitted, in any form or by any means,
electronic, mechanical, photocopying, recording or otherwise,
without the prior written permission of the publishers.

Without limiting the exclusive rights of any author, contributor or the publisher,
any unauthorised use of this publication to train generative artificial intelligence
(AI) technologies is expressly prohibited. HarperCollins also exercise their rights
under Article 4(3) of the Digital Single Market Directive 2019/790 and expressly
reserve this publication from the text and data mining exception.

CONTENTS

Introduction	vii
The Arcadian Deer	1
The Case of the City Clerk	25
The Soul of the Croupier	45
The Stymphalean Birds	67
The Companion	95
Have You Got Everything You Want?	119
The Man from the Sea	137
The Girdle of Hyppolita	173
The Last Séance	193
The Oracle at Delphi	213
The World's End	229
The Chocolate Box	255
Bibliography	275

INTRODUCTION

'Girls and Boys Come Out to Play'

We arrived at Pau. The Hotel Beausejour bus was waiting so we piled into it, our eighteen pieces of luggage coming separately, and in due course arrived at the hotel. It had a large terrace outside it facing the Pyrenees.

'There!' said father. 'See? There are the Pyrenees. The snow mountains.'

I looked. It was one of the great disillusionments of my life, a disillusionment that I have never forgotten. Where was that soaring height going up, up, up into the sky, far above my head—something beyond contemplation or understanding? Instead, I saw, some distance away on the horizon, what looked like a row of teeth standing up, it seemed, about an inch or two from the plain below. *Those?* Were those *mountains*? I said nothing, but even now I can still feel that terrible disappointment.

We must have spent about six months at Pau. It was an entirely new life for me. My father and mother and Madge were soon caught up in a whirl of activity. Father had several American friends staying there, he made a lot of hotel acquaintances, and we also had brought letters of introduction to people in various hotels and pensions.

To look after me, mother engaged a kind of daily

nursery governess—actually an English girl, but one who had lived in Pau all her life and who spoke French as easily as English, if not, in fact, rather better. The idea was that I should learn French from her. This plan did not turn out as expected. Miss Markham called for me every morning and took me for a walk. In its course she drew my attention to various objects and repeated their names in French. '*Un chien.*' '*Une maison.*' '*Un gendarme.*' '*Le boulanger.*' I repeated these dutifully, but naturally when I had a question to ask I asked it in English and Miss Markham replied in English. As far as I can remember I was rather bored during my day; interminable walks in the company of Miss Markham, who was nice, kind, conscientious and dull.

My mother soon decided that I should never learn French with Miss Markham, and that I must have regular French lessons from a Frenchwoman who would come every afternoon. The new acquisition was called Mademoiselle Mauhourat. She was large, buxom and dressed in a multiplicity of little capes, brown in colour.

All rooms of that period were overcrowded, of course. There was too much furniture in them, too many ornaments and so on. Mlle Mauhourat was a flouncer. She flounced about the room, jerking her shoulders, gesticulating with her hands and elbows, and sooner or later she invariably knocked an ornament off the table and broke it. It became quite a family joke. Father said, 'She reminds me of that bird you had, Agatha. Daphne. Always big and awkward and knocking her seed pans over.'

Mlle Mauhourat was particularly full of gush, and gush made me feel shy. I found it increasingly difficult to respond to her little cooing squeals of: '*Oh, la chère mignonne! Quelle est gentille, cette petite! Oh, la chère mignonne! Nous allons prendre des leçons très amusantes, n'est ce pas?'* I looked at her politely but with a cold eye. Then, receiving a firm look from my mother, I muttered unconvincingly, '*Oui, merci*', which was about the limit of my French at that time.

The French lessons went on amiably. I was docile as usual, but apparently bone-headed as well. Mother, who liked quick results, was dissatisfied with my progress.

'She's not getting on as she should, Fred,' she complained to my father.

My father, always amiable, said, 'Oh, give her time, Clara, give her time. The woman's only been here ten days.'

But my mother was not one to give anybody time. The climax came when I had a slight childish illness. It started, I suppose, with local flu and led to catarrhal trouble. I was feverish, out of sorts, and in this convalescent stage with still a slight temperature I could not stand the sight of Mlle Mauhourat.

'Please,' I would beg, 'please don't let me have a lesson this afternoon. I don't want to.'

Mother was always kind enough when there was real cause. She agreed. In due course Mlle Mauhourat, capes and all, arrived. My mother explained that I had a temperature, was staying indoors, and perhaps it would be better not to have a lesson that day. Mlle Mauhourat was off at once, fluttering over me, jerking her elbows, waving her capes, breathing down my neck. '*Oh, la pauvre mignonne, la pauvre petite mignonne.*' She would read to me, she said. She would tell me stories. She would amuse '*la pauvre petite*'.

I cast the most agonising glances at mother. I couldn't bear it. I couldn't bear another moment of it! Mlle Mauhourat's voice went on, high-pitched, squeaky—

everything I most disliked in a voice. My eyes implored: 'Take her away. Please take her *away*.' Firmly, my mother drew Mlle Mauhourat towards the door.

'I think Agatha had better be kept quite quiet this afternoon,' she said. She ushered Mlle Mauhourat out, then she returned and shook her head at me. 'It's all very well,' she said, 'but you must not make such terrible *faces*.'

'Faces?' I said.

'Yes. All that grimacing and looking at me. Mlle Mauhourat could see perfectly that you wanted her to go away.'

I was upset. I had not meant to be impolite.

'But, Mummy,' I said, 'those weren't *French* faces that I was making. They were *English* faces.'

My mother was much amused, and explained to me that making faces was a kind of international language which was understood by people of all countries. However, she told my father that Mlle Mauhourat was not being much of a success and she was going to look elsewhere. My father said it would be just as well if we did not lose too many more china ornaments. He added, 'If I were in Agatha's place, *I* should find that woman insupportable, just as she does.'

Freed from the ministrations of Miss Markham and Mlle Mauhourat, I began to enjoy myself. Staying in the hotel was Mrs Selwyn, the widow or perhaps the daughter-in-law of Bishop Selwyn, and her two daughters, Dorothy and Mary. Dorothy (Dar) was a year older than I was, Mary a year younger. Pretty soon we were inseparable.

Agatha Christie

The Arcadian Deer

Hercule Poirot stamped his feet, seeking to warm them. He blew upon his fingers. Flakes of snow melted and dripped from the corners of his moustache.

There was a knock at the door and a chambermaid appeared. She was a slow-breathing thickset country girl and she stared with a good deal of curiosity at Hercule Poirot. It was possible that she had not seen anything quite like him before.

She asked: 'Did you ring?'

'I did. Will you be so good as to light a fire?'

She went out and came back again immediately with paper and sticks. She knelt down in front of the big Victorian grate and began to lay a fire.

Hercule Poirot continued to stamp his feet, swing his arms and blow on his fingers.

He was annoyed. His car—an expensive Messarro Gratz—had not behaved with that mechanical perfection which he expected of a car. His chauffeur, a young man who enjoyed a handsome salary, had not succeeded in putting things right. The car had staged a final refusal in a secondary road a mile and a half from anywhere with a fall of snow beginning. Hercule Poirot, wearing his usual smart patent leather shoes, had been forced to walk that mile and a half to reach the riverside village of Hartly Dene—a village which, though showing every sign of animation in summer-time, was completely moribund in winter. The Black Swan had registered something like dismay at the arrival of a guest. The landlord had been almost eloquent as he pointed out that the local garage could supply a car in which the gentleman could continue his journey.

Hercule Poirot repudiated the suggestion. His Latin thrift was offended. Hire a car? He already *had* a car—a large car—an expensive car. In that car and no other he proposed to continue his journey back to town. And in any case, even if repairs to it could be quickly effected, he was not going on in this snow until next morning. He demanded a room, a fire and a meal. Sighing, the landlord showed him to the room, sent the maid to supply the fire and then retired to discuss with his wife the problem of the meal.

An hour later, his feet stretched out towards the comforting blaze, Hercule Poirot reflected leniently on the dinner he had just eaten. True, the steak had been both tough and full of gristle, the brussels-sprouts had been large, pale, and definitely watery, the potatoes had had hearts of stone. Nor was there much to be said for the portion of stewed apple and custard which had followed. The cheese had been hard, and the biscuits soft. Nevertheless, thought Hercule Poirot, looking graciously at the leaping flames, and sipping delicately at a cup of liquid mud euphemistically called coffee, it was better to be full than empty, and after tramping snowbound lanes in patent leather shoes, to sit in front of a fire was Paradise!

There was a knock on the door and the chambermaid appeared.

'Please, sir, the man from the garage is here and would like to see you.'

Hercule Poirot replied amiably:

'Let him mount.'

The girl giggled and retired. Poirot reflected kindly that her account of him to her friends would provide entertainment for many winter days to come.

There was another knock—a different knock—and Poirot called:

'Come in.'

He looked up with approval at the young man who entered and stood there looking ill at ease, twisting his cap in his hands.

Here, he thought, was one of the handsomest specimens of humanity he had ever seen, a simple young man with the outward semblance of a Greek god.

The young man said in a low husky voice:

'About the car, sir, we've brought it in. And we've got at the trouble. It's a matter of an hour's work or so.'

Poirot said:

'What is wrong with it?'

The young man plunged eagerly into technical details. Poirot nodded his head gently, but he was not listening. Perfect physique was a thing he admired greatly. There were, he considered, too many rats in spectacles about. He said to himself approvingly: 'Yes, a Greek god—a young shepherd in Arcady.'

The young man stopped abruptly. It was then that Hercule Poirot's brows knitted themselves for a second. His first reaction had been æsthetic, his second mental. His eyes narrowed themselves curiously, as he looked up.

He said:

'I comprehend. Yes, I comprehend.' He paused and then added: 'My chauffeur, he has already told me that which you have just said.'

He saw the flush that came to the other's cheek, saw the fingers grip the cap nervously.

The young man stammered:

'Yes—er—yes, sir. I know.'

Hercule Poirot went on smoothly:

'But you thought that you would also come and tell me yourself?'

'Er—yes, sir, I thought I'd better.'

'That,' said Hercule Poirot, 'was very conscientious of you. Thank you.'

There was a faint but unmistakable note of dismissal in the last words but he did not expect the other to go and he was right. The young man did not move.

His fingers moved convulsively, crushing the tweed cap, and he said in a still lower embarrassed voice:

'Er—excuse me, sir—but it's true, isn't it, that you're the detective gentleman—you're Mr Hercules Pwarrit?' He said the name very carefully.

Poirot said: 'That is so.'

Red crept up the young man's face. He said:

'I read a piece about you in the paper.'

'Yes?'

The boy was now scarlet. There was distress in his

eyes—distress and appeal. Hercule Poirot came to his aid. He said gently:

'Yes? What is it you want to ask me?'

The words came with a rush now.

'I'm afraid you may think it's awful cheek of me, sir. But your coming here by chance like this—well, it's too good to be missed. Having read about you and the clever things you've done. Anyway, I said as after all I might as well ask you. There's no harm in asking, is there?'

Hercule Poirot shook his head. He said:

'You want my help in some way?'

The other nodded. He said, his voice husky and embarrassed:

'It's—it's about a young lady. If—if you could find her for me.'

'Find her? Has she disappeared, then?'

'That's right, sir.'

Hercule Poirot sat up in his chair. He said sharply:

'I could help you, perhaps, yes. But the proper people for you to go to are the police. It is their job and they have far more resources at their disposal than I have.'

The boy shuffled his feet. He said awkwardly:

'I couldn't do that, sir. It's not like that at all. It's all rather peculiar, so to speak.'

Hercule Poirot stared at him. Then he indicated a chair.

'*Eh bien,* then, sit down—what is your name?'

'Williamson, sir, Ted Williamson.'

'Sit down, Ted. And tell me all about it.'

'Thank you sir.' He drew forward the chair and sat down carefully on the edge of it. His eyes had still that appealing doglike look.

Hercule Poirot said gently:

'Tell me.'

Ted Williamson drew a deep breath.

'Well, you see, sir, it was like this. I never saw her but the once. And I don't know her right name nor anything. But it's queer like, the whole thing, and my letter coming back and everything.'

'Start,' said Hercule Poirot, 'at the beginning. Do not hurry yourself. Just tell me everything that occurred.'

'Yes, sir. Well, perhaps you know Grasslawn, sir, that big house down by the river past the bridge?'

'I know nothing at all.'

'Belongs to Sir George Sanderfield, it does. He uses it in the summer-time for week-ends and parties—rather a gay lot he has down as a rule. Actresses and that. Well, it was last June—and the wireless was out of order and they sent me up to see to it.'

Poirot nodded.

'So I went along. The gentleman was out on the river with his guests and the cook was out and his manservant had gone along to serve the drinks and all that on the launch. There was only this girl in the house—she was the lady's-maid to one of the guests. She let me in and showed me where the set was, and stayed there while I was working on it. And so we got to talking and all that... Nita her name was, so she told me, and she was lady's-maid to a Russian dancer who was staying there.'

'What nationality was she, English?'

'No, sir, she'd be French, I think. She'd a funny sort of accent. But she spoke English all right. She—she was friendly and after a bit I asked her if she could come out that night and go to the pictures, but she said her lady would be needing her. But then she said as how she could get off early in the afternoon because as how they wasn't going to be back off the river till late. So the long and the short of it was that I took the afternoon off without asking (and nearly got the sack for it too) and we went for a walk along by the river.'

He paused. A little smile hovered on his lips. His eyes were dreamy. Poirot said gently:

'And she was pretty, yes?'

'She was just the loveliest thing you ever saw. Her hair was like gold—it went up each side like wings—and she had a gay kind of way of tripping along. I—I—well, I fell for her right away, sir. I'm not pretending anything else.'

Poirot nodded. The young man went on:

'She said as how her lady would be coming down again in a fortnight and we fixed up to meet again then.' He paused. 'But she never came. I waited for her at the spot she'd said, but not a sign of her, and at last I made bold to go up to the house and ask for her. The Russian lady was staying there all right and her maid too, they said. Sent for her, they did, but when she came, why, it wasn't Nita at all! Just a dark catty-looking girl—a bold lot if there ever was one. Marie, they called her. "You want to see me?" she says, simpering all over. She must have seen I was took aback. I said was she the Russian lady's maid and something about her not being the one I'd seen before, and then she laughed and said that the last maid had been sent away sudden. "Sent away?" I said. "What for?" She sort of shrugged her shoulders and stretched out her hands. "How should I know?" she said. "I was not there."

'Well, sir, it took me aback. At the moment I couldn't think of anything to say. But afterwards I plucked up the courage and I got to see this Marie again and asked her to get me Nita's address. I didn't let on to her that I didn't even know Nita's last name. I promised her a present if she did what I asked—she was the kind as wouldn't do anything for you for nothing. Well, she got it all right for me—an address in North London, it was, and I wrote to Nita there—but the letter came back after a bit—sent back through the post office with *no longer at this address* scrawled on it.'

Ted Williamson stopped. His eyes, those deep blue steady eyes, looked across at Poirot. He said:

'You see how it is, sir? It's not a case for the police. But I want to find her. And I don't know how to set about it. If—if you could find her for me.' His colour deepened. 'I've—I've a bit put by. I could manage five pounds—or even ten.'

Poirot said gently:

'We need not discuss the financial side for the moment. First reflect on this point—this girl, this Nita—she knew your name and where you worked?'

'Oh yes, sir.'

'She could have communicated with you if she had wanted to?'

Ted said more slowly:

'Yes, sir.'

'Then do you not think—perhaps—'

Ted Williamson interrupted him.

'What you're meaning, sir, is that I fell for her but she didn't fall for me? Maybe that's true in a way... But she liked me—she *did* like me—it wasn't just a bit of fun to her. And I've been thinking, sir, as there might be a *reason* for all this. You see, sir, it was a funny crowd she was mixed up in. She might be in a bit of trouble, if you know what I mean.'

'You mean she might have been going to have a child? Your child?'

'Not mine, sir.' Ted flushed. 'There wasn't nothing wrong between us.'

Poirot looked at him thoughtfully. He murmured:

'And if what you suggest is true—you still want to find her?'

The colour surged up in Ted Williamson's face. He said:

'Yes, I do, and that's flat! I want to marry her if she'll have me. And that's no matter what kind of a jam she's in! If you'll only try and find her for me, sir?'

Hercule Poirot smiled. He said, murmuring to himself:

'"Hair like wings of gold." Yes, I think this is the third Labour of Hercules... If I remember rightly, that happened in Arcady...'

II

Hercule Poirot looked thoughtfully at the sheet of paper on which Ted Williamson had laboriously inscribed a name and address.

Miss Valetta, 17 Upper Renfrew Lane, N15.

He wondered if he would learn anything at that address. Somehow he fancied not. But it was the only help Ted could give him.

No. 17 Upper Renfrew Lane was a dingy but respectable street. A stout woman with bleary eyes opened the door to Poirot's knock.

'Miss Valetta?'

'Gone away a long time ago, she has.'

Poirot advanced a step into the doorway just as the door was about to close.

'You can give me, perhaps, her address?'

'Couldn't say, I'm sure. She didn't leave one.'

'When did she go away?'

'Last summer it was.'

'Can you tell me exactly *when*?'

A gentle clicking noise came from Poirot's right hand where two half-crowns jostled each other in friendly fashion.

The bleary-eyed woman softened in an almost magical manner. She became graciousness itself.

'Well, I'm sure I'd like to help you, sir. Let me see now. August, no, before that—July—yes, July it must have been. About the first week in July. Went off in a hurry, she did. Back to Italy, I believe.'

'She was an Italian, then?'

'That's right, sir.'

'And she was at one time lady's maid to a Russian dancer, was she not?'

'That's right. Madame Semoulina or some such name. Danced at the Thespian in this Bally everyone's so wild about. One of the stars, she was.'

Poirot said:

'Do you know why Miss Valetta left her post?'

The woman hesitated a moment before saying:

'I couldn't say, I'm sure.'

'She was dismissed, was she not?'

'Well—I believe there was a bit of a dust up! But mind you, Miss Valetta didn't let on much about it. *She* wasn't one to give things away. But she looked wild about it. Wicked temper she had—real Italian—her black eyes all snapping and looking as if she'd like to put a knife into you. I wouldn't have crossed her when she was in one of her moods!'

'And you are quite sure you do not know Miss Valetta's present address?'

The half-crowns clinked again encouragingly.

The answer rang true enough.

'I wish I did, sir. I'd be only too glad to tell you. But there—she went off in a hurry and there it is!'

Poirot said to himself thoughtfully:

'Yes, there it is...'

III

Ambrose Vandel, diverted from his enthusiastic account of the *décor* he was designing for a forthcoming ballet, supplied information easily enough.

'Sanderfield? George Sanderfield? Nasty fellow. Rolling in money but they say he's a crook. Dark horse! Affair with a dancer? But of course, my dear—he had an affair with *Katrina*. Katrina Samoushenka. You *must* have seen her? Oh, my dear—too delicious. Lovely technique. *The Swan of Tuolela*—you must have seen *that? My décor!* And that other thing of Debussy or is it Mannine *"La Biche au Bois"*? She danced it with Michael Novgin. He's *so* marvellous, isn't he?'

'And she was a friend of Sir George Sanderfield?'

'Yes, she used to week-end with him at his house on the river. Marvellous parties I believe he gives.'

'Would it be possible, *mon cher,* for you to introduce me to Mademoiselle Samoushenka?'

'But, my dear, she isn't *here* any longer. She went to Paris or somewhere quite suddenly. You know, they do say that *she* was a Bolshevik spy or something—not that I believed it *myself*—you know people love saying things like that. Katrina always pretended that she was a White Russian— her father was a Prince or a Grand Duke— the usual thing! It goes *down* so much better.' Vandel paused and returned to the absorbing subject of himself. 'Now as I was saying, if you want to get the *spirit* of Bathsheba you've got to steep yourself in the Semitic tradition. I express it by—'

He continued happily.

IV

The interview that Hercule Poirot managed to arrange with Sir George Sanderfield did not start too auspiciously.

The 'dark horse', as Ambrose Vandel had called him, was slightly ill at ease. Sir George was a short square man with dark coarse hair and a roll of fat in his neck.

He said:

'Well, M. Poirot, what can I do for you? Er—we haven't met before, I think?'

'No, we have not met.'

'Well, what is it? I confess, I'm quite curious.'

'Oh, it is very simple—a mere matter of information.'

The other gave an uneasy laugh.

'Want me to give you some inside dope, eh? Didn't know you were interested in finance.'

'It is not a matter of *les affaires*. It is a question of a certain lady.'

'Oh, a woman.' Sir George Sanderfield leant back in his armchair. He seemed to relax. His voice held an easier note.

Poirot said:

'You were acquainted, I think, with Mademoiselle Katrina Samoushenka?'

Sanderfield laughed.

'Yes. An enchanting creature. Pity she's left London.'

'Why did she leave London?'

'My dear fellow, *I* don't know. Row with the management, I believe. She was temperamental, you know—very Russian in her moods. I'm sorry that I can't help you but I haven't the least idea where she is now. I haven't kept up with her at all.'

There was a note of dismissal in his voice as he rose to his feet.

Poirot said:

'But it is not Mademoiselle Samoushenka that I am anxious to trace.'

'Isn't it?'

'No, it is a question of her maid.'

'Her *maid*?' Sanderfield stared at him.

Poirot said:

'Do you—perhaps—remember her maid?'

All Sanderfield's uneasiness had returned. He said awkwardly:

'Good Lord, no, how should I? I remember she *had* one, of course... Bit of a bad lot, too, I should say. Sneaking, prying sort of girl. If I were you I shouldn't put any faith in a word that girl says. She's the kind of girl who's a born liar.'

Poirot murmured:

'So actually, you remember quite a lot about her?'

Sanderfield said hastily:

'Just an impression, that's all... Don't even remember her name. Let me see, Marie something or other—no, I'm afraid I can't help you to get hold of her. Sorry.'

Poirot said gently:

'I have already got the name of Marie Hellin from the Thespian Theatre—and her address. But I am speaking, Sir George, of the maid who was with Mademoiselle Samoushenka *before* Marie Hellin. I am speaking of Nita Valetta.'

Sanderfield stared. He said:

'Don't remember her at all. Marie's the only one *I* remember. Little dark girl with a nasty look in her eye.'

Poirot said:

'The girl I mean was at your house Grasslawn last June.'

Sanderfield said sulkily:

'Well, all I can say is I don't remember her. Don't believe she had a maid with her. I think you're making a mistake.'

Hercule Poirot shook his head. He did not think he was making a mistake.

V

Marie Hellin looked swiftly at Poirot out of small intelligent eyes and as swiftly looked away again. She said in smooth, even tones:

'But I remember *perfectly*, Monsieur. I was engaged by Madame Samoushenka the last week in June. Her former maid had departed in a hurry.'

'Did you ever hear why that maid left?'

'She went—suddenly—that is all I know! It may have been illness—something of that kind. Madame did not say.'

Poirot said:

'Did you find your mistress easy to get on with?'

The girl shrugged her shoulders.

'She had great moods. She wept and laughed in turns. Sometimes she was so despondent she would not speak or eat. Sometimes she was wildly gay. They are like that, these dancers. It is temperament.'

'And Sir George?'

The girl looked up alertly. An unpleasant gleam came into her eyes.

'Ah, Sir George Sanderfield? You would like to know about *him*? Perhaps it is that that you really want to know? The other was only an excuse, eh? Ah, Sir George, I could tell you some curious things about him, I could tell you—'

Poirot interrupted:

'It is not necessary.'

She stared at him, her mouth open. Angry disappointment showed in her eyes.

VI

'I always say you know everything, Alexis Pavlovitch.'

Hercule Poirot murmured the words with his most flattering intonation.

He was reflecting to himself that his third Labour of Hercules had necessitated more travelling and more interviews than could have been imagined possible. This little matter of a missing lady's-maid was proving one of the longest and most difficult problems he had ever tackled. Every clue, when examined, led exactly nowhere.

It had brought him this evening to the Samovar Restaurant in Paris whose proprietor, Count Alexis Pavlovitch, prided himself on knowing everything that went on in the artistic world.

He nodded now complacently:

'Yes, yes, my friend, *I* know—I always know. You ask me where she is gone—the little Samoushenka, the exquisite dancer? Ah! she was the real thing, that little one.' He kissed his fingertips. 'What fire—what abandon! She would have gone far—she would have been the Première Ballerina of her day—and then suddenly it all ends—she creeps away—to the end of the world—and soon, ah! so soon, they forget her.'

'Where is she then?' demanded Poirot.

'In Switzerland. At Vagray les Alpes. It is there that they go, those who have the little dry cough and who grow thinner and thinner. She will die, yes, she will die! She has a fatalistic nature. She will surely die.'

Poirot coughed to break the tragic spell. He wanted information.

'You do not, by chance, remember a maid she had? A maid called Nita Valetta?'

'Valetta? Valetta? I remember seeing a maid once—at the station when I was seeing Katrina off to London. She was an Italian from Pisa, was she not? Yes, I am sure she was an Italian who came from Pisa.'

Hercule Poirot groaned.

'In that case,' he said, 'I must now journey to Pisa.'

VII

Hercule Poirot stood in the Campo Santo at Pisa and looked down on a grave.

So it was here that his quest had come to an end—here by this humble mound of earth. Underneath it lay the joyous creature who had stirred the heart and imagination of a simple English mechanic.

Was this perhaps the best end to that sudden strange romance? Now the girl would live always in the young man's memory as he had seen her for those few enchanted hours of a June afternoon. The clash of opposing nationalities, of different standards, the pain of disillusionment, all that was ruled out for ever.

Hercule Poirot shook his head sadly. His mind went back to his conversation with the Valetta family. The mother, with her broad peasant face, the upright grief-stricken father, the dark hard-lipped sister.

'It was sudden, Signor, it was very sudden. Though for many years she had had pains on and off... The doctor gave us no choice—he said there must be an operation immediately for the appendicitis. He took her off to the hospital then and there. *Si, si,* it was under the anæsthetic she died. She never recovered consciousness.'

The mother sniffed, murmuring:

'Bianca was always such a clever girl. It is terrible that she should have died so young...'

Hercule Poirot repeated to himself:

'She died young...'

That was the message he must take back to the young man who had asked his help so confidingly.

'She is not for you, my friend. She died young.'

His quest had ended—here where the leaning Tower was silhouetted against the sky and the first spring flowers were showing pale and creamy with their promise of life and joy to come.

Was it the stirring of spring that made him feel so rebelliously disinclined to accept this final verdict? Or was it something else? Something stirring at the back of his brain—words—a phrase—a name? Did not the whole thing finish too neatly—dovetail too obviously?

Hercule Poirot sighed. He must take one more journey to put things beyond any possible doubt. He must go to Vagray les Alpes.

VIII

Here, he thought, really was the world's end. This shelf of snow—these scattered huts and shelters in each of which lay a motionless human being fighting an insidious death.

So he came at last to Katrina Samoushenka. When he saw her, lying there with hollow cheeks in each of which was a vivid red stain, and long thin emaciated hands stretched out on the coverlet, a memory stirred in him. He had not remembered her name, but he *had* seen her dance—had been carried away and fascinated by the supreme art that can make you forget art.

He remembered Michael Novgin, the Hunter, leaping and twirling in that outrageous and fantastic forest that the brain of Ambrose Vandel had conceived. And he remembered the lovely flying Hind, eternally pursued, eternally desirable—a golden beautiful creature with horns on her head and twinkling bronze feet. He remembered her final collapse, shot and wounded, and Michael Novgin standing bewildered, with the body of the slain deer in his arms.

Katrina Samoushenka was looking at him with faint curiosity. She said:

'I have never seen you before, have I? What is it you want of me?'

Hercule Poirot made her a little bow.

'First, Madame, I wish to thank you—for your art which made for me once an evening of beauty.'

She smiled faintly.

'But also I am here on a matter of business. I have been looking, Madame, for a long time for a certain maid of yours—her name was Nita.'

'Nita?'

She stared at him. Her eyes were large and startled. She said:

'What do you know about—Nita?'

'I will tell you.'

He told her of the evening when his car had broken down and of Ted Williamson standing there twisting his cap between his fingers and stammering out his love and his pain. She listened with close attention.

She said when he had finished:

'It is touching, that—yes, it is touching...'

Hercule Poirot nodded.

'Yes,' he said. 'It is a tale of Arcady, is it not? What can you tell me, Madame, of this girl?'

Katrina Samoushenka sighed.

'I had a maid—Juanita. She was lovely, yes—gay, light of heart. It happened to her what happens so often to those the gods favour. She died young.'

They had been Poirot's own words—final words—irrevocable words—Now he heard them again—and yet he persisted. He asked:

'She is dead?'

'Yes, she is dead.'

Hercule Poirot was silent for a minute, then he said:

'There is one thing I do not quite understand. I asked Sir George Sanderfield about this maid of yours and he seemed afraid. Why was that?'

There was a faint expression of disgust on the dancer's face.

'You just said a maid of mine. He thought you meant Marie—the girl who came to me after Juanita left. She tried to blackmail him, I believe, over something that she found out about him. She was an odious girl—inquisitive, always prying into letters and locked drawers.'

Poirot murmured:

'Then that explains that.'

He paused a minute, then he went on, still persistent:

'Juanita's other name was Valetta and she died of an operation for appendicitis in Pisa. Is that correct?'

He noted the hesitation, hardly perceptible but nevertheless there, before the dancer bowed her head.

'Yes, that is right...'

Poirot said meditatively:

'And yet—there is still a little point—her people spoke of her, not as Juanita but as *Bianca*.'

Katrina shrugged her thin shoulders. She said: 'Bianca—Juanita, does it matter? I suppose her real name was Bianca but she thought the name of Juanita was more romantic and so chose to call herself by it.'

'Ah, you think that?' He paused and then, his voice changing, he said: 'For me, there is another explanation.'

'What is it?'

Poirot leaned forward. He said:

'The girl that Ted Williamson saw had hair that he described as being like wings of gold.'

He leaned still a little further forward. His finger just touched the two springing waves of Katrina's hair.

'Wings of gold, horns of gold? It is as you look at it, it is whether one sees you as devil or as angel! You might be either. Or are they perhaps only the golden horns of the stricken deer?'

Katrina murmured:

'The stricken deer...' and her voice was the voice of one without hope.

Poirot said:

'All along Ted Williamson's description has worried me—it brought something to my mind—that something was *you,* dancing on your twinkling bronze feet through the forest. Shall I tell you what *I* think, Mademoiselle? I think there was a week when you had *no* maid, when you went down alone to Grasslawn, for Bianca Valetta had returned to Italy and you had not yet engaged a new maid. Already you were feeling the illness which has since overtaken you, and you stayed in the house one day when the others went on an all day excursion on the river. There was a ring at the door and you went to it and you saw—*shall I tell you what you saw? You saw a young man who was as simple as a child and as handsome as a god! And you invented for him a girl—not Juanita—but Incognita—and for a few hours you walked with him in Arcady...*'

There was a long pause. Then Katrina said in a low hoarse voice:

'In one thing at least I have told you the truth. I have given you the right end to the story. Nita will die young.'

'*Ah non!*' Hercule Poirot was transformed. He struck his hand on the table. He was suddenly prosaic, mundane, practical.

He said:

'It is quite unnecessary! *You need not die.* You can fight for your life, can you not, as well as another?'

She shook her head—sadly, hopelessly—

'What life is there for me?'

'Not the life of the stage, *bien entendu!* But think, there is another life. Come now, Mademoiselle, be honest, was your father really a Prince or a Grand Duke, or even a General?'

She laughed suddenly. She said:

'He drove a lorry in Leningrad!'

'Very good! And why should you not be the wife of a garage hand in a country village? And have children as beautiful as gods, and with feet, perhaps, that will dance as you once danced.'

Katrina caught her breath.

'But the whole idea is fantastic!'

'Nevertheless,' said Hercule Poirot with great selfsatisfaction, 'I believe it is going to come true!'

The Case of the City Clerk

Mr Parker Pyne leaned back thoughtfully in his swivel chair and surveyed his visitor. He saw a small sturdily built man of forty-five with wistful, puzzled, timid eyes that looked at him with a kind of anxious hopefulness.

'I saw your advertisement in the paper,' said that little man nervously.

'You are in trouble, Mr Roberts?'

'No, not in trouble exactly.'

'You are unhappy?'

'I shouldn't like to say that either. I've a great deal to be thankful for.'

'We all have,' said Mr Parker Pyne. 'But when we have to remind ourselves of the fact it is a bad sign.'

'I know,' said the little man eagerly. 'That's just it! You've hit the nail on the head, sir.'

'Supposing you tell me all about yourself,' suggested Mr Parker Pyne.

'There's not much to tell, sir. As I say, I've a great deal to be thankful for. I have a job; I've managed to save a little money; the children are strong and healthy.'

'So you want—what?'

'I—I don't know.' He flushed. 'I expect that sounds foolish to you, sir.'

'Not at all,' said Mr Parker Pyne.

By skilled questioning he elicited further confidences. He heard of Mr Roberts' employment in a well-known firm and of his slow but steady rise. He heard of his marriage; of the struggle to present a decent appearance, to educate the children and have them 'looking nice'; of the plotting and planning and skimping and saving to put aside a few pounds each year. He heard, in fact, the saga of a life of ceaseless effort to survive.

'And—well, you see how it is,' confessed Mr Roberts. 'The wife's away. Staying with her mother with the two children. Little change for them and a rest for her. No room for me and we can't afford to go elsewhere. And being alone and reading the paper, I saw your advertisement and it set me thinking. I'm forty-eight. I just wondered . . . Things going on everywhere,' he ended, with all his wistful suburban soul in his eyes.

'You want,' said Mr Pyne, 'to live gloriously for ten minutes?'

'Well, I shouldn't put it like that. But perhaps you're right. Just to get out of the rut. I'd go back to it thankful afterwards—if only I had something to think about.' He looked at the other man anxiously. 'I suppose there's nothing possible, sir? I'm afraid—I'm afraid I couldn't afford to pay much.'

'How much could you afford?'

'I could manage five pounds, sir.' He waited, breathless.

'Five pounds,' said Mr Parker Pyne. 'I fancy—I just fancy we might be able to manage something for five pounds. Do you object to danger?' he added sharply.

A tinge of colour came into Mr Roberts' sallow face. 'Danger, did you say, sir? Oh, no, not at all. I—I've never done anything dangerous.'

Mr Parker Pyne smiled. 'Come to see me again tomorrow and I'll tell you what I can do for you.'

The Bon Voyageur is a little-known hostelry. It is a restaurant frequented by a few habitués. They dislike newcomers.

To the Bon Voyageur came Mr Pyne and was greeted with respectful recognition. 'Mr Bonnington here?' he asked.

'Yes, sir. He's at his usual table.'

'Good. I'll join him.'

Mr Bonnington was a gentleman of military appearance with a somewhat bovine face. He greeted his friend with pleasure.

'Hallo, Parker. Hardly ever see you nowadays. Didn't know you came here.'

'I do now and then. Especially when I want to lay my hand on an old friend.'

'Meaning me?'

'Meaning you. As a matter of fact, Lucas, I've been thinking over what we were talking about the other day.'

'The Peterfield business? Seen the latest in the papers? No, you can't have. It won't be in till this evening.'

'What is the latest?'

'They murdered Peterfield last night,' said Mr Bonnington, placidly eating salad.

'Good heavens!' cried Mr Pyne.

'Oh, I'm not surprised,' said Mr Bonnington. 'Pigheaded

old man, Peterfield. Wouldn't listen to us. Insisted on keeping the plans in his own hands.'

'Did they get them?'

'No; it seems some woman came round and gave the professor a recipe for boiling a ham. The old ass, absent-minded as usual, put the recipe for the ham in his safe and the plans in the kitchen.'

'Fortunate.'

'Almost providential. But I still don't know who's going to take 'em to Geneva. Maitland's in the hospital. Carslake's in Berlin. I can't leave. It means young Hooper.' He looked at his friend.

'You're still of the same opinion?' asked Mr Parker Pyne.

'Absolutely. He's been got at! I know it. I haven't a shadow of proof, but I tell you, Parker, I know when a chap's crooked! And I want those plans to get to Geneva. The League needs 'em. For the first time an invention isn't going to be sold to a nation. It's going to be handed over voluntarily to the League.

'It's the finest peace gesture that's ever been attempted, and it's got to be put through. And Hooper's crooked. You'll see, he'll be drugged on the train! If he goes in a plane it'll come down at some convenient spot! But confound it all, I can't pass him over. Discipline! You've got to have discipline! That's why I spoke to you the other day.'

'You asked me whether I knew of anyone.'

'Yes. Thought you might in your line of business. Some fire eater spoiling for a row. Whoever *I* send stands a good chance of being done in. Your man would probably not be suspected at all. But he's got to have nerve.'

'I think I know of someone who would do,' said Mr Parker Pyne.

'Thank God there are still chaps who will take a risk. Well, it's agreed then?'

'It's agreed,' said Mr Parker Pyne.

Mr Parker Pyne was summing up instructions. 'Now, that's quite clear? You will travel in a first-class sleeper to Geneva. You leave London at ten forty-five, via Folkestone and Boulogne, and you get into your first-class sleeper at Boulogne. You arrive at Geneva at eight the following morning. Here is the address at which you will report. Please memorize it and I will destroy it. Afterwards go to this hotel and await further instructions. Here is sufficient money in French and Swiss notes and currency. You understand?'

'Yes, sir.' Roberts' eyes were shining with excitement. 'Excuse me, sir, but am I allowed to—er—know anything of what it is I am carrying?'

Mr Parker Pyne smiled beneficently. 'You are carrying a cryptogram which reveals the secret hiding-place of the crown jewels of Russia,' he said solemnly. 'You can understand, naturally, that Bolshevist agents will be alert to intercept you. If it is necessary for you to talk about yourself, I should recommend that you say you have come into money and are enjoying a little holiday abroad.'

Mr Roberts sipped a cup of coffee and looked out over the Lake of Geneva. He was happy but at the same time he was disappointed.

He was happy because, for the first time in his life, he

was in a foreign country. Moreover, he was staying in the kind of hotel he would never stay in again, and not for one moment had he had to worry about money! He had a room with private bathroom, delicious meals and attentive service. All these things Mr Roberts had enjoyed very much indeed.

He was disappointed because so far nothing that could be described as adventure had come his way. No disguised Bolshevists or mysterious Russians had crossed his path. A pleasant chat on the train with a French commercial traveller who spoke excellent English was the only human intercourse that had come his way. He had secreted the papers in his sponge bag as he had been told to do and had delivered them according to instructions. There had been no dangers to overcome, no hair's breadth escapes. Mr Roberts was disappointed.

It was at that moment that a tall, bearded man murmured *'Pardon,'* and sat down on the other side of the little table. 'You will excuse me,' he said, 'but I think you know a friend of mine. "P.P." are the initials.'

Mr Roberts was pleasantly thrilled. Here, at last, was a mysterious Russian. 'Qu-quite right.'

'Then I think we understand each other,' said the stranger.

Mr Roberts looked at him searchingly. This was far more like the real thing. The stranger was a man of about fifty, of distinguished though foreign appearance. He wore an eye-glass, and a small coloured ribbon in his button-hole.

'You have accomplished your mission in the most satisfactory manner,' said the stranger. 'Are you prepared to undertake a further one?'

'Certainly. Oh, yes.'

'Good. You will book a sleeper on the Geneva–Paris train for tomorrow night. You will ask for Berth Number Nine.'

'Supposing it is not free?'

'It will be free. That will have been seen to.'

'Berth Number Nine,' repeated Roberts. 'Yes, I've got that.'

'During the course of your journey someone will say to you, "Pardon, Monsieur, but I think you were recently at Grasse?" To that you will reply "Yes, last month." The person will then say, "Are you interested in scent?" And you will reply, "Yes, I am a manufacturer of synthetic Oil of Jasmine." After that you will place yourself entirely at the disposal of the person who has spoken to you. By the way, are you armed?'

'No,' said Mr Roberts in a flutter. 'No; I never thought—that is—'

'That can soon be remedied,' said the bearded man. He glanced around. No one was near them. Something hard and shining was pressed into Mr Roberts' hand. 'A small weapon but efficacious,' said the stranger, smiling.

Mr Roberts, who had never fired a revolver in his life, slipped it gingerly into a pocket. He had an uneasy feeling that it might go off at any minute.

They went over the passwords again. Then Roberts' new friend rose.

'I wish you good luck,' he said. 'May you come through safely. You are a brave man, Mr Roberts.'

'Am I?' thought Roberts, when the other had departed. 'I'm sure I don't want to get killed. That would never do.'

A pleasant thrill shot down his spine, slightly adulterated by a thrill that was not quite so pleasant.

He went to his room and examined the weapon. He was still uncertain about its mechanism and hoped he would not be called upon to use it.

He went out to book his seat.

The train left Geneva at nine-thirty. Roberts got to the station in good time. The sleeping-car conductor took his ticket and his passport, and stood aside while an underling swung Roberts' suitcase on to the rack. There was other luggage there: a pigskin case and a Gladstone bag.

'Number Nine is the lower berth,' said the conductor.

As Roberts turned to leave the carriage he ran into a big man who was entering. They drew apart with apologies—Roberts' in English and the stranger's in French. He was a big burly man, with a closely shaven head and thick eye-glasses through which his eyes seemed to peer suspiciously.

'An ugly customer,' said the little man to himself.

He sensed something vaguely sinister about his travelling companion. Was it to keep a watch on this man that he had been told to ask for Berth Number Nine? He fancied it might be.

He went out again into the corridor. There was still ten minutes before the train was due to start and he thought he would walk up and down the platform. Half-way along the passage he stood back to allow a lady to pass him. She was just entering the train and the conductor preceded her, ticket in hand. As she passed Roberts she dropped her handbag. The Englishman picked it up and handed it to her.

'Thank you, Monsieur.' She spoke in English but her voice was foreign, a rich low voice very seductive in quality. As she was about to pass on, she hesitated and murmured: 'Pardon, Monsieur, but I think you were recently at Grasse?'

Roberts' heart leaped with excitement. He was to place himself at the disposal of this lovely creature—for she *was* lovely, of that there was no doubt. She wore a travelling coat of fur, a chic hat. There were pearls round her neck. She was dark and her lips were scarlet.

Roberts made the required answer. 'Yes, last month.'

'You are interested in scent?'

'Yes, I am a manufacturer of synthetic Oil of Jasmine.'

She bent her head and passed on, leaving a mere whisper behind her. 'In the corridor as soon as the train starts.'

The next ten minutes seemed an age to Roberts. At last the train started. He walked slowly along the corridor. The lady in the fur coat was struggling with a window. He hurried to her assistance.

'Thank you, Monsieur. Just a little air before they insist on closing everything.' And then in a soft, low, rapid voice: 'After the frontier, when our fellow traveller is asleep—not before—go into the washing place and through it into the compartment on the other side. You understand?'

'Yes.' He let down the window and said in a louder voice: 'Is that better, Madame?'

'Thank you very much.'

He retired to his compartment. His travelling companion was already stretched out in the upper berth. His preparations for the night had obviously been simple. The removal of boots and a coat, in fact.

Roberts debated his own costume. Clearly, if he were going into a lady's compartment he could not undress.

He found a pair of slippers, substituting them for his boots, and then lay down, switching out the light. A few minutes later, the man above began to snore.

Just after ten o'clock they reached the frontier. The door was thrown open; a perfunctory question was asked. Had Messieurs anything to declare? The door was closed again. Presently the train drew out of Bellegarde.

The man in the upper berth was snoring again. Roberts allowed twenty minutes to elapse, then he slipped to his feet and opened the door of the lavatory compartment. Once inside, he bolted the door behind him and eyed the door on the farther side. It was not bolted. He hesitated. Should he knock?

Perhaps it would be absurd to knock. But he didn't quite like entering without knocking. He compromised, opened the door gently about an inch and waited. He even ventured on a small cough.

The response was prompt. The door was pulled open, he was seized by the arm, pulled through into the farther compartment, and the girl closed and bolted the door behind him.

Roberts caught his breath. Never had he imagined anything so lovely. She was wearing a long foamy garment of cream chiffon and lace. She leaned against the door into the corridor, panting. Roberts had often read of beautiful hunted creatures at bay. Now for the first time, he saw one—a thrilling sight.

'Thank God!' murmured the girl.

She was quite young, Roberts noted, and her loveliness was such that she seemed to him like a being from another world. Here was romance at last—and he was in it!

She spoke in a low, hurried voice. Her English was good but the inflection was wholly foreign. 'I am so glad you have come,' she said. 'I have been horribly frightened. Vassilievitch is on the train. You understand what that means?'

Roberts did not understand in the least what it meant, but he nodded.

'I thought I had given them the slip. I might have known better. What are we to do? Vassilievitch is in the next carriage to me. Whatever happens, he must not get the jewels.'

'He's not going to murder you and he's not going to get the jewels,' said Robert with determination.

'Then what am I to do with them?'

Roberts looked past her to the door. 'The door's bolted,' he said.

The girl laughed. 'What are locked doors to Vassilievitch?'

Roberts felt more and more as though he were in the middle of one of his favourite novels. 'There's only one thing to be done. Give them to me.'

She looked at him doubtfully. 'They are worth a quarter of a million.'

Roberts flushed. 'You can trust me.'

The girl hesitated a moment longer, then: 'Yes, I will trust you,' she said. She made a swift movement. The next minute she was holding out to him a rolled-up pair of stockings—stockings of cobweb silk. 'Take them, my friend,' she said to the astonished Roberts.

He took them and at once he understood. Instead of being light as air, the stockings were unexpectedly heavy.

'Take them to your compartment,' she said. 'You can give them to me in the morning—if—if I am still here.'

Roberts coughed. 'Look here,' he said. 'About you.' He paused. 'I—I must keep guard over you.' Then he flushed in an agony of propriety. 'Not in here, I mean. I'll stay in there.' He nodded towards the lavatory compartment.

'If you like to stay here—' She glanced at the upper unoccupied berth.

Roberts flushed to the roots of his hair. 'No, no,' he protested. 'I shall be all right in there. If you need me, call out.'

'Thank you, my friend,' said the girl softly.

She slipped into the lower berth, drew up the covers and smiled at him gratefully. He retreated into the washroom.

Suddenly—it must have been a couple of hours later—he thought he heard something. He listened—nothing. Perhaps he had been mistaken. And yet it certainly seemed to him that he had heard a faint sound from the next carriage. Supposing—just supposing . . .

He opened the door softly. The compartment was as he had left it, with the tiny blue light in the ceiling. He stood there with his eyes straining through the dimness till they got accustomed to it. The girl was not there!

He switched the light full on. The compartment was empty. Suddenly he sniffed. Just a whiff but he recognized it—the sweet, sickly odour of chloroform!

He stepped from the compartment (unlocked now, he noted) out into the corridor and looked up and down it. Empty! His eyes fastened on the door next to the girl's. She had said that Vassilievitch was in the next compartment. Gingerly Roberts tried the handle. The door was bolted on the inside.

What should he do? Demand admittance? But the man would refuse—and after all, the girl might not be there! And if she were, would she thank him for making a public business of the matter? He had gathered that secrecy was essential in the game they were playing.

A perturbed little man wandered slowly along the corridor. He paused at the end compartment. The door was open, and the conductor lay there sleeping. And above him, on a hook, *hung his brown uniform coat and peaked cap.*

In a flash Roberts had decided on his course of action. In another minute he had donned the coat and cap, and was hurrying back along the corridor. He stopped at the door next to that of the girl, summoned all his resolution and knocked peremptorily.

When the summons was not answered, he knocked again.

'Monsieur,' he said in his best accent.

The door opened a little way and a head peered out—the head of a foreigner, clean-shaven except for a black moustache. It was an angry, malevolent face.

'*Qu'est-ce-qu'il y a?*' he snapped.

'*Votre passeport, monsieur.*' Roberts stepped back and beckoned.

The other hesitated, then stepped out into the corridor. Roberts had counted on his doing that. If he had the girl inside, he naturally would not want the conductor to come in. Like a flash, Roberts acted. With all his force he shoved the foreigner aside—the man was unprepared and the swaying of the train helped—bolted into the carriage himself, shut the door and locked it.

Lying across the end of the berth was the girl, a gag across her mouth and her wrists tied together. He freed her quickly and she fell against him with a sigh.

'I feel so weak and ill,' she murmured. 'It was chloroform, I think. Did he—did he get them?'

'No.' Roberts tapped his pocket. 'What are we going to do now?' he asked.

The girl sat up. Her wits were returning. She took in his costume.

'How clever of you. Fancy thinking of that! He said that he would kill me if I did not tell him where the jewels were. I have been so afraid—and then you came.' Suddenly she laughed. 'But we have outwitted him! He will not dare to do anything. He cannot even try to get back into his own compartment.

'We must stay here till morning. Probably he will leave the train at Dijon; we are due to stop there in about half an hour. He will telegraph to Paris and they will pick up our trail there. In the meantime, you had better throw that coat and cap out of the window. They might get you into trouble.'

Roberts obeyed.

'We must not sleep,' the girl decided. 'We must stay on guard till morning.'

It was a strange, exciting vigil. At six o'clock in the morning, Roberts opened the door carefully and looked out. No one was about. The girl slipped quickly into her own compartment. Roberts followed her in. The place had clearly been ransacked. He regained his own carriage through the washroom. His fellow-traveller was still snoring.

They reached Paris at seven o'clock. The conductor was declaiming at the loss of his coat and cap. He had not yet discovered the loss of a passenger.

Then began a most entertaining chase. The girl and Roberts took taxi after taxi across Paris. They entered hotels and restaurants by one door and left them by another. At last the girl gave a sign.

'I feel sure we are not followed now,' she said. 'We have shaken them off.'

They breakfasted and drove to Le Bourget. Three hours later they were at Croydon. Roberts had never flown before.

At Croydon a tall gentleman with a far-off resemblance to Mr Roberts' mentor at Geneva was waiting for them. He greeted the girl with especial respect.

'The car is here, madam,' he said.

'This gentleman will accompany us, Paul,' said the girl. And to Roberts: 'Count Paul Stepanyi.'

The car was a vast limousine. They drove for about an hour, then they entered the grounds of a country house and pulled up at the door of an imposing mansion. Mr Roberts was taken to a room furnished as a study. There he handed over the precious pair of stockings. He was left alone for a while. Presently Count Stepanyi returned.

'Mr Roberts,' he said, 'our thanks and gratitude are due to you. You have proved yourself a brave and resourceful man.' He held out a red morocco case. 'Permit me to confer upon you the Order of St Stanislaus—tenth class with laurels.'

As in a dream Roberts opened the case and looked at the jewelled order. The old gentleman was still speaking.

'The Grand Duchess Olga would like to thank you herself before you depart.'

He was led to a big drawing-room. There, very beautiful in a flowing robe, stood his travelling companion.

She made an imperious gesture of the hand, and the other man left them.

'I owe you my life, Mr Roberts,' said the grand duchess.

She held out her hand. Roberts kissed it. She leaned suddenly towards him.

'You are a brave man,' she said.

His lips met hers; a waft of rich Oriental perfume surrounded him.

For a moment he held that slender, beautiful form in his arms . . .

He was still in a dream when somebody said to him: 'The car will take you anywhere you wish.'

An hour later, the car came back for the Grand Duchess Olga. She got into it and so did the white-haired man. He had removed his beard for coolness. The car set down the Grand Duchess Olga at a house in Streatham. She entered it and an elderly woman looked up from a tea table.

'Ah, Maggie, dear, so there you are.'

In the Geneva–Paris express this girl was the Grand Duchess Olga; in Mr Parker Pyne's office she was Madeleine de Sara, and in the house at Streatham she was Maggie Sayers, fourth daughter of an honest, hard-working family.

How are the mighty fallen!

Mr Parker Pyne was lunching with his friend. 'Congratulations,' said the latter, 'your man carried the thing through without a hitch. The Tormali gang must be wild to think the plans of that gun have gone to the League. Did you tell your man what he was carrying?'

'No. I thought it better to—er—embroider.'

'Very discreet of you.'

'It wasn't exactly discretion. I wanted him to enjoy himself. I fancied he might find a gun a little tame. I wanted him to have some adventures.'

'Tame?' said Mr Bonnington, staring at him. 'Why, that lot would murder him as soon as look at him.'

'Yes,' said Mr Parker Pyne mildly. 'But I didn't want him to be murdered.'

'Do you make a lot of money in your business, Parker?' asked Mr Bonnington.

'Sometimes I lose it,' said Mr Parker Pyne. 'That is, if it is a deserving case.'

Three angry gentlemen were abusing one another in Paris.

'That confounded Hooper!' said one. 'He let us down.'

'The plans were not taken by anyone from the office,' said the second. 'But they went Wednesday, I am assured of that. And so I say *you* bungled it.'

'I didn't,' said the third sulkily; 'there was no Englishman on the train except a little clerk. He'd never heard of Peterfield or of the gun. I know. I tested him. Peterfield and the gun meant nothing to him.' He laughed. 'He had a Bolshevist complex of some kind.'

Mr Roberts was sitting in front of a gas fire. On his knee was a letter from Mr Parker Pyne. It enclosed a cheque for fifty pounds 'from certain people who are delighted with the way a certain commission was executed.'

On the arm of his chair was a library book. Mr Roberts opened it at random. 'She crouched against the door like a beautiful, hunted creature at bay.'

Well, he knew all about that.

He read another sentence: 'He sniffed the air. The faint, sickly odour of chloroform came to his nostrils.'

That he knew all about too.

'He caught her in his arms and felt the responsive quiver of her scarlet lips.'

Mr Roberts gave a sigh. It wasn't a dream. It had all happened. The journey out had been dull enough, but the journey home! He had enjoyed it. But he was glad to be home again. He felt vaguely that life could not be lived indefinitely at such a pace. Even the Grand Duchess Olga— even that last kiss—partook already of the unreal quality of a dream.

Mary and the children would be home tomorrow. Mr Roberts smiled happily.

She would say: 'We've had such a nice holiday. I hated thinking of you all alone here, poor old boy.' And he'd say: 'That's all right, old girl. I had to go to Geneva for the firm on business—delicate bit of negotiations—and look what they've sent me.' And he'd show her the cheque for fifty pounds.

He thought of the Order of St Stanislaus, tenth class with laurels. He'd hidden it, but supposing Mary found it! It would take a bit of explaining . . .

Ah, that was it—he'd tell her he'd picked it up abroad. A curio.

He opened his book again and read happily. No longer was there a wistful expression on his face.

He, too, was of that glorious company to whom Things Happened.

The Soul of the Croupier

Mr Satterthwaite was enjoying the sunshine on the terrace at Monte Carlo.

Every year regularly on the second Sunday in January, Mr Satterthwaite left England for the Riviera. He was far more punctual than any swallow. In the month of April he returned to England, May and June he spent in London, and had never been known to miss Ascot. He left town after the Eton and Harrow match, paying a few country house visits before repairing to Deauville or Le Touquet. Shooting parties occupied most of September and October, and he usually spent a couple of months in town to wind up the year. He knew everybody and it may safely be said that everybody knew him.

This morning he was frowning. The blue of the sea was admirable, the gardens were, as always, a delight, but the people disappointed him—he thought them an ill-dressed, shoddy crowd. Some, of course, were gamblers, doomed souls who could not keep away. Those Mr Satterthwaite tolerated. They were a necessary background. But he missed the usual leaven of the *élite*—his own people.

'It's the exchange,' said Mr Satterthwaite gloomily. 'All sorts of people come here now who could never have afforded it before. And then, of course, I'm getting old . . . All the young people—the people coming on— they go to these Swiss places.'

But there were others that he missed, the well-dressed Barons and Counts of foreign diplomacy, the Grand Dukes and the Royal Princes. The only Royal Prince he had seen so far was working a lift in one of the less well-known hotels. He missed, too, the beautiful and expensive ladies. There was still a few of them, but not nearly as many as there used to be.

Mr Satterthwaite was an earnest student of the drama called Life, but he liked his material to be highly coloured. He felt discouragement sweep over him. Values were changing—and he—was too old to change.

It was at that moment that he observed the Countess Czarnova coming towards him.

Mr Satterthwaite had seen the Countess at Monte Carlo for many seasons now. The first time he had seen her she had been in the company of a Grand Duke. On the next occasion she was with an Austrian Baron. In successive years her friends had been of Hebraic extraction wearing rather flamboyant jewellery. For the last year or two she was much seen with very young men, almost boys.

She was walking with a very young man now. Mr Satterthwaite happened to know him, and he was sorry. Franklin Rudge was a young American, a typical product of one of the Middle West States, eager to register impression, crude, but loveable, a curious mixture of native shrewdness and idealism. He was in Monte Carlo with a party of other young Americans of both sexes, all much of the same type. It was their first glimpse of the Old World and they were outspoken in criticism and in appreciation.

On the whole they disliked the English people in the hotel, and the English people disliked them. Mr Satterthwaite, who prided himself on being a cosmopolitan, rather liked them. Their directness and vigour appealed to him, though their occasional solecisms made him shudder.

It occurred to him that the Countess Czarnova was a most unsuitable friend for young Franklin Rudge.

He took off his hat politely as they came abreast of him, and the Countess gave him a charming bow and smile.

She was a very tall woman, superbly made. Her hair was black, so were her eyes, and her eyelashes and eyebrows were more superbly black than any Nature had ever fashioned.

Mr Satterthwaite, who knew far more of feminine secrets than it is good for any man to know, rendered immediate homage to the art with which she was made up. Her complexion appeared to be flawless, of a uniform creamy white. The very faint bistre shadows under her eyes were most effective. Her mouth was neither crimson nor scarlet, but a subdued wine colour. She was dressed in a very daring creation of black and white and carried a parasol of the shade of pinky red which is most helpful to the complexion.

Franklin Rudge was looking happy and important.

'There goes a young fool,' said Mr Satterthwaite to himself. 'But I suppose it's no business of mine and anyway he wouldn't listen to me. Well, well, I've bought experience myself in my time.'

But he still felt rather worried, because there was a very attractive little American girl in the party, and he was sure that she would not like Franklin Rudge's friendship with the Countess at all.

He was just about to retrace his steps in the opposite direction when he caught sight of the girl in question coming up one of the paths towards him. She wore a well-cut tailor-made 'suit' with a white muslin shirt waist, she had on good, sensible walking shoes, and carried a guide-book. There are some Americans who pass through Paris and emerge clothed as the Queen of Sheba, but Elizabeth Martin was not one of them. She was 'doing Europe' in a stern, conscientious spirit. She had high ideas of culture and art and she was anxious to get as much as possible for her limited store of money.

It is doubtful if Mr Satterthwaite thought of her as either cultured or artistic. To him she merely appeared very young.

'Good morning, Mr Satterthwaite,' said Elizabeth. 'Have you seen Franklin—Mr Rudge—anywhere about?'

'I saw him just a few minutes ago.'

'With his friend the Countess, I suppose,' said the girl sharply.

'Er—with the Countess, yes,' admitted Mr Satterthwaite.

'That Countess of his doesn't cut any ice with me,' said the girl in a rather high, shrill voice. 'Franklin's just crazy about her. *Why* I can't think.'

'She's got a very charming manner, I believe,' said Mr Satterthwaite cautiously.

'Do you know her?'

'Slightly.'

'I'm right down worried about Franklin,' said Miss Martin. 'That boy's got a lot of sense as a rule. You'd never think he'd fall for this sort of siren stuff. And he won't hear a thing, he gets madder than a hornet if anyone tries to say a word to him. Tell me, anyway—is she a real Countess?'

'I shouldn't like to say,' said Mr Satterthwaite. 'She may be.'

'That's the real Ha Ha English manner,' said Elizabeth with signs of displeasure. 'All I can say is that in Sargon Springs—that's our home town, Mr Satterthwaite—that Countess would look a mighty queer bird.'

Mr Satterthwaite thought it possible. He forebore to point out that they were not in Sargon Springs but in the principality of Monaco, where the Countess happened to synchronize with her environment a great deal better than Miss Martin did.

He made no answer and Elizabeth went on towards the Casino. Mr Satterthwaite sat on a seat in the sun, and was presently joined by Franklin Rudge.

Rudge was full of enthusiasm.

'I'm enjoying myself,' he announced with naïve enthusiasm. 'Yes, sir! This is what I call seeing life—rather a different kind of life from what we have in the States.'

The elder man turned a thoughtful face to him.

'Life is lived very much the same everywhere,' he said rather wearily. 'It wears different clothes—that's all.'

Franklin Rudge stared.

'I don't get you.'

'No,' said Mr Satterthwaite. 'That's because you've got a long way to travel yet. But I apologize. No elderly man should permit himself to get into the habit of preaching.'

'Oh! that's all right.' Rudge laughed, displaying the beautiful teeth of all his countrymen. 'I don't say, mind you, that I'm not disappointed in the Casino. I thought the gambling would be different—something much more feverish. It seems just rather dull and sordid to me.'

'Gambling is life and death to the gambler, but it has no great spectacular value,' said Mr Satterthwaite. 'It is more exciting to read about than to see.'

The young man nodded his agreement.

'You're by way of being rather a big bug socially, aren't you?' he asked with a diffident candour that made it impossible to take offence. 'I mean, you know all the Duchesses and Earls and Countesses and things.'

'A good many of them,' said Mr Satterthwaite. 'And also the Jews and the Portuguese and the Greeks and the Argentines.'

'Eh?' said Mr Rudge.

'I was just explaining,' said Mr Satterthwaite, 'that I move in English society.'

Franklin Rudge meditated for a moment or two.

'You know the Countess Czarnova, don't you?' he said at length.

'Slightly,' said Mr Satterthwaite, making the same answer he had made to Elizabeth.

'Now there's a woman whom it's been very interesting to meet. One's inclined to think that the aristocracy of Europe is played out and effete. That may be true of the men, but the women are different. Isn't it a pleasure to meet an exquisite creature like the Countess? Witty, charming, intelligent, generations of civilization behind her, an aristocrat to her finger-tips!'

'Is she?' asked Mr Satterthwaite.

'Well, isn't she? You know what her family are?'

'No,' said Mr Satterthwaite. 'I'm afraid I know very little about her.'

'She was a Radzynski,' explained Franklin Rudge. 'One of the oldest families in Hungary. She's had the most extraordinary life. You know that great rope of pearls she wears?'

Mr Satterthwaite nodded.

'That was given her by the King of Bosnia. She smuggled some secret papers out of the kingdom for him.'

'I heard,' said Mr Satterthwaite, 'that the pearls had been given her by the King of Bosnia.'

The fact was indeed a matter of common gossip, it being reported that the lady had been a *chère amie* of His Majesty's in days gone by.

'Now I'll tell you something more.'

Mr Satterthwaite listened, and the more he listened the more he admired the fertile imagination of the Countess Czarnova. No vulgar 'siren stuff' (as Elizabeth Martin had put it) for her. The young man was shrewd enough in that way, clean living and idealistic. No, the Countess moved austerely through a labyrinth of diplomatic intrigues. She had enemies, detractors—naturally! It was a glimpse, so the young American was made to feel, into the life of the old régime with the Countess as the central figure, aloof, aristocratic, the friend of counsellors and princes, a figure to inspire romantic devotion.

'And she's had any amount to contend against,' ended

the young man warmly. 'It's an extraordinary thing but she's never found a woman who would be a real friend to her. Women have been against her all her life.'

'Probably,' said Mr Satterthwaite.

'Don't you call it a scandalous thing?' demanded Rudge hotly.

'N—no,' said Mr Satterthwaite thoughtfully. 'I don't know that I do. Women have got their own standards, you know. It's no good our mixing ourselves up in their affairs. They must run their own show.'

'I don't agree with you,' said Rudge earnestly. 'It's one of the worst things in the world today, the unkindness of woman to woman. You know Elizabeth Martin? Now she agrees with me in theory absolutely. We've often discussed it together. She's only a kid, but her ideas are all right. But the moment it comes to a practical test—why, she's as bad as any of them. Got a real down on the Countess without knowing a darned thing about her, and won't listen when I try to tell her things. It's all *wrong,* Mr Satterthwaite. I believe in democracy—and—what's that but brotherhood between men and sisterhood between women?'

He paused earnestly. Mr Satterthwaite tried to think of any circumstances in which a sisterly feeling might arise between the Countess and Elizabeth Martin and failed.

'Now the Countess, on the other hand,' went on Rudge, 'admires Elizabeth immensely, and thinks her charming in every way. Now what does that show?'

'It shows,' said Mr Satterthwaite dryly, 'that the Countess has lived a considerable time longer than Miss Martin has.'

Franklin Rudge went off unexpectedly at a tangent.

'Do you know how old she is? She told me. Rather sporting of her. I should have guessed her to be twenty-nine, but she told me of her own accord that she was thirty-five. She doesn't look it, does she?'

Mr Satterthwaite, whose private estimate of the lady's age was between forty-five and forty-nine, merely raised his eyebrows.

'I should caution you against believing all you are told at Monte Carlo,' he murmured.

He had enough experience to know the futility of arguing with the lad. Franklin Rudge was at a pitch of white hot chivalry when he would have disbelieved any statement that was not backed with authoritative proof.

'Here is the Countess,' said the boy, rising.

She came up to them with the languid grace that so became her. Presently they all three sat down together. She was very charming to Mr Satterthwaite, but in rather an aloof manner. She deferred to him prettily, asking his opinion, and treating him as an authority on the Riviera.

The whole thing was cleverly managed. Very few minutes had elapsed before Franklin Rudge found himself gracefully but unmistakably dismissed, and the Countess and Mr Satterthwaite were left *tête-à-tête*.

She put down her parasol and began drawing patterns with it in the dust.

'You are interested in the nice American boy, Mr Satterthwaite, are you not?'

Her voice was low with a caressing note in it.

'He's a nice young fellow,' said Mr Satterthwaite, noncommittally.

'I find him sympathetic, yes,' said the Countess reflectively. 'I have told him much of my life.'

'Indeed,' said Mr Satterthwaite.

'Details such as I have told to few others,' she continued dreamily. 'I have had an extraordinary life, Mr Satterthwaite. Few would credit the amazing things that have happened to me.'

Mr Satterthwaite was shrewd enough to penetrate her meaning. After all, the stories that she had told to Franklin Rudge *might* be the truth. It was extremely unlikely, and in the last degree improbable, but it was *possible* . . . No one could definitely say: 'That is not so—'

He did not reply, and the Countess continued to look out dreamily across the bay.

And suddenly Mr Satterthwaite had a strange and new impression of her. He saw her no longer as a harpy, but as a desperate creature at bay, fighting tooth and nail. He stole a sideways glance at her. The parasol was down, he could see the little haggard lines at the corners of her eyes. In one temple a pulse was beating.

It flowed through him again and again—that increasing certitude. She was a creature desperate and driven. She would be merciless to him or to anyone who stood between her and Franklin Rudge. But he still felt he hadn't got the hang of the situation. Clearly she had plenty of money. She was always beautifully dressed, and her jewels were marvellous. There could be no real urgency of that kind. Was it love? Women of her age did, he well knew, fall in love with boys. It might be that. There was, he felt sure, something out of the common about the situation.

Her *tête-à-tête* with him was, he recognized, a throwing down of the gauntlet. She had singled him out as her chief enemy. He felt sure that she hoped to goad him into speaking slightingly of her to Franklin Rudge. Mr Satterthwaite smiled to himself. He was too old a bird for that. He knew when it was wise to hold one's tongue.

He watched her that night in the Cercle Privé, as she tried her fortunes at roulette.

Again and again she staked, only to see her stake swept away. She bore her losses well, with the stoical *sang froid* of the old *habitué*. She staked *en plein* once or twice, put the maximum on red, won a little on the middle dozen and then lost it again, finally she backed *manque* six times and lost every time. Then with a little graceful shrug of the shoulders she turned away.

She was looking unusually striking in a dress of gold tissue with an underlying note of green. The famous Bosnian pearls were looped round her neck and long pearl ear-rings hung from her ears.

Mr Satterthwaite heard two men near him appraise her.

'The Czarnova,' said one, 'she wears well, does she not? The Crown jewels of Bosnia look fine on her.'

The other, a small Jewish-looking man, stared curiously after her.

'So those are the pearls of Bosnia, are they?' he asked. '*En vérité*. That is odd.'

He chuckled softly to himself.

Mr Satterthwaite missed hearing more, for at the moment he turned his head and was overjoyed to recognize an old friend.

'My dear Mr Quin.' He shook him warmly by the

hand. 'The last place I should ever have dreamed of seeing you.'

Mr Quin smiled, his dark attractive face lighting up.

'It should not surprise you,' he said. 'It is Carnival time. I am often here in Carnival time.'

'Really? Well, this is a great pleasure. Are you anxious to remain in the rooms? I find them rather warm.'

'It will be pleasanter outside,' agreed the other. 'We will walk in the gardens.'

The air outside was sharp, but not chill. Both men drew deep breaths.

'That is better,' said Mr Satterthwaite.

'Much better,' agreed Mr Quin. 'And we can talk freely. I am sure that there is much that you want to tell me.'

'There is indeed.'

Speaking eagerly, Mr Satterthwaite unfolded his perplexities. As usual he took pride in his power of conveying atmosphere. The Countess, young Franklin, uncompromising Elizabeth—he sketched them all in with a deft touch.

'You have changed since I first knew you,' said Mr Quin, smiling, when the recital was over.

'In what way?'

'You were content then to look on at the drama that life offered. Now—you want to take part—to act.'

'It is true,' confessed Mr Satterthwaite. 'But in this case I do not know what to do. It is all very perplexing. Perhaps—' He hesitated. 'Perhaps you will help me?'

'With pleasure,' said Mr Quin. 'We will see what we can do.'

Mr Satterthwaite had an odd sense of comfort and reliance.

The following day he introduced Franklin Rudge and Elizabeth Martin to his friend Mr Harley Quin. He was pleased to see that they got on together. The Countess was not mentioned, but at lunch time he heard news that aroused his attention.

'Mirabelle is arriving in Monte this evening,' he confided excitedly to Mr Quin.

'The Parisian stage favourite?'

'Yes. I daresay you know—it's common property—she is the King of Bosnia's latest craze. He has showered jewels on her, I believe. They say she is the most exacting and extravagant woman in Paris.'

'It should be interesting to see her and the Countess Czarnova meet tonight.'

'Exactly what I thought.'

Mirabelle was a tall, thin creature with a wonderful head of dyed fair hair. Her complexion was a pale mauve with orange lips. She was amazingly chic. She was dressed in something that looked like a glorified bird of paradise, and she wore chains of jewels hanging down her bare back. A heavy bracelet set with immense diamonds clasped her left ankle.

She created a sensation when she appeared in the Casino.

'Your friend the Countess will have a difficulty in outdoing this,' murmured Mr Quin in Mr Satterthwaite's ear.

The latter nodded. He was curious to see how the Countess comported herself.

She came late, and a low murmur ran round as she walked unconcernedly to one of the centre roulette tables.

She was dressed in white—a mere straight slip of maro-cain such as a débutante might have worn and her gleaming white neck and arms were unadorned. She wore not a single jewel.

'It is clever, that,' said Mr Satterthwaite with instant approval. 'She disdains rivalry and turns the tables on her adversary.'

He himself walked over and stood by the table. From time to time he amused himself by placing a stake. Sometimes he won, more often he lost.

There was a terrific run on the last dozen. The numbers 31 and 34 turned up again and again. Stakes flocked to the bottom of the cloth.

With a smile Mr Satterthwaite made his last stake for the evening, and placed the maximum on Number 5.

The Countess in her turn leant forward and placed the maximum on Number 6.

'*Faites vos jeux*,' called the croupier hoarsely. '*Rien ne va plus. Plus rien.*'

The ball span, humming merrily. Mr Satterthwaite thought to himself: '*This means something different to each of us. Agonies of hope and despair, boredom, idle amusement, life and death.*'

Click!

The croupier bent forward to see.

'*Numéro cinque, rouge, impair et manque.*'

Mr Satterthwaite had won!

The croupier, having raked in the other stakes, pushed forward Mr Satterthwaite's winnings. He put out his hand to take them. The Countess did the same. The croupier looked from one to the other of them.

'A *madame*,' he said brusquely.

The Countess picked up the money. Mr Satterthwaite drew back. He remained a gentleman. The Countess looked him full in the face and he returned her glance. One or two of the people round pointed out to the croupier that he had made a mistake, but the man shook his head impatiently. He had decided. That was the end. He raised his raucous cry:

'Faites vos jeux, Messieurs et Mesdames.'

Mr Satterthwaite rejoined Mr Quin. Beneath his impeccable demeanour, he was feeling extremely indignant. Mr Quin listened sympathetically.

'Too bad,' he said, 'but these things happen.

'We are to meet your friend Franklin Rudge later. I am giving a little supper party.'

The three met at midnight, and Mr Quin explained his plan.

'It is what is called a "Hedges and Highways" party,' he explained. 'We choose our meeting place, then each one goes out and is bound in honour to invite the first person he meets.'

Franklin Rudge was amused by the idea.

'Say, what happens if they won't accept?'

'You must use your utmost powers of persuasion.'

'Good. And where's the meeting place?'

'A somewhat Bohemian café—where one can take strange guests. It is called Le Caveau.'

He explained its whereabouts, and the three parted. Mr Satterthwaite was so fortunate as to run straight into Elizabeth Martin and he claimed her joyfully. They reached Le Caveau and descended into a kind of cellar where they found a table spread for supper and lit by old-fashioned candles in candlesticks.

'We are the first,' said Mr Satterthwaite. 'Ah! here comes Franklin—'

He stopped abruptly. With Franklin was the Countess. It was an awkward moment. Elizabeth displayed less graciousness than she might have done. The Countess, as a woman of the world, retained the honours.

Last of all came Mr Quin. With him was a small, dark man, neatly dressed, whose face seemed familiar to Mr Satterthwaite. A moment later he recognized him. It was the croupier who earlier in the evening had made such a lamentable mistake.

'Let me introduce you to the company, M. Pierre Vaucher,' said Mr Quin.

The little man seemed confused. Mr Quin performed the necessary introductions easily and lightly. Supper was brought—an excellent supper. Wine came—very excellent wine. Some of the frigidity went out of the atmosphere. The Countess was very silent, so was Elizabeth. Franklin Rudge became talkative. He told various stories—not humorous stories, but serious ones. And quietly and assiduously Mr Quin passed round the wine.

'I'll tell you—and this is a true story—about a man who made good,' said Franklin Rudge impressively.

For one coming from a Prohibition country he had shown no lack of appreciation of champagne.

He told his story—perhaps at somewhat unnecessary length. It was, like many true stories, greatly inferior to fiction.

As he uttered the last word, Pierre Vaucher, opposite him, seemed to wake up. He also had done justice to the champagne. He leaned forward across the table.

'I, too, will tell you a story,' he said thickly. 'But mine

is the story of a man who did not make good. It is the story of a man who went, not up, but down the hill. And, like yours, it is a true story.'

'Pray tell it to us, monsieur,' said Mr Satterthwaite courteously.

Pierre Vaucher leant back in his chair and looked at the ceiling.

'It is in Paris that the story begins. There was a man there, a working jeweller. He was young and light-hearted and industrious in his profession. They said there was a future before him. A good marriage was already arranged for him, the bride not too bad-looking, the dowry most satisfactory. And then, what do you think? One morning he sees a girl. Such a miserable little wisp of a girl, messieurs. Beautiful? Yes, perhaps, if she were not half starved. But anyway, for this young man, she has a magic that he cannot resist. She has been struggling to find work, she is virtuous—or at least that is what she tells him. I do not know if it is true.'

The Countess's voice came suddenly out of the semi-darkness.

'Why should it not be true? There are many like that.'

'Well, as I say, the young man believed her. And he married her—an act of folly! His family would have no more to say to him. He had outraged their feelings. He married—I will call her Jeanne—it was a good action. He told her so. He felt that she should be very grateful to him. He had sacrificed much for her sake.'

'A charming beginning for the poor girl,' observed the Countess sarcastically.

'He loved her, yes, but from the beginning she maddened him. She had moods—tantrums—she would be cold to him one day, passionate the next. At last he saw the truth. She had never loved him. She had married him so as to keep body and soul together. That truth hurt him, it hurt him horribly, but he tried his utmost to let nothing appear on the surface. And he still felt he deserved gratitude and obedience to his wishes. They quarrelled. She reproached him—Mon Dieu, what did she not reproach him with?

'You can see the next step, can you not? The thing that was bound to come. She left him. For two years he was alone, working in his little shop with no news of her. He had one friend—absinthe. The business did not prosper so well.

'And then one day he came into the shop to find her sitting there. She was beautifully dressed. She had rings on her hands. He stood considering her. His heart was beating—but beating! He was at a loss what to do. He would have liked to have beaten her, to have clasped her in his arms, to have thrown her down on the floor and trampled on her, to have thrown himself at her feet. He did none of those things. He took up his pincers and went on with his work. "Madame desires?" he asked formally.

'That upset her. She did not look for that, see you. "Pierre," she said, "I have come back." He laid aside his pincers and looked at her. "You wish to be forgiven?" he said. "You want me to take you back? You are sincerely repentant?" "Do you want me back?" she murmured. Oh! very softly she said it.

'He knew she was laying a trap for him. He longed to seize her in his arms, but he was too clever for that. He pretended indifference.

'"I am a Christian man," he said. "I try to do what the Church directs." "Ah!" he thought, "I will humble her, humble her to her knees."

'But Jeanne, that is what I will call her, flung back her head and laughed. Evil laughter it was. "I mock myself at you, little Pierre," she said. "Look at these rich clothes, these rings and bracelets. I came to show myself to you. I thought I would make you take me in your arms and when you did so, then—*then* I would spit in your face and tell you how I hated you!"

'And on that she went out of the shop. Can you believe, messieurs, that a woman could be as evil as all that—to come back only to torment me?'

'No,' said the Countess. 'I would not believe it, and any man who was not a fool would not believe it either. But all men are blind fools.'

Pierre Vaucher took no notice of her. He went on.

'And so that young man of whom I tell you sank lower and lower. He drank more absinthe. The little shop was sold over his head. He became of the dregs, of the gutter. Then came the war. Ah! it was good, the war. It took that man out of the gutter and taught him to be a brute beast no longer. It drilled him—and sobered him. He endured cold and pain and the fear of death—but he did not die and when the war ended, he was a man again.

'It was then, messieurs, that he came South. His lungs had been affected by the gas, they said he must find work in the South. I will not weary you with all the things he did. Suffice it to say that he ended up as a croupier, and there—there in the Casino one evening, he saw her again—the woman who had ruined his life. She did not recognize him, but he recognized her. She appeared to be rich and to lack for nothing—but messieurs, the eyes of a croupier are sharp. There came an evening when she placed her last stake in the world on the table. Ask me not how I know—I do know—one feels these things. Others might not believe. She still had rich clothes— why not pawn them, one would say? But to do that— pah! your credit is gone at once. Her jewels? Ah no! Was I not a jeweller in my time? Long ago the real jewels have gone. The pearls of a King are sold one by one, are replaced with false. And meantime one must eat and pay one's hotel bill. Yes, and the rich men—well, they have seen one about for many years. Bah! they say—she is over fifty. A younger chicken for my money.'

A long shuddering sigh came out of the windows where the Countess leant back.

'Yes. It was a great moment, that. Two nights I have watched her. Lose, lose, and lose again. And now the end. She put all on one number. Beside her, an English milord stakes the maximum also—on the next number. The ball rolls . . . The moment has come, she has lost . . .

'Her eyes meet mine. What do I do? I jeopardize my place in the Casino. I rob the English milord. *"à Madame"* I say, and pay over the money.'

'Ah!' There was a crash, as the Countess sprang to her feet and leant across the table, sweeping her glass on to the floor.

'Why?' she cried. 'That's what I want to know, *why* did you do it?'

There was a long pause, a pause that seemed interminable, and still those two facing each other across the table looked and looked . . . It was like a duel.

A mean little smile crept across Pierre Vaucher's face. He raised his hands.

'Madame,' he said, 'there is such a thing as pity . . .'

'Ah!'

She sank down again.

'I see.'

She was calm, smiling, herself again.

'An interesting story, M. Vaucher, is it not? Permit me to give you a light for your cigarette.'

She deftly rolled up a spill, and lighted it at the candle and held it towards him. He leaned forward till the flame caught the tip of the cigarette he held between his lips.

Then she rose unexpectedly to her feet.

'And now I must leave you all. Please—I need no one to escort me.'

Before one could realize it she was gone. Mr Satterthwaite would have hurried out after her, but he was arrested by a startled oath from the Frenchman.

'A thousand thunders!'

He was staring at the half-burned spill which the Countess had dropped on the table. He unrolled it.

'Mon Dieu!' he muttered. 'A fifty thousand franc bank note. You understand? Her winnings tonight. All that she had in the world. And she lighted my cigarette with it! Because she was too proud to accept—pity. Ah! proud, she was always proud as the Devil. She is unique—wonderful.'

He sprang up from his seat and darted out. Mr Satterthwaite and Mr Quin had also risen. The waiter approached Franklin Rudge.

'La note, monsieur,' he observed unemotionally.

Mr Quin rescued it from him quickly.

'I feel kind of lonesome, Elizabeth,' remarked Franklin Rudge. 'These foreigners—they beat the band! I don't understand them. What's it all mean, anyhow?'

He looked across at her.

'Gee, it's good to look at anything so hundred per cent American as you.' His voice took on the plaintive note of a small child. 'These foreigners are so *odd*.'

They thanked Mr Quin and went out into the night together. Mr Quin picked up his change and smiled across at Mr Satterthwaite, who was preening himself like a contented bird.

'Well,' said the latter. 'That's all gone off splendidly. Our pair of love birds will be all right now.'

'Which ones?' asked Mr Quin.

'Oh!' said Mr Satterthwaite, taken aback. 'Oh! yes, well, I suppose you are right, allowing for the Latin point of view and all that—'

He looked dubious.

Mr Quin smiled, and a stained glass panel behind him invested him for just a moment in a motley garment of coloured light.

The Stymphalean Birds

Harold Waring noticed them first walking up the path from the lake. He was sitting outside the hotel on the terrace. The day was fine, the lake was blue, and the sun shone. Harold was smoking a pipe and feeling that the world was a pretty good place.

His political career was shaping well. An under-secretaryship at the age of thirty was something to be justly proud of. It had been reported that the Prime Minister had said to someone that 'young Waring would go far'. Harold was, not unnaturally, elated. Life presented itself to him in rosy colours. He was young, sufficiently good-looking, in first-class condition, and quite unencumbered with romantic ties.

He had decided to take a holiday in Herzoslovakia so as to get right off the beaten track and have a real rest from everyone and everything. The hotel at Lake Stempka, though small, was comfortable and not overcrowded. The few people there were mostly foreigners. So far the only other English people were an elderly woman, Mrs Rice, and her married daughter, Mrs Clayton. Harold liked them both. Elsie Clayton was pretty in a rather old-fashioned style. She made up very little, if at all, and was gentle and rather shy. Mrs Rice was what is called a woman of character. She was tall, with a deep voice and a masterful manner, but she had a sense of humour and was good company. Her life was clearly bound up in that of her daughter.

Harold had spent some pleasant hours in the company of mother and daughter, but they did not attempt to monopolize him and relations remained friendly and unexacting between them.

The other people in the hotel had not aroused Harold's notice. Usually they were hikers, or members of a motor-coach tour. They stayed a night or two and then went on. He had hardly noticed any one else—until this afternoon.

They came up the path from the lake very slowly and it just happened that at the moment when Harold's attention was attracted to them, a cloud came over the sun. He shivered a little.

Then he stared. Surely there was something odd about these two women? They had long, curved noses, like birds, and their faces, which were curiously alike, were quite immobile. Over their shoulders they wore loose cloaks that flapped in the wind like the wings of two big birds.

Harold thought to himself.

'They *are* like birds—' he added almost without volition, *'birds of ill omen.'*

The women came straight up on the terrace and passed close by him. They were not young—perhaps nearer fifty than forty, and the resemblance between them was so close that they were obviously sisters. Their expression was forbidding. As they passed Harold the eyes of both of them rested on him for a minute. It was a curious, appraising glance—almost inhuman.

Harold's impression of evil grew stronger. He noticed the hand of one of the two sisters, a long claw-like hand... Although the sun had come out, he shivered once again.

He thought:

'Horrible creatures. Like birds of prey...'

He was distracted from these imaginings by the emergence of Mrs Rice from the hotel. He jumped up and drew forward a chair. With a word of thanks she sat down and, as usual, began to knit vigorously.

Harold asked:

'Did you see those two women who just went into the hotel?'

'With cloaks on? Yes, I passed them.'

'Extraordinary creatures, didn't you think?'

'Well—yes, perhaps they are rather odd. They only arrived yesterday, I think. Very alike—they must be twins.'

Harold said:

'I may be fanciful, but I distinctly felt there was something evil about them.'

'How curious. I must look at them more closely and see if I agree with you.'

She added: 'We'll find out from the concierge who they are. Not English, I imagine?'

'Oh no.'

Mrs Rice glanced at her watch. She said:

'Tea-time. I wonder if you'd mind going in and ringing the bell, Mr Waring?'

'Certainly, Mrs Rice.'

He did so and then as he returned to his seat he asked:

'Where's your daughter this afternoon?'

'Elsie? We went for a walk together. Part of the way round the lake and then back through the pinewoods. It really was lovely.'

A waiter came out and received orders for tea. Mrs Rice went on, her needles flying vigorously:

'Elsie had a letter from her husband. She mayn't come down to tea.'

'Her husband?' Harold was surprised. 'Do you know, I always thought she was a widow.'

Mrs Rice shot him a sharp glance. She said drily:

'Oh no, Elsie isn't a widow.' She added with emphasis: 'Unfortunately!'

Harold was startled.

Mrs Rice, nodding her head grimly, said:

'Drink is responsible for a lot of unhappiness, Mr Waring.'

'Does he drink?'

'Yes. And a good many other things as well. He's insanely jealous and has a singularly violent temper.' She sighed. 'It's a difficult world, Mr Waring. I'm devoted to Elsie, she's my only child—and to see her unhappy isn't an easy thing to bear.'

Harold said with real emotion:

'She's such a gentle creature.'

'A little too gentle, perhaps.'

'You mean—'

Mrs Rice said slowly:

'A happy creature is more arrogant. Elsie's gentleness

comes, I think, from a sense of defeat. Life has been too much for her.'

Harold said with some slight hesitation:

'How—did she come to marry this husband of hers?'

Mrs Rice answered:

'Philip Clayton was a very attractive person. He had (still has) great charm, he had a certain amount of money—and there was no one to advise us of his real character. I had been a widow for many years. Two women, living alone, are not the best judges of a man's character.'

Harold said thoughtfully:

'No, that's true.'

He felt a wave of indignation and pity sweep over him. Elsie Clayton could not be more than twenty-five at the most. He recalled the clear friendliness of her blue eyes, the soft droop of her mouth. He realized, suddenly, that his interest in her went a little beyond friendship.

And she was tied to a brute.

II

That evening, Harold joined mother and daughter after dinner. Elsie Clayton was wearing a soft dull pink dress. Her eyelids, he noticed, were red. She had been crying.

Mrs Rice said briskly:

'I've found out who your two harpies are, Mr Waring. Polish ladies—of very good family, so the concierge says.'

Harold looked across the room to where the Polish ladies were sitting. Elsie said with interest:

'Those two women over there? With the henna-dyed hair? They look rather horrible somehow—I don't know why.'

Harold said triumphantly:

'That's just what I thought.'

Mrs Rice said with a laugh:

'I think you are both being absurd. You can't possibly tell what people are like just by looking at them.'

Elsie laughed.

She said:

'I suppose one can't. All the same *I* think they're vultures!'

'Picking out dead men's eyes!' said Harold.

'Oh, don't,' cried Elsie.

Harold said quickly:

'Sorry.'

Mrs Rice said with a smile:

'Anyway they're not likely to cross *our* path.'

Elsie said:

'*We* haven't got any guilty secrets!'

'Perhaps Mr Waring has,' said Mrs Rice with a twinkle. Harold laughed, throwing his head back.

He said:

'Not a secret in the world. My life's an open book.'

And it flashed across his mind:

'What fools people are who leave the straight path. A clear conscience—that's all one needs in life. With that you can face the world and tell everyone who interferes with you to go to the devil!'

He felt suddenly very much alive—very strong—very much master of his fate!

III

Harold Waring, like many other Englishmen, was a bad linguist. His French was halting and decidedly British in intonation. Of German and Italian he knew nothing.

Up to now, these linguistic disabilities had not worried him. In most hotels on the Continent, he had always found, everyone spoke English, so why worry?

But in this out-of-the-way spot, where the native language was a form of Slovak and even the concierge only spoke German it was sometimes galling to Harold when one of his two women friends acted as interpreter for him. Mrs Rice, who was fond of languages, could even speak a little Slovak.

Harold determined that he would set about learning German. He decided to buy some text books and spend a couple of hours each morning in mastering the language.

The morning was fine and after writing some letters, Harold looked at his watch and saw that there was still time for an hour's stroll before lunch. He went down towards the lake and then turned aside into the pine woods. He had walked there for perhaps five minutes when he heard an unmistakable sound. Somewhere not far away a woman was sobbing her heart out.

Harold paused a minute, then he went in the direction of the sound. The woman was Elsie Clayton and she was sitting on a fallen tree with her face buried in her hands and her shoulders quivering with the violence of her grief.

Harold hesitated a minute, then he came up to her. He said gently:

'Mrs Clayton—Elsie?'

She started violently and looked up at him. Harold sat down beside her.

He said with real sympathy:

'Is there anything I can do? Anything at all?'

She shook her head.

'No—no—you're very kind. But there's nothing that anyone can do for me.'

Harold said rather diffidently:

'Is it to do with—your husband?'

She nodded. Then she wiped her eyes and took out her powder compact, struggling to regain command of herself. She said in a quavering voice:

'I didn't want Mother to worry. She's so upset when she sees me unhappy. So I came out here to have a good cry. It's silly, I know. Crying doesn't help. But—sometimes—one just feels that life is quite unbearable.'

Harold said:

'I'm terribly sorry.'

She threw him a grateful glance. Then she said hurriedly:

'It's my own fault, of course. I married Philip of my own free will. It—it's turned out badly, I've only myself to blame.'

Harold said:

'It's very plucky of you to put it like that.'

Elsie shook her head.

'No, I'm not plucky. I'm not brave at all. I'm an awful coward. That's partly the trouble with Philip. I'm terrified of him—absolutely terrified—when he gets in one of his rages.'

Harold said with feeling:

'You ought to leave him!'

'I daren't. He—he wouldn't let me.'

'Nonsense! What about a divorce?'

She shook her head slowly.

'I've no grounds.' She straightened her shoulders. 'No, I've got to carry on. I spend a fair amount of time with Mother, you know. Philip doesn't mind that. Especially when we go somewhere off the beaten track like this.' She added, the colour rising in her cheeks, 'You see, part of the trouble is that he's insanely jealous. If—if I so much as speak to another man he makes the most frightful scenes.'

Harold's indignation rose. He had heard many women complain of the jealousy of a husband, and whilst professing sympathy, had been secretly of the opinion that the husband was amply justified. But Elsie Clayton was not one of those women. She had never thrown him so much as a flirtatious glance.

Elsie drew away from him with a slight shiver. She glanced up at the sky.

'The sun's gone in. It's quite cold. We'd better get back to the hotel. It must be nearly lunch time.'

They got up and turned in the direction of the hotel. They had walked for perhaps a minute when they overtook a figure going in the same direction. They recognized her by the flapping cloak she wore. It was one of the Polish sisters.

They passed her, Harold bowing slightly. She made no response but her eyes rested on them both for a minute and there was a certain appraising quality in the glance which made Harold feel suddenly hot. He wondered if the woman had seen him sitting by Elsie on the tree trunk. If so, she probably thought...

Well, she looked as though she thought. A wave of indignation overwhelmed him! What foul minds some women had!

Odd that the sun had gone in and that they should both have shivered—perhaps just at the moment that that woman was watching them...

Somehow, Harold felt a little uneasy.

IV

That evening, Harold went to his room a little after ten. The English maid had arrived and he had received a number of letters, some of which needed immediate answers.

He got into his pyjamas and a dressing-gown and sat down at the desk to deal with his correspondence. He had written three letters and was just starting on the fourth when the door was suddenly flung open and Elsie Clayton staggered into the room.

Harold jumped up, startled. Elsie had pushed the door to behind her and was standing clutching at the chest of drawers. Her breath was coming in great gasps, her face was the colour of chalk. She looked frightened to death.

She gasped out: 'It's my husband! He arrived unexpectedly. I—I think he'll kill me. He's mad—quite mad. I came to you. Don't—don't let him find me.'

She took a step or two forward, swaying so much that she almost fell. Harold put out an arm to support her.

As he did so, the door was flung open and a man stood in the doorway. He was of medium height with thick eyebrows and a sleek, dark head. In his hand he carried a heavy car spanner. His voice rose high and shook with rage. He almost screamed the words.

'So that Polish woman was right! You *are* carrying on with this fellow!'

Elsie cried:

'No, no, Philip. It's not true. You're wrong.'

Harold thrust the girl swiftly behind him, as Philip Clayton advanced on them both. The latter cried:

'Wrong, am I? When I find you here in his room? You she-devil, I'll kill you for this.'

With a swift, sideways movement he dodged Harold's arm. Elsie, with a cry, ran round the other side of Harold, who swung round to fend the other off.

But Philip Clayton had only one idea, to get at his wife. He swerved round again. Elsie, terrified, rushed out of the room. Philip Clayton dashed after her, and Harold, with not a moment's hesitation, followed him.

Elsie had darted back into her own bedroom at the end of the corridor. Harold could hear the sound of the key turning in the lock, but it did not turn in time. Before the lock could catch Philip Clayton wrenched the door open. He disappeared into the room and Harold heard Elsie's frightened cry. In another minute Harold burst in after them.

Elsie was standing at bay against the curtains of the window. As Harold entered Philip Clayton rushed at her brandishing the spanner. She gave a terrified cry, then snatching up a heavy paper-weight from the desk beside her, she flung it at him.

Clayton went down like a log. Elsie screamed. Harold stopped petrified in the doorway. The girl fell on her knees beside her husband. He lay quite still where he had fallen.

Outside in the passage, there was the sound of the bolt of one of the doors being drawn back. Elsie jumped up and ran to Harold.

'Please—please—' Her voice was low and breathless. 'Go back to your room. They'll come—they'll find you here.'

Harold nodded. He took in the situation like lightning. For the moment, Philip Clayton was *hors de combat*. But Elsie's scream might have been heard. If he were found in her room it could only cause embarrassment and misunderstanding. Both for her sake and his own there must be no scandal.

As noislessly as possible, he sprinted down the passage and back into his room. Just as he reached it, he heard the sound of an opening door.

He sat in his room for nearly half an hour, waiting. He dared not go out. Sooner or later, he felt sure, Elsie would come.

There was a light tap on his door. Harold jumped up to open it.

It was not Elsie who came in but her mother and Harold was aghast at her appearance. She looked suddenly years older. Her grey hair was dishevelled and there were deep black circles under her eyes.

He sprang up and helped her to a chair. She sat down, her breath coming painfully. Harold said quickly:

'You look all in, Mrs Rice. Can I get you something?'

She shook her head.

'No. Never mind me. I'm all right, really. It's only the shock. Mr Waring, a terrible thing has happened.'

Harold asked:

'Is Clayton seriously injured?'

She caught her breath.

'Worse than that. *He's dead...*'

V

The room spun round.

A feeling as of icy water trickling down his spine rendered Harold incapable of speech for a moment or two.

He repeated dully:

'Dead?'

Mrs Rice nodded.

She said, and her voice had the flat level tones of complete exhaustion:

'The corner of that marble paper-weight caught him right on the temple and he fell back with his head on the iron fender. I don't know which it was that killed him—but he is certainly dead. I have seen death often enough to know.'

Disaster—that was the word that rang insistently in Harold's brain. Disaster, disaster, disaster...

He said vehemently:

'It was an accident. I saw it happen.'

Mrs Rice said sharply:

'Of course it was an accident. *I* know that. But—but—is anyone else going to think so? I'm—frankly, I'm frightened, Harold! This isn't England.'

Harold said slowly:

'I can confirm Elsie's story.'

Mrs Rice said:

'Yes, and she can confirm yours. That—that is just it!'

Harold's brain, naturally a keen and cautious one, saw her point. He reviewed the whole thing and appreciated the weakness of their position.

He and Elsie had spent a good deal of their time together. Then there was the fact that they had been seen together in the pinewoods by one of the Polish women under rather compromising circumstances. The Polish ladies apparently spoke no English, but they might nevertheless understand it a little. The woman might have known the meaning of words like 'jealousy' and 'husband' if she had chanced to overhear their conversation. Anyway it was clear that it was something she had said to Clayton that had aroused his jealousy. And now—his death. When Clayton had died, he, Harold, *had been in Elsie Clayton's room*. There was nothing to show that he had not deliberately assaulted Philip Clayton with the paper-weight. Nothing to show that the jealous husband had not actually found them together. There was only his word and Elsie's. Would they be believed?

A cold fear gripped him.

He did not imagine—no, he really did *not* imagine—that either he or Elsie was in danger of being condemned to death for a murder they had not committed. Surely, in any case, it could be only a charge of manslaughter brought against them. (Did they have manslaughter in these foreign countries?) But even if they were acquitted of blame there would have to be an inquiry—it would be reported in all the papers. *An English man and woman accused—jealous husband—rising politician.* Yes, it would mean the end of his political career. It would never survive a scandal like that.

He said on an impulse:

'Can't we get rid of the body somehow? Plant it somewhere?'

Mrs Rice's astonished and scornful look made him blush. She said incisively:

'My dear Harold, this isn't a detective story! To attempt a thing like that would be quite crazy.'

'I suppose it would.' He groaned. 'What can we do? My God, what can we do?'

Mrs Rice shook her head despairingly. She was frowning, her mind working painfully.

Harold demanded:

'Isn't there anything we can do? Anything to avoid this frightful disaster?'

There, it was out—disaster! Terrible—unforeseen—utterly damning.

They stared at each other. Mrs Rice said hoarsely:

'Elsie—my little girl. I'd do anything. It will kill her if she has to go through a thing like this.' And she added: 'You too, your career—everything.'

Harold managed to say:

'Never mind me.'

But he did not really mean it.

Mrs Rice went on bitterly:

'And all so unfair—so utterly untrue! It's not as though there had ever been anything between you. *I* know that well enough.'

Harold suggested, catching at a straw:

'You'll be able to say that at least—that it was all perfectly all right.'

Mrs Rice said bitterly:

'Yes, if they believe me. But you know what these people out here are like!'

Harold agreed gloomily. To the Continental mind, there would undoubtedly be a guilty connection between himself and Elsie, and all Mrs Rice's denials would be taken as a mother lying herself black in the face for her daughter.

Harold said gloomily:

'Yes, we're not in England, worse luck.'

'Ah!' Mrs Rice lifted her head. *'That's* true... It's not England. I wonder now if something *could* be done—'

'Yes?' Harold looked at her eagerly.

Mrs Rice said abruptly:

'How much money have you got?'

'Not much with me.' He added, 'I could wire for money, of course.'

Mrs Rice said grimly:

'We may need a good deal. But I think it's worth trying.'

Harold felt a faint lifting of despair. He said:

'What is your idea?'

Mrs Rice spoke decisively.

'We haven't a chance of concealing the death *ourselves,* but I do think there's just a chance of hushing it up *officially!*'

'You really think so?' Harold was hopeful but slightly incredulous.

'Yes, for one thing the manager of the hotel will be on our side. He'd much rather have the thing hushed up. It's my opinion that in these out of the way curious little Balkan countries you can bribe anyone and everyone—and the police are probably more corrupt than anyone else!'

Harold said slowly:

'Do you know, I believe you're right.'

Mrs Rice went on:

'Fortunately, I don't think anyone in the hotel *heard* anything.'

'Who has the room next to Elsie's on the other side from yours?'

'The two Polish ladies. They didn't hear anything. They'd have come out into the passage if they had. Philip arrived late, nobody saw him but the night porter. Do you know, Harold, I believe it will be possible to hush the whole thing up—and get Philip's death certified as due to natural causes! It's just a question of bribing high enough—and finding the right man—probably the Chief of Police!'

Harold smiled faintly. He said:

'It's rather Comic Opera, isn't it? Well, after all, we can but try.'

VI

Mrs Rice was energy personified. First the manager was summoned. Harold remained in his room, keeping out of it. He and Mrs Rice had agreed that the story told had better be that of a quarrel between husband and wife. Elsie's youth and prettiness would command more sympathy.

On the following morning various police officials arrived and were shown up to Mrs Rice's bedroom. They left at midday. Harold had wired for money but otherwise had taken no part in the proceedings—indeed he would have been unable to do so since none of these official personages spoke English.

At twelve o'clock Mrs Rice came to his room. She looked white and tired, but the relief on her face told its own story. She said simply:

'It's worked!'

'Thank heaven! You've been really marvellous! It seems incredible!'

Mrs Rice said thoughtfully:

'By the ease with which it went, you might almost think it was quite normal. They practically held out their hands right away. It's—it's rather disgusting, really!'

Harold said dryly:

'This isn't the moment to quarrel with the corruption of the public services. How much?'

'The tariff's rather high.'

She read out a list of figures.

'The Chief of Police.
The *Commissaire*.
The *Agent*.
The Doctor.
The Hotel Manager.
The Night Porter.'

Harold's comment was merely:

'The night porter doesn't get much, does he? I suppose it's mostly a question of gold lace.'

Mrs Rice explained:

'The manager stipulated that the death should not have taken place in his hotel at all. The official story will be that Philip had a heart attack in the train. He went along the corridor for air—you know how they always leave those doors open—and he fell out on the line. It's wonderful what the police can do when they try!'

'Well,' said Harold. 'Thank God *our* police force isn't like that.'

And in a British and superior mood he went down to lunch.

VII

After lunch Harold usually joined Mrs Rice and her daughter for coffee. He decided to make no change in his usual behaviour.

This was the first time he had seen Elsie since the night before. She was very pale and was obviously still suffering from shock, but she made a gallant endeavour to behave as usual, uttering small commonplaces about the weather and the scenery.

They commented on a new guest who had just arrived, trying to guess his nationality. Harold thought a moustache like that must be French—Elsie said German—and Mrs Rice thought he might be Spanish.

There was no one else but themselves on the terrace with the exception of the two Polish ladies who were sitting at the extreme end, both doing fancy-work.

As always when he saw them, Harold felt a queer

shiver of apprehension pass over him. Those still faces, those curved beaks of noses, those long claw-like hands...

A page boy approached and told Mrs Rice she was wanted. She rose and followed him. At the entrance to the hotel they saw her encounter a police official in full uniform.

Elsie caught her breath.

'You don't think—anything's gone wrong?'

Harold reassured her quickly.

'Oh, no, no, nothing of that kind.'

But he himself knew a sudden pang of fear.

He said:

'Your mother's been wonderful!'

'I know. Mother is a great fighter. She'll never sit down under defeat.' Elsie shivered. 'But it is all horrible, isn't it?'

'Now, don't dwell on it. It's all over and done with.'

Elsie said in a low voice:

'I can't forget that—that it was *I* who killed him.'

Harold said urgently:

'Don't think of it that way. It was an accident. You know that really.'

Her face grew a little happier. Harold added:

'And anyway it's past. The past is the past. Try never to think of it again.'

Mrs Rice came back. By the expression on her face they saw that all was well.

'It gave me quite a fright,' she said almost gaily. 'But it was only a formality about some papers. Everything's all right, my children. We're out of the shadow. I think we might order ourselves a liqueur on the strength of it.'

The liqueur was ordered and came. They raised their glasses.

Mrs Rice said: 'To the Future!'

Harold smiled at Elsie and said:

'To your happiness!'

She smiled back at him and said as she lifted her glass:

'And to you—to your success! I'm sure you're going to be a very great man.'

With the reaction from fear they felt gay, almost light-headed. The shadow had lifted! All was well...

From the far end of the terrace the two bird-like women rose. They rolled up their work carefully. They came across the stone flags.

With little bows they sat down by Mrs Rice. One of them began to speak. The other one let her eyes rest on Elsie and Harold. There was a little smile on her lips. It was not, Harold thought, a nice smile...

He looked over at Mrs Rice. She was listening to the Polish woman and though he couldn't understand a word, the expression on Mrs Rice's face was clear enough. All the old anguish and despair came back. She listened and occasionally spoke a brief word.

Presently the two sisters rose, and with stiff little bows went into the hotel.

Harold leaned forward. He said hoarsely:

'What is it?'

Mrs Rice answered him in the quiet hopeless tones of despair.

'Those women are going to blackmail us. They heard everything last night. And now we've tried to hush it up, it makes the whole thing a thousand times worse...'

VIII

Harold Waring was down by the lake. He had been walking feverishly for over an hour, trying by sheer physical energy to still the clamour of despair that had attacked him.

He came at last to the spot where he had first noticed the two grim women who held his life and Elsie's in their evil talons. He said aloud:

'Curse them! Damn them for a pair of devilish blood-sucking harpies!'

A slight cough made him spin round. He found himself facing the luxuriantly moustached stranger who had just come out from the shade of the trees.

Harold found it difficult to know what to say. This little man must have almost certainly overheard what he had just said.

Harold, at a loss, said somewhat ridiculously:

'Oh—er—good afternoon.'

In perfect English the other replied:

'But for you, I fear, it is not a good afternoon?'

'Well—er—I—' Harold was in difficulties again.

The little man said:

'You are, I think, in trouble, Monsieur? Can I be of any assistance to you?'

'Oh no thanks, no thanks! Just blowing off steam, you know.'

The other said gently:

'But I think, you know, that I *could* help you. I am correct, am I not, in connecting your troubles with two ladies who were sitting on the terrace just now?'

Harold stared at him.

'Do you know anything about them?' He added: 'Who are you, anyway?'

As though confessing to royal birth the little man said modestly:

'*I am Hercule Poirot.* Shall we walk a little way into the wood and you shall tell me your story? As I say, I think I can aid you.'

To this day, Harold is not quite certain what made him suddenly pour out the whole story to a man to whom he had only spoken a few minutes before. Perhaps it was overstrain. Anyway, it happened. He told Hercule Poirot the whole story.

The latter listened in silence. Once or twice he nodded his head gravely. When Harold came to a stop the other spoke dreamily.

'The Stymphalean Birds, with iron beaks, who feed on human flesh and who dwell by the Stymphalean Lake . . .

Yes, it accords very well.'

'I beg your pardon,' said Harold staring.

Perhaps, he thought, this curious-looking little man was mad!

Hercule Poirot smiled.

'I reflect, that is all. I have my own way of looking at things, you understand. Now as to this business of yours. You are very unpleasantly placed.'

Harold said impatiently:

'I don't need you to tell me that!'

Hercule Poirot went on:

'It is a serious business, blackmail. These harpies will force you to pay—and pay—and pay again! And if you defy them, well, what happens?'

Harold said bitterly:

'The whole thing comes out. My career's ruined, and a wretched girl who's never done anyone any harm will be put through hell, and God knows what the end of it all will be!'

'Therefore,' said Hercule Poirot, 'something must be done!'

Harold said baldly: 'What?'

Hercule Poirot leaned back, half-closing his eyes. He said (and again a doubt about his sanity crossed Harold's mind):

'It is the moment for the castanets of bronze.'

Harold said:

'Are you quite mad?'

The other shook his head. He said:

'*Mais non!* I strive only to follow the example of my great predecessor, Hercules. Have a few hours' patience, my friend. By tomorrow I may be able to deliver you from your persecutors.'

IX

Harold Waring came down the following morning to find Hercule Poirot sitting alone on the terrace. In spite of himself Harold had been impressed by Hercule Poirot's promises.

He came up to him now and asked anxiously:

'Well?'

Hercule Poirot beamed upon him.

'It is well.'

'What do you mean?'

'Everything has settled itself satisfactorily.'

'But what has *happened*?'

Hercule Poirot replied dreamily:

'I have employed the castanets of bronze. Or, in modern parlance, I have caused metal wires to hum—in short I have employed the telegraph! Your Stymphalean Birds, Monsieur, have been removed to where they will be unable to exercise their ingenuity for some time to come.'

'They were wanted by the police? They have been arrested?'

'Precisely.'

Harold drew a deep breath.

'How marvellous! I never thought of that.' He got up. 'I must find Mrs Rice and Elsie and tell them.'

'They know.'

'Oh good.' Harold sat down again. 'Tell me just what—'

He broke off.

Coming up the path from the lake were two figures with flapping cloaks and profiles like birds.

He exclaimed:

'I thought you said they had been taken away!'

Hercule Poirot followed his glance.

'Oh, those ladies? They are very harmless; Polish ladies of good family, as the porter told you. Their appearance is, perhaps, not very pleasing but that is all.'

'But I don't *understand*'

'No, you do not understand! It is the *other* ladies who were wanted by the police—the resourceful Mrs Rice and the lachrymose Mrs Clayton! It is *they* who are well-known birds of prey. Those two, they make their living by blackmail, *mon cher*.'

Harold had a sensation of the world spinning round him. He said faintly:

'But the man—the man who was killed?'

'No one was killed. There was no man!'

'But I *saw* him!'

'Oh no. The tall deep-voiced Mrs Rice is a very successful male impersonator. It was she who played the part of the husband—without her grey wig and suitably made up for the part.'

He leaned forward and tapped the other on the knee.

'You must not go through life being too credulous, my friend. The police of a country are not so easily bribed—they are probably not to be bribed at all—certainly not when it is a question of murder! These women trade on the average Englishman's ignorance of foreign languages. Because she speaks French or German, it is always this Mrs Rice who interviews the manager and takes charge of the affair. The police arrive and go to *her* room, yes! But what actually passes? *You* do not know. Perhaps she says she has lost a brooch—something of that kind. Any excuse to arrange for the police to come *so that you shall see them*. For the rest, what actually happens? You wire for money, a lot of money, and you hand it over to Mrs Rice who is in charge of all the negotiations! And that is that! But they are greedy, these birds of prey. They have seen that you have taken an unreasonable aversion to these two unfortunate Polish ladies. The ladies in question come and hold a perfectly innocent conversation with Mrs Rice and she cannot resist repeating the game. She knows you cannot understand what is being said.

'So you will have to send for more money which Mrs Rice will pretend to distribute to a fresh set of people.'

Harold drew a deep breath. He said:

'And Elsie—Elsie?'

Hercule Poirot averted his eyes.

'She played her part very well. She always does. A most accomplished little actress. Everything is very pure—very innocent. She appeals, not to sex, but to chivalry.'

Hercule Poirot added dreamily:

'That is always successful with Englishmen.'

Harold Waring drew a deep breath. He said crisply:

'I'm going to set to work and learn every European language there is! Nobody's going to make a fool of me a second time!'

The Companion

'Now, Dr Lloyd,' said Miss Helier. 'Don't *you* know any creepy stories?'

She smiled at him—the smile that nightly bewitched the theatre-going public. Jane Helier was sometimes called the most beautiful woman in England, and jealous members of her own profession were in the habit of saying to each other: 'Of course Jane's not an *artist*. She can't *act*—if you know what I mean. It's those eyes!'

And those 'eyes' were at this minute fixed appealingly on the grizzled elderly bachelor doctor who, for the last five years, had ministered to the ailments of the village of St Mary Mead.

With an unconscious gesture, the doctor pulled down his waistcoat (inclined of late to be uncomfortably tight) and racked his brains hastily, so as not to disappoint the lovely creature who addressed him so confidently.

'I feel,' said Jane dreamily, 'that I would like to wallow in crime this evening.'

'Splendid,' said Colonel Bantry, her host. 'Splendid, splendid.' And he laughed a loud hearty military laugh. 'Eh, Dolly?'

His wife, hastily recalled to the exigencies of social life (she had been planning her spring border) agreed enthusiastically.

'Of course it's splendid,' she said heartily but vaguely. 'I always thought so.'

'Did you, my dear?' said old Miss Marple, and her eyes twinkled a little.

'We don't get much in the creepy line—and still less in the criminal line—in St Mary Mead, you know, Miss Helier,' said Dr Lloyd.

'You surprise me,' said Sir Henry Clithering. The ex-Commissioner of Scotland Yard turned to Miss Marple. 'I always understood from our friend here that St Mary Mead is a positive hotbed of crime and vice.'

'Oh, Sir Henry!' protested Miss Marple, a spot of colour coming into her cheeks. 'I'm sure I never said anything of the kind. The only thing I ever said was that human nature is much the same in a village as anywhere else, only one has opportunities and leisure for seeing it at closer quarters.'

'But *you* haven't always lived here,' said Jane Helier, still addressing the doctor. 'You've been in all sorts of queer places all over the world—places where things *happen*!'

'That is so, of course,' said Dr Lloyd, still thinking desperately. 'Yes, of course . . . Yes . . . Ah! I have it!'

He sank back with a sigh of relief.

'It is some years ago now—I had almost forgotten. But the facts were really very strange—very strange indeed. And the final coincidence which put the clue into my hand was strange also.'

Miss Helier drew her chair a little nearer to him,

applied some lipstick and waited expectantly. The others also turned interested faces towards him.

'I don't know whether any of you know the Canary Islands,' began the doctor.

'They must be wonderful,' said Jane Helier. 'They're in the South Seas, aren't they? Or is it the Mediterranean?'

'I've called in there on my way to South Africa,' said the Colonel. 'The Peak of Tenerife is a fine sight with the setting sun on it.'

'The incident I am describing happened in the island of Grand Canary, not Tenerife. It is a good many years ago now. I had had a breakdown in health and was forced to give up my practice in England and go abroad. I practised in Las Palmas, which is the principal town of Grand Canary. In many ways I enjoyed the life out there very much. The climate was mild and sunny, there was excellent surf bathing (and I am an enthusiastic bather) and the sea life of the port attracted me. Ships from all over the world put in at Las Palmas. I used to walk along the mole every morning far more interested than any member of the fair sex could be in a street of hat shops.

'As I say, ships from all over the world put in at Las Palmas. Sometimes they stay a few hours, sometimes a day or two. In the principal hotel there, the Metropole, you will see people of all races and nationalities—birds of passage. Even the people going to Tenerife usually come here and stay a few days before crossing to the other island.

'My story begins there, in the Metropole Hotel, one Thursday evening in January. There was a dance going on and I and a friend had been sitting at a small table watching the scene. There were a fair sprinkling of English and other nationalities, but the majority of the dancers were Spanish; and when the orchestra struck up a tango, only half a dozen couples of the latter nationality took the floor. They all danced well and we looked on and admired. One woman in particular excited our lively admiration. Tall, beautiful and sinuous, she moved with the grace of a half-tamed leopardess. There was something dangerous about her. I said as much to my friend and he agreed.

"'Women like that,' he said, 'are bound to have a history. Life will not pass them by.'

"'Beauty is perhaps a dangerous possession,' I said.

"'It's not only beauty,' he insisted. 'There is something else. Look at her again. Things are bound to happen to that woman, or because of her. As I said, life will not pass her by. Strange and exciting events will surround her. You've only got to look at her to know it.'

'He paused and then added with a smile:

"'Just as you've only got to look at those two women over there, and know that nothing out of the way could ever happen to either of them! They are made for a safe and uneventful existence.'

'I followed his eyes. The two women he referred to were travellers who had just arrived—a Holland Lloyd boat had put into port that evening, and the passengers were just beginning to arrive.

'As I looked at them I saw at once what my friend meant. They were two English ladies—the thoroughly nice travelling English that you do find abroad. Their ages, I should say, were round about forty. One was fair and a little—just a little—too plump; the other was dark and a little—again just a little—inclined to scragginess. They were what is called well-preserved, quietly and inconspicuously dressed in well-cut tweeds, and innocent of any kind of make-up. They had that air of quiet assurance which is the birthright of well-bred Englishwomen. There was nothing remarkable about either of them. They were like thousands of their sisters. They would doubtless see what they wished to see, assisted by Baedeker, and be blind to everything else. They would use the English library and attend the English Church in any place they happened to be, and it was quite likely that one or both of them sketched a little. And as my friend said, nothing exciting or remarkable would ever happen to either of them, though they might quite likely travel half over the world. I looked from them back to our sinuous Spanish woman with her half-closed smouldering eyes and I smiled.'

'Poor things,' said Jane Helier with a sigh. 'But I do think it's so silly of people not to make the most of themselves. That woman in Bond Street—Valentine—is really wonderful. Audrey Denman goes to her; and have you seen her in "The Downward Step"? As the schoolgirl in the first act she's really marvellous. And yet Audrey is fifty if she's a day. As a matter of fact I happen to know she's really nearer sixty.'

'Go on,' said Mrs Bantry to Dr Lloyd. 'I love stories about sinuous Spanish dancers. It makes me forget how old and fat I am.'

'I'm sorry,' said Dr Lloyd apologetically. 'But you see, as a matter of fact, this story isn't about the Spanish woman.'

'It isn't?'

'No. As it happens my friend and I were wrong. Nothing in the least exciting happened to the Spanish beauty. She married a clerk in a shipping office, and by the time I left the island she had had five children and was getting very fat.'

'Just like that girl of Israel Peters,' commented Miss Marple. 'The one who went on the stage and had such good legs that they made her principal boy in the pantomime. Everyone said she'd come to no good, but she married a commercial traveller and settled down splendidly.'

'The village parallel,' murmured Sir Henry softly.

'No,' went on the doctor. 'My story is about the two English ladies.'

'Something happened to them?' breathed Miss Helier.

'Something happened to them—and the very next day, too.'

'Yes?' said Mrs Bantry encouragingly.

'Just for curiosity, as I went out that evening I glanced at the hotel register. I found the names easily enough. Miss Mary Barton and Miss Amy Durrant of Little Paddocks, Caughton Weir, Bucks. I little thought then how soon I was to encounter the owners of those names again—and under what tragic circumstances.

'The following day I had arranged to go for a picnic with some friends. We were to motor across the island, taking our lunch, to a place called (as far as I remember—it is so long ago) Las Nieves, a well-sheltered bay where we could bathe if we felt inclined. This programme we duly carried out, except that we were somewhat late in starting, so that we stopped on the way and picnicked, going on to Las Nieves afterwards for a bathe before tea.

'As we approached the beach, we were at once aware of a tremendous commotion. The whole population of the small village seemed to be gathered on the shore. As soon as they saw us they rushed towards the car and began explaining excitedly. Our Spanish not being very good, it took me a few minutes to understand, but at last I got it.

'Two of the mad English ladies had gone in to bathe, and one had swum out too far and got into difficulties. The other had gone after her and had tried to bring her in, but her strength in turn had failed and she too would have drowned had not a man rowed out in a boat and brought in rescuer and rescued—the latter beyond help.

'As soon as I got the hang of things I pushed the crowd aside and hurried down the beach. I did not at first recognize the two women. The plump figure in the black stockinet costume and the tight green rubber bathing cap awoke no chord of recognition as she looked up anxiously. She was kneeling beside the body of her friend, making somewhat amateurish attempts at artificial respiration. When I told her that I was a doctor she gave a sigh of relief, and I ordered her off at once to one of the cottages for a rub down and dry clothing. One of the ladies in my party went with her. I myself worked unavailingly on the body of the drowned woman in vain. Life was only too clearly extinct, and in the end I had reluctantly to give in.

'I rejoined the others in the small fisherman's cottage and there I had to break the sad news. The survivor was attired now in her own clothes, and I immediately recognized her as one of the two arrivals of the night before. She received the sad news fairly calmly, and it was evidently the horror of the whole thing that struck her more than any great personal feeling.

'"Poor Amy," she said. "Poor, poor Amy. She had been looking forward to the bathing here so much. And she was a good swimmer too. I can't understand it. What do you think it can have been, doctor?"

'"Possibly cramp. Will you tell me exactly what happened?"

'"We had both been swimming about for some time—twenty minutes, I should say. Then I thought I would go in, but Amy said she was going to swim out once more. She did so, and suddenly I heard her call and realized she was crying for help. I swam out as fast as I could. She was still afloat when I got to her, but she clutched at me wildly and we both went under. If it hadn't been for that man coming out with his boat I should have been drowned too."

'"That has happened fairly often," I said. "To save anyone from drowning is not an easy affair."

'"It seems so awful," continued Miss Barton. "We only arrived yesterday, and were so delighting in the sunshine and our little holiday. And now this—this terrible tragedy occurs."

'I asked her then for particulars about the dead woman, explaining that I would do everything I could for her, but that the Spanish authorities would require full information. This she gave me readily enough.

'The dead woman, Miss Amy Durrant, was her companion and had come to her about five months previously. They had got on very well together, but Miss Durrant had spoken very little about her people. She had been left an orphan at an early age and had been brought up by an uncle and had earned her own living since she was twenty-one.

'And so that was that,' went on the doctor. He paused and said again, but this time with a certain finality in his voice, 'And so that was that.'

'I don't understand,' said Jane Helier. 'Is that all? I mean, it's very tragic, I suppose, but it isn't—well, it isn't what I call *creepy*.'

'I think there's more to follow,' said Sir Henry.

'Yes,' said Dr Lloyd, 'there's more to follow. You see, right at the time there was one queer thing. Of course I asked questions of the fishermen, etc., as to what they'd seen. They were eye-witnesses. And one woman had rather a funny story. I didn't pay any attention to it at the time, but it came back to me afterwards. She insisted, you see, that Miss Durrant wasn't in difficulties when she called out. The other swam out to her and, according to this woman, deliberately held Miss Durrant's head under water. I didn't, as I say, pay much attention. It was such a fantastic story, and these things look so differently from the shore. Miss Barton might have tried to make her friend lose consciousness, realizing that the latter's panic-stricken clutching would drown them both. You see, according to the Spanish woman's story, it looked as though—well, as though Miss Barton was deliberately trying to drown her companion.

'As I say, I paid very little attention to this story at the time. It came back to me later. Our great difficulty was to find out anything about this woman, Amy Durrant. She didn't seem to have any relations. Miss Barton and I went through her things together. We found one address and wrote there, but it proved to be simply a room she had taken in which to keep her things. The landlady knew nothing, had only seen her when she took the room. Miss Durrant had remarked at the time that she always liked to have one place she could call her own to which she could return at any moment. There were one or two nice pieces of old furniture and some bound numbers of Academy pictures, and a trunk full of pieces of material bought at sales, but no personal belongings. She had mentioned to the landlady that her father and mother had died in India when she was a child and that she had been brought up by an uncle who was a clergyman, but she did not say if he was her father's or her mother's brother, so the name was no guide.

'It wasn't exactly mysterious, it was just unsatisfactory. There must be many lonely women, proud and reticent, in just that position. There were a couple of photographs amongst her belongings in Las Palmas—rather old and faded and they had been cut to fit the frames they were in, so that there was no photographer's name upon them, and there was an old daguerreotype which might have been her mother or more probably her grandmother.

'Miss Barton had had two references with her. One she had forgotten, the other name she recollected after an effort. It proved to be that of a lady who was now abroad, having gone to Australia. She was written to. Her answer, of course, was a long time in coming, and I may say that when it did arrive there was no particular help to be gained from it. She said Miss Durrant had been with her as companion and had been most efficient and that she was a very charming woman, but that she knew nothing of her private affairs or relations.

'So there it was—as I say, nothing unusual, really. It was just the two things together that aroused my uneasiness. This Amy Durrant of whom no one knew anything, and the Spanish woman's queer story. Yes, and I'll add a third thing: When I was first bending over the body and Miss Barton was walking away towards the huts, she looked back. Looked back with an expression on her face that I can only describe as one of poignant anxiety—a kind of anguished uncertainty that imprinted itself on my brain.

'It didn't strike me as anything unusual at the time. I put it down to her terrible distress over her friend. But, you see, later I realized that they weren't on those terms. There was no devoted attachment between them, no terrible grief. Miss Barton was fond of Amy Durrant and shocked by her death—that was all.

'But, then, why that terrible poignant anxiety? That was the question that kept coming back to me. I had not been mistaken in that look. And almost against my will, an answer began to shape itself in my mind. Supposing the Spanish woman's story were true; supposing that Mary Barton wilfully and in cold blood tried to drown Amy Durrant. She succeeds in holding her under water whilst pretending to be saving her. She is rescued by a boat. They are on a lonely beach far from anywhere. And then I appear—the last thing she expects. A doctor! And an English doctor! She knows well enough that people who have been under water far longer than Amy Durrant have been revived by artificial respiration. But she has to play her part—to go off leaving me alone with her victim. And as she turns for one last look, a terrible poignant anxiety shows in her face. Will Amy Durrant come back to life *and tell what she knows?*'

'Oh!' said Jane Helier. 'I'm thrilled now.'

'Viewed in that aspect the whole business seemed more sinister, and the personality of Amy Durrant became more mysterious. Who was Amy Durrant? Why should she, an insignificant paid companion, be murdered by her employer? What story lay behind that fatal bathing expedition? She had entered Mary Barton's employment only a few months before. Mary Barton had brought her abroad, and the very day after they landed the tragedy had occurred. And they were both nice, commonplace, refined Englishwomen! The whole thing was fantastic, and I told myself so. I had been letting my imagination run away with me.'

'You didn't do anything, then?' asked Miss Helier.

'My dear young lady, what could I do? There was no evidence. The majority of the eye-witnesses told the same story as Miss Barton. I had built up my own suspicions out of a fleeting expression which I might possibly have imagined. The only thing I could and did do was to see that the widest inquiries were made for the relations of Amy Durrant. The next time I was in England I even went and saw the landlady of her room, with the results I have told you.'

'But you felt there was something wrong,' said Miss Marple.

Dr Lloyd nodded.

'Half the time I was ashamed of myself for thinking so. Who was I to go suspecting this nice, pleasant-mannered English lady of a foul and cold-blooded crime? I did my best to be as cordial as possible to her during the short time she stayed on the island. I helped her with the Spanish authorities. I did everything I could do as an Englishman to help a compatriot in a foreign country; and yet I am convinced that she knew I suspected and disliked her.'

'How long did she stay out there?' asked Miss Marple.

'I think it was about a fortnight. Miss Durrant was buried there, and it must have been about ten days later when she took a boat back to England. The shock had upset her so much that she felt she couldn't spend the winter there as she had planned. That's what she said.'

'Did it seem to have upset her?' asked Miss Marple.

The doctor hesitated.

'Well, I don't know that it affected her appearance at all,' he said cautiously.

'She didn't, for instance, grow fatter?' asked Miss Marple.

'Do you know—it's a curious thing your saying that. Now I come to think back, I believe you're right. She—yes, she did seem, if anything, to be putting on weight.'

'How horrible,' said Jane Helier with a shudder. 'It's like—it's like fattening on your victim's blood.'

'And yet, in another way, I may be doing her an injustice,' went on Dr Lloyd. 'She certainly said something before she left, which pointed in an entirely different direction. There may be, I think there are, consciences which work very slowly—which take some time to awaken to the enormity of the deed committed.

'It was the evening before her departure from the Canaries. She had asked me to go and see her, and had thanked me very warmly for all I had done to help her.

I, of course, made light of the matter, said I had only done what was natural under the circumstances, and so on. There was a pause after that, and then she suddenly asked me a question.

"'Do you think,' she asked, 'that one is ever justified in taking the law into one's own hands?'"

'I replied that that was rather a difficult question, but that on the whole, I thought not. The law was the law, and we had to abide by it.

"'Even when it is powerless?'"

"'I don't quite understand.'"

"'It's difficult to explain; but one might do something that is considered definitely wrong—that is considered a crime, even, for a good and sufficient reason.'"

'I replied drily that possibly several criminals had thought that in their time, and she shrank back.

"'But that's horrible,' she murmured. 'Horrible.'"

'And then with a change of tone she asked me to give her something to make her sleep. She had not been able to sleep properly since—she hesitated—since that terrible shock.

"'You're sure it is that? There is nothing worrying you? Nothing on your mind?'"

"'On my mind? What should be on my mind?'"

'She spoke fiercely and suspiciously.

"'Worry is a cause of sleeplessness sometimes,' I said lightly.

'She seemed to brood for a moment.

"'Do you mean worrying over the future, or worrying over the past, which can't be altered?'"

"'Either.'"

"'Only it wouldn't be any good worrying over the

past. You couldn't bring back—Oh! what's the use! One mustn't think. One must not think."

'I prescribed her a mild sleeping draught and made my adieu. As I went away I wondered not a little over the words she had spoken. "You couldn't bring back—" What? Or *who*?

'I think that last interview prepared me in a way for what was to come. I didn't expect it, of course, but when it happened, I wasn't surprised. Because, you see, Mary Barton struck me all along as a conscientious woman—not a weak sinner, but a woman with convictions, who would act up to them, and who would not relent as long as she still believed in them. I fancied that in the last conversation we had she was beginning to doubt her own convictions. I know her words suggested to me that she was feeling the first faint beginnings of that terrible soul-searcher—remorse.

'The thing happened in Cornwall, in a small watering-place, rather deserted at that season of the year. It must have been—let me see—late March. I read about it in the papers. A lady had been staying at a small hotel there—a Miss Barton. She had been very odd and peculiar in her manner. That had been noticed by all. At night she would walk up and down her room, muttering to herself, and not allowing the people on either side of her to sleep. She had called on the vicar one day and had told him that she had a communication of the gravest importance to make to him. She had, she said, committed a crime. Then, instead of proceeding, she had stood up abruptly and said she would call another day. The vicar put her down as being slightly mental, and did not take her self-accusation seriously.

'The very next morning she was found to be missing from her room. A note was left addressed to the coroner. It ran as follows:

> *'I tried to speak to the vicar yesterday, to confess all, but was not allowed. She would not let me. I can make amends only one way—a life for a life; and my life must go the same way as hers did. I, too, must drown in the deep sea. I believed I was justified. I see now that that was not so. If I desire Amy's forgiveness I must go to her. Let no one be blamed for my death—Mary Barton.*

'Her clothes were found lying on the beach in a secluded cove nearby, and it seemed clear that she had undressed there and swum resolutely out to sea where the current was known to be dangerous, sweeping one down the coast.

'The body was not recovered, but after a time leave was given to presume death. She was a rich woman, her estate being proved at a hundred thousand pounds. Since she died intestate it all went to her next of kin—a family of cousins in Australia. The papers made discreet references to the tragedy in the Canary Islands, putting forward the theory that the death of Miss Durrant had unhinged her friend's brain. At the inquest the usual verdict of *Suicide whilst temporarily insane* was returned.

'And so the curtain falls on the tragedy of Amy Durrant and Mary Barton.'

There was a long pause and then Jane Helier gave a great gasp.

'Oh, but you mustn't stop there—just at the most interesting part. Go on.'

'But you see, Miss Helier, this isn't a serial story. This is real life; and real life stops just where it chooses.'

'But I don't want it to,' said Jane. 'I want to know.'

'This is where we use our brains, Miss Helier,' explained Sir Henry. 'Why did Mary Barton kill her companion? That's the problem Dr Lloyd has set us.'

'Oh, well,' said Miss Helier, 'she might have killed her for lots of reasons. I mean—oh, I don't know. She might have got on her nerves, or else she got jealous, although Dr Lloyd doesn't mention any men, but still on the boat out—well, you know what everyone says about boats and sea voyages.'

Miss Helier paused, slightly out of breath, and it was borne in upon her audience that the outside of Jane's charming head was distinctly superior to the inside.

'I would like to have a lot of guesses,' said Mrs Bantry. 'But I suppose I must confine myself to one. Well, I think that Miss Barton's father made all his money out of ruining Amy Durrant's father, so Amy determined to have her revenge. Oh, no, that's the wrong way round. How tiresome! Why does the rich employer kill the humble companion? I've got it. Miss Barton had a young brother who shot himself for love of Amy Durrant. Miss Barton waits her time. Amy comes down in the world. Miss B. engages her as companion and takes her to the Canaries and accomplishes her revenge. How's that?'

'Excellent,' said Sir Henry. 'Only we don't know that Miss Barton ever had a young brother.'

'We deduce that,' said Mrs Bantry. 'Unless she had a young brother there's no motive. So she must have had a young brother. Do you see, Watson?'

'That's all very fine, Dolly,' said her husband. 'But it's only a guess.'

'Of course it is,' said Mrs Bantry. 'That's all we can do—guess. We haven't got any clues. Go on, dear, have a guess yourself.'

'Upon my word, I don't know what to say. But I think there's something in Miss Helier's suggestion that they fell out about a man. Look here, Dolly, it was probably some high church parson. They both embroidered him a cope or something, and he wore the Durrant woman's first. Depend upon it, it was something like that. Look how she went off to a parson at the end. These women all lose their heads over a good-looking clergyman. You hear of it over and over again.'

'I think I must try to make my explanation a little more subtle,' said Sir Henry, 'though I admit it's only a guess. I suggest that Miss Barton was always mentally unhinged. There are more cases like that than you would imagine. Her mania grew stronger and she began to believe it her duty to rid the world of certain persons—possibly what is termed unfortunate females. Nothing much is known about Miss Durrant's past. So very possibly she *had* a past—an "unfortunate" one. Miss Barton learns of this and decides on extermination. Later, the righteousness of her act begins to trouble her and she is overcome by remorse. Her end shows her to be completely unhinged. Now, do say you agree with me, Miss Marple.'

'I'm afraid I don't, Sir Henry,' said Miss Marple, smiling apologetically. 'I think her end shows her to have been a very clever and resourceful woman.'

Jane Helier interrupted with a little scream.

'Oh! I've been so stupid. May I guess again? Of course it must have been that. Blackmail! The companion woman was blackmailing her. Only I don't see why Miss Marple says it was clever of her to kill herself. I can't see that at all.'

'Ah!' said Sir Henry. 'You see, Miss Marple knew a case just like it in St Mary Mead.'

'You always laugh at me, Sir Henry,' said Miss Marple reproachfully. 'I must confess it does remind me, just a little, of old Mrs Trout. She drew the old age pension, you know, for three old women who were dead, in different parishes.'

'It sounds a most complicated and resourceful crime,' said Sir Henry. 'But it doesn't seem to me to throw any light upon our present problem.'

'Of course not,' said Miss Marple. 'It wouldn't—to you. But some of the families were very poor, and the old age pension was a great boon to the children. I know it's difficult for anyone outside to understand. But what I really meant was that the whole thing hinged upon one old woman being so like any other old woman.'

'Eh?' said Sir Henry, mystified.

'I always explain things so badly. What I mean is that when Dr Lloyd described the two ladies first, he didn't know which was which, and I don't suppose anyone else in the hotel did. They would have, of course, after a day or so, but the very next day one of the two was drowned, and if the one who was left said she was Miss Barton, I don't suppose it would ever occur to anyone that she mightn't be.'

'You think—Oh! I see,' said Sir Henry slowly.

'It's the only natural way of thinking of it. Dear Mrs

Bantry began that way just now. Why *should* the rich employer kill the humble companion? It's so much more likely to be the other way about. I mean—that's the way things happen.'

'Is it?' said Sir Henry. 'You shock me.'

'But of course,' went on Miss Marple, 'she would have to wear Miss Barton's clothes, and they would probably be a little tight on her, so that her general appearance would look as though she had got a little fatter. That's why I asked that question. A gentleman would be sure to think it was the lady who had got fatter, and not the clothes that had got smaller—though that isn't quite the right way of putting it.'

'But if Amy Durrant killed Miss Barton, what did she gain by it?' asked Mrs Bantry. 'She couldn't keep up the deception for ever.'

'She only kept it up for another month or so,' pointed out Miss Marple. 'And during that time I expect she travelled, keeping away from anyone who might know her. That's what I meant by saying that one lady of a certain age looks so like another. I don't suppose the different photograph on her passport was ever noticed—you know what passports are. And then in March, she went down to this Cornish place and began to act queerly and draw attention to herself so that when people found her clothes on the beach and read her last letter they shouldn't think of the commonsense conclusion.'

'Which was?' asked Sir Henry.

'No *body*,' said Miss Marple firmly. 'That's the thing that would stare you in the face, if there weren't such a lot of red herrings to draw you off the trail—including the suggestion of foul play and remorse. *No body.* That was the real significant fact.'

'Do you mean—' said Mrs Bantry—'do you mean that there wasn't any remorse? That there wasn't—that she didn't drown herself?'

'Not she!' said Miss Marple. 'It's just Mrs Trout over again. Mrs Trout was very good at red herrings, but she met her match in me. And I can see through your remorse-driven Miss Barton. Drown herself? Went off to Australia, if I'm any good at guessing.'

'You are, Miss Marple,' said Dr Lloyd. 'Undoubtedly you are. Now it again took me quite by surprise. Why, you could have knocked me down with a feather that day in Melbourne.'

'Was that what you spoke of as a final coincidence?'

Dr Lloyd nodded.

'Yes, it was rather rough luck on Miss Barton—or Miss Amy Durrant—whatever you like to call her. I became a ship's doctor for a while, and landing in Melbourne, the first person I saw as I walked down the street was the lady I thought had been drowned in Cornwall. She saw the game was up as far as I was concerned, and she did the bold thing—took me into her confidence. A curious woman, completely lacking, I suppose, in some moral sense. She was the eldest of a family of nine, all wretchedly poor. They had applied once for help to their rich cousin in England and been repulsed, Miss Barton having quarrelled with their father. Money was wanted desperately, for the three youngest children were delicate and wanted expensive medical treatment. Amy Barton then and there seems to have decided on her plan of cold-blooded murder. She set out for England, working her passage over as a children's nurse. She obtained the situation of companion to Miss Barton, calling herself Amy Durrant. She engaged a room and put some furniture into it so as to create more of a personality for herself. The drowning plan was a sudden inspiration. She had been waiting for some opportunity to present itself. Then she staged the final scene of the drama and returned to Australia, and in due time she and her brothers and sisters inherited Miss Barton's money as next of kin.'

'A very bold and perfect crime,' said Sir Henry. 'Almost *the* perfect crime. If it had been Miss Barton who had died in the Canaries, suspicion might attach to Amy Durrant and her connection with the Barton family might have been discovered; but the change of identity and the double crime, as you may call it, effectually did away with that. Yes, almost the perfect crime.'

'What happened to her?' asked Mrs Bantry. 'What did you do in the matter, Dr Lloyd?'

'I was in a very curious position, Mrs Bantry. Of evidence as the law understands it, I still had very little. Also, there were certain signs, plain to me as a medical man, that though strong and vigorous in appearance, the lady was not long for this world. I went home with her and saw the rest of the family—a charming family, devoted to their eldest sister and without an idea in their heads that she might prove to have committed a crime. Why bring sorrow on them when I could prove nothing? The lady's admission to me was unheard by anyone else. I let Nature take its course. Miss Amy Barton died six months after my meeting with her. I have often wondered if she was cheerful and unrepentant up to the last.'

'Surely not,' said Mrs Bantry.

'I expect so,' said Miss Marple. 'Mrs Trout was.'

Jane Helier gave herself a little shake.

'Well,' she said. 'It's very, very thrilling. I don't quite understand now who drowned which. And how does this Mrs Trout come into it?'

'She doesn't, my dear,' said Miss Marple. 'She was only a person—not a very nice person—in the village.'

'Oh!' said Jane. 'In the village. But nothing ever happens in a village, does it?' She sighed. 'I'm sure I shouldn't have any brains at all if I lived in a village.'

Have You Got Everything You Want?

'*Par ici, Madame.*'

A tall woman in a mink coat followed her heavily encumbered porter along the platform of the Gare de Lyon.

She wore a dark-brown knitted hat pulled down over one eye and ear. The other side revealed a charming tip-tilted profile and little golden curls clustering over a shell-like ear. Typically an American, she was altogether a very charming-looking creature and more than one man turned to look at her as she walked past the high carriages of the waiting train.

Large plates were stuck in holders on the sides of the carriages.

PARIS–ATHÈNES. PARIS–BUCHAREST. PARIS–STAMBOUL.

At the last named the porter came to an abrupt halt. He undid the strap which held the suitcases together and they slipped heavily to the ground. '*Voici, Madame.*'

The *wagon-lit* conductor was standing beside the steps. He came forward, remarking, '*Bonsoir, Madame,*' with an *empressement* perhaps due to the richness and perfection of the mink coat.

The woman handed him her sleeping-car ticket of flimsy paper.

'Number Six,' he said. 'This way.'

He sprang nimbly into the train, the woman following him. As she hurried down the corridor after him, she nearly collided with a portly gentleman who was emerging from the compartment next to hers. She had a momentary glimpse of a large bland face with benevolent eyes.

'*Voici, Madame.*'

The conductor displayed the compartment. He threw up the window and signalled to the porter. The lesser employee took in the baggage and put it up in the racks. The woman sat down.

Beside her on the seat she had placed a small scarlet case and her handbag. The carriage was hot, but it did not seem to occur to her to take off her coat. She stared out of the window with unseeing eyes. People were hurrying up and down the platform. There were sellers of newspapers, of pillows, of chocolate, of fruit, of mineral waters. They held up their wares to her, but her eyes looked blankly through them. The Gare de Lyon had faded from her sight. On her face were sadness and anxiety.

'If Madame will give me her passport?'

The words made no impression on her. The conductor, standing in the doorway, repeated them. Elsie Jeffries roused herself with a start.

'I beg your pardon?'

'Your passport, Madame.'

She opened her bag, took out the passport and gave it to him.

'That will be all right, Madame, I will attend to everything.' A slight significant pause. 'I shall be going with Madame as far as Stamboul.'

Elsie drew out a fifty-franc note and handed it to him. He accepted it in a business-like manner, and inquired when she would like her bed made up and whether she was taking dinner.

These matters settled, he withdrew and almost immediately the restaurant man came rushing down the corridor ringing his little bell frantically, and bawling out, *'Premier service. Premier service.'*

Elsie rose, divested herself of the heavy fur coat, took a brief glance at herself in the little mirror, and picking up her handbag and jewel case stepped out into the corridor. She had gone only a few steps when the restaurant man came rushing along on his return journey. To avoid him, Elsie stepped back for a moment into the doorway of the adjoining compartment, which was now empty. As the man passed and she prepared to continue her journey to the dining car, her glance fell idly on the label of a suitcase which was lying on the seat.

It was a stout pigskin case, somewhat worn. On the label were the words: 'J. Parker Pyne, passenger to Stamboul.' The suitcase itself bore the initials 'P.P.'

A startled expression came over the girl's face. She hesitated a moment in the corridor, then going back to her own compartment she picked up a copy of *The Times* which she had laid down on the table with some magazines and books.

She ran her eye down the advertisement columns on the front page, but what she was looking for was not there. A slight frown on her face, she made her way to the restaurant car.

The attendant allotted her a seat at a small table already tenanted by one person—the man with whom she had nearly collided in the corridor. In fact, the owner of the pigskin suitcase.

Elsie looked at him without appearing to do so. He seemed very bland, very benevolent, and in some way impossible to explain, delightfully reassuring. He behaved in reserved British fashion, and it was not until the fruit was on the table that he spoke.

'They keep these places terribly hot,' he said.

'I know,' said Elsie. 'I wish one could have the window open.'

He gave a rueful smile. 'Impossible! Every person present except ourselves would protest.'

She gave an answering smile. Neither said any more.

Coffee was brought and the usual indecipherable bill. Having laid some notes upon it, Elsie suddenly took her courage in both hands.

'Excuse me,' she murmured. 'I saw your name upon your suitcase—Parker Pyne. Are you—are you, by any chance—?'

She hesitated and he came quickly to her rescue.

'I believe I am. That is'—he quoted from the advertisement which Elsie had noticed more than once in *The Times,* and for which she had searched vainly just now: '"Are you happy? If not, consult Mr Parker Pyne." Yes, I'm that one, all right.'

'I see,' said Elsie. 'How—how extraordinary!'

He shook his head. 'Not really. Extraordinary from your point of view, but not from mine.' He smiled reassuringly, then leaned forward. Most of the other diners had left the car. 'So you are unhappy?' he said.

'I—' began Elsie, and stopped.

'You would not have said "How extraordinary" otherwise,' he pointed out.

Elsie was silent a minute. She felt strangely soothed by the mere presence of Mr Parker Pyne. 'Ye—es,' she admitted at last. 'I am—unhappy. At least, I am worried.'

He nodded sympathetically.

'You see,' she continued, 'a very curious thing has happened—and I don't know in the least what to make of it.'

'Suppose you tell me about it,' suggested Mr Pyne.

Elsie thought of the advertisement. She and Edward had often commented on it and laughed. She had never thought that she . . . perhaps she had better not . . . if Mr Parker Pyne were a charlatan . . . but he looked—nice!

Elsie made her decision. Anything to get this worry off her mind.

'I'll tell you. I'm going to Constantinople to join my husband. He does a lot of Oriental business, and this year he found it necessary to go there. He went a fortnight ago. He was to get things ready for me to join him. I've been very excited at the thought of it. You see, I've never been abroad before. We've been in England six months.'

'You and your husband are both American?'

'Yes.'

'And you have not, perhaps, been married very long?'
'We've been married a year and a half.'
'Happily?'
'Oh, yes! Edward's a perfect angel.' She hesitated. 'Not, perhaps, very much go to him. Just a little—well, I'd call it straitlaced. Lot of puritan ancestry and all that. But he's a *dear*,' she added hastily.

Mr Parker Pyne looked at her thoughtfully for a moment or two, then he said, 'Go on.'

'It was about a week after Edward had started. I was writing a letter in his study, and I noticed that the blotting paper was all new and clean, except for a few lines of writing across it. I'd just been reading a detective story with a clue in a blotter and so, just for fun, I held it up to a mirror. It really *was* just fun, Mr Pyne—I mean, he's such a mild lamb one wouldn't dream of anything of that kind.'

'Yes, yes; I quite understand.'

'The thing was quite easy to read. First there was the word "wife" then "Simplon Express", and lower down, "just before Venice would be the best time".' She stopped.

'Curious,' said Mr Pyne. 'Distinctly curious. It was your husband's handwriting?'

'Oh, yes. But I've cudgelled my brains and I cannot see under what circumstances he would write a letter with just those words in it.'

'"Just before Venice would be the best time",' repeated Mr Parker Pyne. 'Distinctly curious.'

Mrs Jeffries was leaning forward looking at him with a flattering hopefulness. 'What shall I do?' she asked simply.

'I am afraid,' said Mr Parker Pyne, 'that we shall have to wait until before Venice.' He took up a folder from the table. 'Here is the schedule time of our train. It arrives at Venice at two twenty-seven tomorrow afternoon.'

They looked at each other.

'Leave it to me,' said Parker Pyne.

It was five minutes past two. The Simplon Express was eleven minutes late. It had passed Mestre about a quarter of an hour before.

Mr Parker Pyne was sitting with Mrs Jeffries in her compartment. So far the journey had been pleasant and uneventful. But now the moment had arrived when, if anything was going to happen, it presumably would happen. Mr Parker Pyne and Elsie faced each other. Her heart was beating fast, and her eyes sought him in a kind of anguished appeal for reassurance.

'Keep perfectly calm,' he said. 'You are quite safe. I am here.'

Suddenly a scream broke out from the corridor.

'Oh, look—look! The train is on fire!'

With a bound Elsie and Mr Parker Pyne were in the corridor. An agitated woman with a Slav countenance was pointing a dramatic finger. Out of one of the front compartments smoke was pouring in a cloud. Mr Parker Pyne and Elsie ran along the corridor. Others joined them. The compartment in question was full of smoke. The first comers drew back, coughing. The conductor appeared.

'The compartment is empty!' he cried. 'Do not alarm yourselves, *messieurs et dames*. *Le feu*, it will be controlled.'

A dozen excited questions and answers broke out. The train was running over the bridge that joins Venice to the mainland.

Suddenly Mr Parker Pyne turned, forced his way through the little pack of people behind him and hurried down the corridor to Elsie's compartment. The lady with the Slav face was seated in it, drawing deep breaths from the open window.

'Excuse me, Madame,' said Parker Pyne. 'But this is not your compartment.'

'I know. I know,' said the Slav lady. *'Pardon.* It is the shock, the emotion—my heart.' She sank back on the seat and indicated the open window. She drew in her breath in great gasps.

Mr Parker Pyne stood in the doorway. His voice was fatherly and reassuring. 'You must not be afraid,' he said. 'I do not think for a moment the fire is serious.'

'Not? Ah, what a mercy! I feel restored.' She half-rose. 'I will return to my compartment.'

'Not just yet.' Mr Parker Pyne's hand pressed her gently back. 'I will ask you to wait a moment, Madame.'

'Monsieur, this is an outrage!'

'Madame, you will remain.'

His voice rang out coldly. The woman sat still looking at him. Elsie joined them.

'It seems it was a smoke bomb,' she said breathlessly. 'Some ridiculous practical joke. The conductor is furious. He is asking everybody—' She broke off, staring at the second occupant of the carriage.

'Mrs Jeffries,' said Mr Parker Pyne, 'what do you carry in your little scarlet case?'

'My jewellery.'

'Perhaps you would be so kind as to look and see that everything is there.'

There was immediately a torrent of words from the Slav lady. She broke into French, the better to do justice to her feelings.

In the meantime Elsie had picked up the jewel case. 'Oh!' she cried. 'It's unlocked.'

'. . . *Et je porterai plainte à la Compagnie des Wagons-Lits,*' finished the Slav lady.

'They're gone!' cried Elsie. 'Everything! My diamond bracelet. And the necklace Pop gave me. And the emerald and ruby rings. And some lovely diamond brooches. Thank goodness I was wearing my pearls. Oh, Mr Pyne, what shall we do?'

'If you will fetch the conductor,' said Mr Parker Pyne, 'I will see that this woman does not leave this compartment till he comes.'

'*Scélérat! Monstre!*' shrieked the Slav lady. She went on to further insults. The train drew in to Venice.

The events of the next half-hour may be briefly summarized. Mr Parker Pyne dealt with several different officials in several different languages—and suffered defeat. The suspected lady consented to be searched—and emerged without a stain on her character. The jewels were not on her.

Between Venice and Trieste Mr Parker Pyne and Elsie discussed the case.

'When was the last time you actually saw your jewels?'

'This morning. I put away some sapphire earrings I was wearing yesterday and took out a pair of plain pearl ones.'

'And all the jewellery was there intact?'

'Well, I didn't go through it all, naturally. But it looked the same as usual. A ring or something like that might have been missing, but no more.'

Mr Parker Pyne nodded. 'Now, when the conductor made up the compartment this morning?'

'I had the case with me—in the restaurant car. I always take it with me. I've never left it except when I ran out just now.'

'Therefore,' said Mr Parker Pyne, 'that injured innocent, Madame Subayska, or whatever she calls herself, *must* have been the thief. But what the devil did she do with the things? She was only in here a minute and a half—just time to open the case with a duplicate key and take out the stuff—yes, but what next?'

'Could she have handed them to anyone else?'

'Hardly. I had turned back and was forcing my way along the corridor. If anyone had come out of this compartment I should have seen them.'

'Perhaps she threw them out of the window to someone.'

'An excellent suggestion; only, as it happens, we were passing over the sea at that moment. We were on the bridge.'

'Then she must have hidden them actually in the carriage.'

'Let's hunt for them.'

With true transatlantic energy Elsie began to look about. Mr Parker Pyne participated in the search in a somewhat absent fashion. Reproached for not trying, he excused himself.

'I'm thinking that I must send a rather important telegram at Trieste,' he explained.

Elsie received the explanation coldly. Mr Parker Pyne had fallen heavily in her estimation.

'I'm afraid you're annoyed with me, Mrs Jeffries,' he said meekly.

'Well, you've not been very successful,' she retorted.

'But, my dear lady, you must remember I am not a detective. Theft and crime are not in my line at all. The human heart is my province.'

'Well, I was a bit unhappy when I got on this train,' said Elsie, 'but nothing to what I am now! I could just cry buckets. My lovely, lovely bracelet—and the emerald ring Edward gave me when we were engaged.'

'But surely you are insured against theft?' Mr Parker Pyne interpolated.

'Am I? I don't know. Yes, I suppose I am. But it's the *sentiment* of the thing, Mr Pyne.'

The train slackened speed. Mr Parker Pyne peered out of the window. 'Trieste,' he said. 'I must send my telegram.'

'Edward!' Elsie's face lighted up as she saw her husband hurrying to meet her on the platform at Stamboul. For the moment even the loss of her jewellery faded from her mind. She forgot the curious words she had found on the blotter. She forgot everything except that it was a fortnight since she had seen her husband last, and that in spite of being sober and straitlaced he was really a most attractive person.

They were just leaving the station when Elsie felt a friendly tap on the shoulder and turned to see Mr

Parker Pyne. His bland face was beaming good-naturedly.

'Mrs Jeffries,' he said, 'will you come to see me at the Hotel Tokatlian in half an hour? I think I may have some good news for you.'

Elsie looked uncertainly at Edward. Then she made the introduction. 'This—er—is my husband—Mr Parker Pyne.'

'As I believe your wife wired you, her jewels have been stolen,' said Mr Parker Pyne. 'I have been doing what I can to help her recover them. I think I may have news for her in about half an hour.'

Elsie looked enquiringly at Edward. He replied promptly: 'You'd better go, dear. The Tokatlian, you said, Mr Pyne? Right; I'll see she makes it.'

It was just a half an hour later that Elsie was shown into Mr Parker Pyne's private sitting room. He rose to receive her.

'You've been disappointed in me, Mrs Jeffries,' he said. 'Now, don't deny it. Well, I don't pretend to be a magician but I do what I can. Take a look inside here.'

He passed along the table a small stout cardboard box. Elsie opened it. Rings, brooches, bracelets, necklace—they were all there.

'Mr Pyne, how marvellous! How—how too wonderful!'

Mr Parker Pyne smiled modestly. 'I am glad not to have failed you, my dear young lady.'

'Oh, Mr Pyne, you make me feel just mean! Ever since Trieste I've been horrid to you. And now—this. But how did you get hold of them? When? Where?'

Mr Parker Pyne shook his head thoughtfully. 'It's a long story,' he said. 'You may hear it one day. In fact, you may hear it quite soon.'

'Why can't I hear it now?'

'There are reasons,' said Mr Parker Pyne.

And Elsie had to depart with her curiosity unsatisfied.

When she had gone, Mr Parker Pyne took up his hat and stick and went out into the streets of Pera. He walked along smiling to himself, coming at last to a little café, deserted at the moment, which overlooked the Golden Horn. On the other side, the mosques of Stamboul showed slender minarets against the afternoon sky. It was very beautiful. Mr Pyne sat down and ordered two coffees. They came thick and sweet. He had just begun to sip his when a man slipped into the seat opposite. It was Edward Jeffries.

'I have ordered some coffee for you,' said Mr Parker Pyne, indicating the little cup.

Edward pushed the coffee aside. He leaned forward across the table. 'How did you know?' he asked.

Mr Parker Pyne sipped his coffee dreamily. 'Your wife will have told you about her discovery on the blotter? No? Oh, but she will tell you; it has slipped her mind for the moment.'

He mentioned Elsie's discovery.

'Very well; that linked up perfectly with the curious incident that happened just before Venice. For some reason or other you were engineering the theft of your wife's jewels. But why the phrase "just before Venice would be the best time"? There seemed nonsense in that. Why did you not leave it to your—agent—to choose her own time and place?

'And then, suddenly, I saw the point. *Your wife's jewels were stolen before you yourself left London and were replaced by paste duplicates.* But that solution did not satisfy you. You were a high-minded, conscientious young man. You have a horror of some servant or other innocent person being suspected. A theft must actually occur—at a place and in a manner which will leave no suspicion attached to anybody of your acquaintance or household.

'Your accomplice is provided with a key to the jewel box and a smoke bomb. At the correct moment she gives the alarm, darts into your wife's compartment, unlocks the jewel case and flings the paste duplicates into the sea. She may be suspected and searched, but nothing can be proved against her, since the jewels are not in her possession.

'And now the significance of the place chosen becomes apparent. If the jewels had merely been thrown out by the side of the line, they might have been found. Hence the importance of the one moment when the train is passing over the sea.

'In the meantime, you make your arrangements for selling the jewellery here. You have only to hand over the stones when the robbery has actually taken place. My wire, however, reached you in time. You obeyed my instructions and deposited the box of jewellery at the Tokatlian to await my arrival, knowing that otherwise I should keep my threat of placing the matter in the hands of the police. You also obeyed my instructions in joining me here.'

Edward Jeffries looked at Mr Parker Pyne appealingly. He was a good-looking young man, tall and fair, with a round chin and very round eyes. 'How can I make you understand?' he said hopelessly. 'To you I must seem just a common thief.'

'Not at all,' said Mr Parker Pyne. 'On the contrary, I should say you are almost painfully honest. I am accustomed to the classification of types. You, my dear sir, fall naturally into the category of victims. Now, tell me the whole story.'

'I can tell you in one word—blackmail.'

'Yes?'

'You've seen my wife: you realize what a pure, innocent creature she is—without thought or knowledge of evil.'

'Yes, yes.'

'She has the most marvellously pure ideals. If she were to find out about—about anything I had done, she would leave me.'

'I wonder. But that is not the point. What *have* you done, my young friend? I presume there is some affair with a woman?'

Edward Jeffries nodded.

'Since your marriage—or before?'

'Before—oh, before.'

'Well, well, what happened?'

'Nothing, nothing at all. This is just the cruel part of it. It was at a hotel in the West Indies. There was a very attractive woman—a Mrs Rossiter—staying there. Her husband was a violent man; he had the most savage fits of temper. One night he threatened her with a revolver. She escaped from him and came to my room. She was halfcrazy with terror. She—she asked me to let her stay there till morning. I—what else could I do?'

Mr Parker Pyne gazed at the young man, and the young man gazed back with conscious rectitude. Mr Parker Pyne sighed. 'In other words, to put it plainly, you were had for a mug, Mr Jeffries.'

'Really—'

'Yes, yes. A very old trick—but it often comes off successfully with quixotic young men. I suppose, when your approaching marriage was announced, the screw was turned?'

'Yes. I received a letter. If I did not send a certain sum of money, everything would be disclosed to my prospective father-in-law. How I had—had alienated this young woman's affection from her husband; how she had been seen coming to my room. The husband would bring a suit for divorce. Really, Mr Pyne, the whole thing made me out the most utter blackguard.' He wiped his brow in a harassed manner.

'Yes, yes, I know. And so you paid. And from time to time the screw has been put on again.'

'Yes. This was the last straw. Our business has been badly hit by the slump. I simply could not lay my hands on any ready money. I hit upon this plan.' He picked up his cup of cold coffee, looked at it absently, and drank it. 'What am I to do now?' he demanded pathetically. 'What *am* I to do, Mr Pyne?'

'You will be guided by me,' said Parker Pyne firmly. 'I will deal with your tormentors. As to your wife, you will go straight back to her and tell her the truth—or at least a portion of it. The only point where you will deviate from the truth is concerning the actual facts in the West Indies. You must conceal from her the fact that you were—well, had for a mug, as I said before.'

'But—'

'My dear Mr Jeffries, you do not understand women. If a woman has to choose between a mug and a Don Juan, she will choose Don Juan every time. Your wife, Mr Jeffries, is a charming, innocent, high-minded girl, and the only way she is going to get any kick out of her life with you is to believe that she has reformed a rake.'

Edward Jeffries was staring at him, open-mouthed.

'I mean what I say,' said Mr Parker Pyne. 'At the present moment your wife is in love with you, but I see signs that she may not remain so if you continue to present to her a picture of such goodness and rectitude that it is almost synonymous with dullness.'

Edward winced.

'Go to her, my boy,' said Mr Parker Pyne kindly. 'Confess everything—that is, as many things as you can think of. Then explain that from the moment you met her you gave up all this life. You even stole so that it might not come to her ears. She will forgive you enthusiastically.'

'But when there's nothing really to forgive—'

'What is truth?' said Mr Parker Pyne. 'In my experience it is usually the thing that upsets the apple cart! It is a fundamental axiom of married life that you *must* lie to a woman. She likes it! Go and be forgiven, my boy. And live happily ever afterwards. I dare say your wife will keep a wary eye on you in future whenever a pretty woman comes along—some men would mind that, but I don't think you will.'

'I never want to look at any woman but Elsie,' said Mr Jeffries simply.

'Splendid, my boy,' said Mr Parker Pyne. 'But I shouldn't let her know that if I were you. No woman likes to feel she's taken on too soft a job.'

Edward Jeffries rose. 'You really think—?'

'I *know*,' said Mr Parker Pyne, with force.

The Man from the Sea

Mr Satterthwaite was feeling old. That might not have been surprising since in the estimation of many people he *was* old. Careless youths said to their partners: 'Old Satterthwaite? Oh! he must be a hundred—or at any rate about eighty.' And even the kindest of girls said indulgently, 'Oh! Satterthwaite. Yes, he's quite old. He *must* be sixty.' Which was almost worse, since he was sixty-nine.

In his own view, however, he was not old. Sixty-nine was an interesting age—an age of infinite possibilities—an age when at last the experience of a lifetime was beginning to tell. But to feel old—that was different, a tired discouraged state of mind when one was inclined to ask oneself depressing questions. What was he after all? A little dried-up elderly man, with neither chick nor child, with no human belongings, only a valuable art collection which seemed at the moment strangely unsatisfying. No one to care whether he lived or died . . .

At this point in his meditations Mr Satterthwaite pulled himself up short. What he was thinking was morbid and unprofitable. He knew well enough, who better, that the chances were that a wife would have hated him or alternatively that he would have hated her, that children would have been a constant source of worry and anxiety, and that demands upon his time and affection would have worried him considerably.

'To be safe and comfortable,' said Mr Satterthwaite firmly—that was the thing.

The last thought reminded him of a letter he had received that morning. He drew it from his pocket and re-read it, savouring its contents pleasurably. To begin with, it was from a Duchess, and Mr Satterthwaite liked hearing from Duchesses. It is true that the letter began by demanding a large subscription for charity and but for that would probably never have been written, but the terms in which it was couched were so agreeable that Mr Satterthwaite was able to gloss over the first fact.

So you've deserted the Riviera, wrote the Duchess. *What is this island of yours like? Cheap? Cannotti put up his prices shamefully this year, and I shan't go to the Riviera again. I might try your island next year if you report favourably, though I should hate five days on a boat. Still anywhere you recommend is sure to be pretty comfortable—too much so. You'll get to be one of those people who do nothing but coddle themselves and think of their comfort. There's only one thing that will save you, Satterthwaite, and that is your inordinate interest in other people's affairs . . .*

As Mr Satterthwaite folded the letter, a vision came up vividly before him of the Duchess. Her meanness, her unexpected and alarming kindness, her caustic tongue, her indomitable spirit.

Spirit! Everyone needed spirit. He drew out another letter with a German stamp upon it—written by a young singer in whom he had interested himself. It was a grateful affectionate letter.

'How can I thank you, dear Mr Satterthwaite? It seems too wonderful to think that in a few days I shall be singing Isolde . . .'

A pity that she had to make her *début* as Isolde. A charming, hardworking child, Olga, with a beautiful voice but no temperament. He hummed to himself. 'Nay order him! Pray understand it! I command it. I, Isolde.' No, the child hadn't got it in her—the spirit—the indomitable will—all expressed in that final 'Ich Isoldé!'

Well, at any rate he had done something for somebody. This island depressed him—why, oh! why had he deserted the Riviera which he knew so well and where he was so well known? Nobody here took any interest in him. Nobody seemed to realize that here was *the* Mr Satterthwaite—the friend of Duchesses and Countesses and singers and writers. No one in the island was of any social importance or of any artistic importance either. Most people had been there seven, fourteen, or twenty-one years running and valued themselves and were valued accordingly.

With a deep sigh Mr Satterthwaite proceeded down from the hotel to the small straggling harbour below. His way lay between an avenue of bougainvillaea—a vivid mass of flaunting scarlet, that made him feel older and greyer than ever.

'I'm getting old,' he murmured. 'I'm getting old and tired.'

He was glad when he had passed the bougainvillaea and was walking down the white street with the blue sea at the end of it. A disreputable dog was standing in the middle of the road, yawning and stretching himself in the sun. Having prolonged his stretch to the utmost limits of ecstasy, he sat down and treated himself to a really good scratch. He then rose, shook himself, and looked round for any other good things that life might have to offer.

There was a dump of rubbish by the side of the road and to this he went sniffing in pleasurable anticipation. True enough, his nose had not deceived him! A smell of such rich putrescence that surpassed even his anticipations! He sniffed with growing appreciation, then suddenly abandoning himself, he lay on his back and rolled frenziedly on the delicious dump. Clearly the world this morning was a dog paradise!

Tiring at last, he regained his feet and strolled out once more into the middle of the road. And then, without the least warning, a ramshackle car careered wildly round the corner, caught him full and square and passed on unheeding.

The dog rose to his feet, stood a minute regarding Mr Satterthwaite, a vague dumb reproach in his eyes, then fell over. Mr Satterthwaite went up to him and bent down. The dog was dead. He went on his way, wondering at the sadness and cruelty of life. What a queer dumb look of reproach had been in the dog's eyes. 'Oh! World,' they seemed to say. 'Oh! Wonderful World in which I have trusted. Why have you done this to me?'

Mr Satterthwaite went on, past the palm trees and the straggling white houses, past the black lava beach where the surf thundered and where once, long ago, a well-known English swimmer had been carried out to sea and drowned, past the rock pools where children and elderly ladies bobbed up and down and called it bathing, along the steep road that winds upwards to the top of the cliff. For there on the edge of the cliff was a house, appropriately named La Paz. A white house with faded green shutters tightly closed, a tangled beautiful garden, and a walk between cypress trees that led to a plateau on the edge of the cliff where you looked down—down—down—to the deep blue sea below.

It was to this spot that Mr Satterthwaite was bound. He had developed a great love for the garden of La Paz. He had never entered the villa. It seemed always to be empty. Manuel, the Spanish gardener, wished one good-morning with a flourish and gallantly presented ladies with a bouquet and gentlemen with a single flower as a buttonhole, his dark face wreathed in smiles.

Sometimes Mr Satterthwaite made up stories in his own mind about the owner of the villa. His favourite was a Spanish dancer, once world-famed for her beauty, who hid herself here so that the world should never know that she was no longer beautiful.

He pictured her coming out of the house at dusk and walking through the garden. Sometimes he was tempted to ask Manuel for the truth, but he resisted the temptation. He preferred his fancies.

After exchanging a few words with Manuel and graciously accepting an orange rosebud, Mr Satterthwaite passed on down the cypress walk to the sea. It was rather wonderful sitting there—on the edge of nothing—with that sheer drop below one. It made him think of Tristan and Isolde, of the beginning of the third act with Tristan and Kurwenal—that lonely waiting and of Isolde rushing up from the sea and Tristan dying in her arms. (No, little Olga would never make an Isolde. Isolde of Cornwall, that Royal hater and Royal lover . . .) He shivered. He felt old, chilly, alone . . . What had he had out of life? Nothing—nothing. Not as much as that dog in the street . . .

It was an unexpected sound that roused him from his reverie. Footsteps coming along the cypress walk were inaudible, the first he knew of somebody's presence was the English monosyllable 'Damn.'

He looked round to find a young man staring at him in obvious surprise and disappointment. Mr Satterthwaite recognized him at once as an arrival of the day before who had more or less intrigued him. Mr Satterthwaite called him a young man—because in comparison to most of the die-hards in the Hotel he *was* a young man, but he would certainly never see forty again and was probably drawing appreciably near to his half century. Yet in spite of that, the term young man fitted him—Mr Satterthwaite was usually right about such things—there was an impression of immaturity about him. As there is a touch of puppyhood about many a full grown dog so it was with the stranger.

Mr Satterthwaite thought: 'This chap has really never grown up—not properly, that is.'

And yet there was nothing Peter Pannish about him. He was sleek—almost plump, he had the air of one who has always done himself exceedingly well in the material sense and denied himself no pleasure or satisfaction. He had brown eyes—rather round—fair hair turning grey—a little moustache and rather florid face.

The thing that puzzled Mr Satterthwaite was what had brought him to the island. He could imagine him shooting things, hunting things, playing polo or golf or tennis, making love to pretty women. But in the island there was nothing to hunt or shoot, no games except golf-croquet, and the nearest approach to a pretty woman was represented by elderly Miss Baba Kindersley. There were, of course, artists, to whom the beauty of the scenery made appeal, but Mr Satterthwaite was quite certain that the young man was not an artist. He was clearly marked with the stamp of the Philistine.

While he was resolving these things in his mind, the other spoke, realizing somewhat belatedly that his single ejaculation so far might be open to criticism.

'I beg your pardon,' he said with some embarrassment. 'As a matter of fact, I was—well, startled. I didn't expect anyone to be here.'

He smiled disarmingly. He had a charming smile—friendly—appealing.

'It is rather a lonely spot,' agreed Mr Satterthwaite, as he moved politely a little further up the bench. The other accepted the mute invitation and sat down.

'I don't know about lonely,' he said. 'There always seems to be *someone* here.'

There was a tinge of latent resentment in his voice. Mr Satterthwaite wondered why. He read the other as a friendly soul. Why this insistence on solitude? A rendezvous, perhaps? No—not that. He looked again with carefully veiled scrutiny at his companion. Where had he seen that particular expression before quite lately? That look of dumb bewildered resentment.

'You've been up here before then?' said Mr Satterthwaite, more for the sake of saying something than for anything else.

'I was up here last night—after dinner.'

'Really? I thought the gates were always locked.'

There was a moment's pause and then, almost sullenly, the young man said:

'I climbed over the wall.'

Mr Satterthwaite looked at him with real attention now. He had a sleuth-like habit of mind and he was aware that his companion had only arrived on the preceding afternoon. He had had little time to discover the beauty of the villa by daylight and he had so far spoken to nobody. Yet after dark he had made straight for La Paz. Why? Almost involuntarily Mr Satterthwaite turned his head to look at the green-shuttered villa, but it was as ever serenely lifeless, close shuttered. No, the solution of the mystery was not there.

'And you actually found someone here then?'

The other nodded.

'Yes. Must have been from the other hotel. He had on fancy dress.'

'Fancy dress?'

'Yes. A kind of Harlequin rig.'

'What?'

The query fairly burst from Mr Satterthwaite's lips. His companion turned to stare at him in surprise.

'They often do have fancy dress shows at the hotels, I suppose?'

'Oh! quite,' said Mr Satterthwaite. 'Quite, quite, quite.'

He paused breathlessly, then added:

'You must excuse my excitement. Do you happen to know anything about catalysis?'

The young man stared at him.

'Never heard of it. What is it?'

Mr Satterthwaite quoted gravely: '*A chemical reaction depending for its success on the presence of a certain substance which itself remains unchanged.*'

'Oh,' said the young man uncertainly.

'I have a certain friend—his name is Mr Quin, and he can best be described in the terms of catalysis. His presence is a sign that things are going to happen, because when he is there strange revelations come to light, discoveries are made. And yet—he himself takes no part in the proceedings. I have a feeling that it was my friend you met here last night.'

'He's a very sudden sort of chap then. He gave me quite a shock. One minute he wasn't there and the next minute he was! Almost as though he came up out of the sea.'

Mr Satterthwaite looked along the little plateau and down the sheer drop below.

'That's nonsense, of course,' said the other. 'But it's the feeling he gave me. Of course, really, there isn't the foothold for a fly.' He looked over the edge. 'A straight clear drop. If you went over—well, that would be the end right enough.'

'An ideal spot for a murder, in fact,' said Mr Satterthwaite pleasantly.

The other stared at him, almost as though for the moment he did not follow. Then he said vaguely: 'Oh! yes—of course . . .'

He sat there, making little dabs at the ground with his stick and frowning. Suddenly Mr Satterthwaite got the resemblance he had been seeking. That dumb bewildered questioning. *So had the dog looked who was run over.* His eyes and this young man's eyes asked the same pathetic question with the same reproach. 'Oh! world that I have trusted—what have you done to me?'

He saw other points of resemblance between the two, the same pleasure-loving easy-going existence, the same joyous abandon to the delights of life, the same absence of intellectual questioning. Enough for both to live in the moment—the world was a good place, a place of carnal delights—sun, sea, sky—a discreet garbage heap. And then—what? A car had hit the dog. What had hit the man?

The subject of these cogitations broke in at this point, speaking, however, more to himself than to Mr Satterthwaite.

'One wonders,' he said, 'what it's All For?'

Familiar words—words that usually brought a smile to Mr Satterthwaite's lips, with their unconscious betrayal of the innate egoism of humanity which insists on regarding every manifestation of life as directly designed for its delight or its torment. He did not answer and presently the stranger said with a slight, rather apologetic laugh:

'I've heard it said that every man should build a house, plant a tree and have a son.' He paused and then added: 'I believe I planted an acorn once . . .'

Mr Satterthwaite stirred slightly. His curiosity was aroused—that ever-present interest in the affairs of other people of which the Duchess had accused him was roused. It was not difficult. Mr Satterthwaite had a very feminine side to his nature, he was as good a listener as any woman, and he knew the right moment to put in a prompting word. Presently he was hearing the whole story.

Anthony Cosden, that was the stranger's name, and his life had been much as Mr Satterthwaite had imagined it. He was a bad hand at telling a story but his listener supplied the gaps easily enough. A very ordinary life—an average income, a little soldiering, a good deal of sport whenever sport offered, plenty of friends, plenty of pleasant things to do, a sufficiency of women. The kind of life that practically inhibits thought of any description and substitutes sensation. To speak frankly, an animal's life. 'But there are worse things than that,' thought Mr Satterthwaite from the depths of his experience. 'Oh! many worse things than that . . .' This world had seemed a very good place to Anthony Cosden. He had grumbled because everyone always grumbled but it had never been a serious grumble. And then—*this*.

He came to it at last—rather vaguely and incoherently. Hadn't felt quite the thing—nothing much. Saw his doctor, and the doctor had persuaded him to go to a Harley Street man. And then—the incredible truth. They'd tried to hedge about it—spoke of great care—a quiet life, but they hadn't been able to disguise that that was all eyewash—letting him down lightly. It boiled down to this—six months. That's what they gave him. Six months.

He turned those bewildered brown eyes on Mr Satterthwaite. It was, of course, rather a shock to a fellow. One didn't—one didn't somehow, know what to *do*.

Mr Satterthwaite nodded gravely and understandingly.

It was a bit difficult to take in all at once, Anthony Cosden went on. How to put in the time. Rather a rotten business waiting about to get pipped. He didn't feel really ill—not yet. Though that might come later, so the specialist had said—in fact, it was bound to. It seemed such nonsense to be going to die when one didn't in the least want to. The best thing, he had thought, would be to carry on as usual. But somehow that hadn't worked.

Here Mr Satterthwaite interrupted him. Wasn't there, he hinted delicately, any woman?

But apparently there wasn't. There were women, of course, but not that kind. His crowd was a very cheery crowd. They didn't, so he implied, like corpses. He didn't wish to make a kind of walking funeral of himself. It would have been embarrassing for everybody. So he had come abroad.

'You came to see these islands? But why?' Mr Satterthwaite was hunting for something, something intangible but delicate that eluded him and yet which he was sure was there. 'You've been here before, perhaps?'

'Yes.' He admitted it almost unwillingly. 'Years ago when I was a youngster.'

And suddenly, almost unconsciously so it seemed, he shot a quick glance backward over his shoulder in the direction of the villa.

'I remembered this place,' he said, nodding at the sea. *'One step to eternity!'*

'And that is why you came up here last night,' finished Mr Satterthwaite calmly.

Anthony Cosden shot him a dismayed glance.

'Oh! I say—really—' he protested.

'Last night you found someone here. This afternoon you have found me. Your life has been saved—twice.'

'You may put it that way if you like—but damn it all, it's *my* life. I've a right to do what I like with it.'

'That is a cliché,' said Mr Satterthwaite wearily.

'Of course I see your point,' said Anthony Cosden generously. 'Naturally you've got to say what you can. I'd try to dissuade a fellow myself, even though I knew deep down that he was right. And you know that I'm right. A clean quick end is better than a lingering one—causing trouble and expense and bother to all. In any case it's not as though I had anyone in the world belonging to me . . .'

'If you had—?' said Mr Satterthwaite sharply.

Cosden drew a deep breath.

'I don't know. Even then, I think, this way would be best. But anyway—I haven't . . .'

He stopped abruptly. Mr Satterthwaite eyed him curiously. Incurably romantic, he suggested again that there was, somewhere, some woman. But Cosden negatived it. He oughtn't, he said, to complain. He had had, on the whole, a very good life. It was a pity it was going to be over so soon, that was all. But at any rate he had had, he supposed, everything worth having. Except a son. He would have liked a son. He would like to know now that he had a son living after him. Still, he reiterated the fact, he had had a very good life—

It was at this point that Mr Satterthwaite lost patience. Nobody, he pointed out, who was still in the larval stage, could claim to know anything of life at all. Since the words *larval stage* clearly meant nothing at all to Cosden, he proceeded to make his meaning clearer.

'You have not begun to live yet. You are still at the beginning of life.'

Cosden laughed.

'Why, my hair's grey. I'm forty—'

Mr Satterthwaite interrupted him.

'That has nothing to do with it. Life is a compound of physical and mental experiences. I, for instance, am sixty-nine, and I am really sixty-nine. I have known, either at first or second hand, nearly all the experiences life has to offer. You are like a man who talks of a full year and has seen nothing but snow and ice! The flowers of Spring, the languorous days of Summer, the falling leaves of Autumn—he knows nothing of them—not even that there are such things. And you are going to turn your back on even this opportunity of knowing them.'

'You seem to forget,' said Anthony Cosden dryly, 'that, in any case, I have only six months.'

'Time, like everything else, is relative,' said Mr Satterthwaite. 'That six months might be the longest and most varied experience of your whole life.'

Cosden looked unconvinced.

'In my place,' he said, 'you would do the same.'

Mr Satterthwaite shook his head.

'No,' he said simply. 'In the first place, I doubt if I should have the courage. It needs courage and I am not at all a brave individual. And in the second place—'

'Well?'

'I always want to know what is going to happen tomorrow.'

Cosden rose suddenly with a laugh.

'Well, sir, you've been very good in letting me talk to you. I hardly know why—anyway, there it is. I've said a lot too much. Forget it.'

'And tomorrow, when an accident is reported, I am to leave it at that? To make no suggestion of suicide?'

'That's as you like. I'm glad you realize one thing—that you can't prevent me.'

'My dear young man,' said Mr Satterthwaite placidly, 'I can hardly attach myself to you like the proverbial limpet. Sooner or later you would give me the slip and accomplish your purpose. But you are frustrated at any rate for this afternoon. You would hardly like to go to your death leaving me under the possible imputation of having pushed you over.'

'That is true,' said Cosden. 'If you insist on remaining here—'

'I do,' said Mr Satterthwaite firmly.

Cosden laughed good-humouredly.

'Then the plan must be deferred for the moment. In which case I will go back to the hotel. See you later perhaps.'

Mr Satterthwaite was left looking at the sea.

'And now,' he said to himself softly, 'what next? There must be a next. I wonder . . .'

He got up. For a while he stood at the edge of the plateau looking down on the dancing water beneath. But he found no inspiration there, and turning slowly he walked back along the path between the cypresses and into the quiet garden. He looked at the shuttered, peaceful house and he wondered, as he had often wondered before, who had lived there and what had taken place within those placid walls. On a sudden impulse he walked up some crumbling stone steps and laid a hand on one of the faded green shutters.

To his surprise it swung back at his touch. He hesitated a moment, then pushed it boldly open. The next minute he stepped back with a little exclamation of dismay. A woman stood in the window facing him. She wore black and had a black lace mantilla draped over her head.

Mr Satterthwaite floundered wildly in Italian interspersed with German—the nearest he could get in the hurry of the moment to Spanish. He was desolated and ashamed, he explained haltingly. The Signora must forgive. He thereupon retreated hastily, the woman not having spoken one word.

He was halfway across the courtyard when she spoke—two sharp words like a pistol crack.

'Come back!'

It was a barked-out command such as might have been addressed to a dog, yet so absolute was the authority it conveyed, that Mr Satterthwaite had swung round hurriedly and trotted back to the window almost automatically before it occurred to him to feel any resentment. He obeyed like a dog. The woman was still standing motionless at the window. She looked him up and down appraising him with perfect calmness.

'You are English,' she said. 'I thought so.'

Mr Satterthwaite started off on a second apology.

'If I had known you were English,' he said, 'I could have expressed myself better just now. I offer my most sincere apologies for my rudeness in trying the shutter. I am afraid I can plead no excuse save curiosity. I had a great wish to see what the inside of this charming house was like.'

She laughed suddenly, a deep, rich laugh.

'If you really want to see it,' she said, 'you had better come in.'

She stood aside, and Mr Satterthwaite, feeling pleasurably excited, stepped into the room. It was dark, since the shutters of the other windows were closed, but he could see that it was scantily and rather shabbily furnished and that the dust lay thick everywhere.

'Not here,' she said. 'I do not use this room.'

She led the way and he followed her, out of the room across a passage and into a room the other side. Here the windows gave on the sea and the sun streamed in. The furniture, like that of the other room, was poor in quality, but there were some worn rugs that had been good in their time, a large screen of Spanish leather and bowls of fresh flowers.

'You will have tea with me,' said Mr Satterthwaite's hostess. She added reassuringly: 'It is perfectly good tea and will be made with boiling water.'

She went out of the door and called out something in Spanish, then she returned and sat down on a sofa opposite her guest. For the first time, Mr Satterthwaite was able to study her appearance.

The first effect she had upon him was to make him feel even more grey and shrivelled and elderly than usual by contrast with her own forceful personality. She was a tall woman, very sunburnt, dark and handsome though no longer young. When she was in the room the sun seemed to be shining twice as brightly as when she was out of it, and presently a curious feeling of warmth and aliveness began to steal over Mr Satterthwaite. It was as though he stretched out thin, shrivelled hands to a reassuring flame. He thought, 'She's so much vitality herself that she's got a lot left over for other people.'

He recalled the command in her voice when she had stopped him, and wished that his protégée, Olga, could be imbued with a little of that force. He thought: 'What an Isolde she'd make! And yet she probably hasn't got the ghost of a singing voice. Life is badly arranged.' He was, all the same, a little afraid of her. He did not like domineering women.

She had clearly been considering him as she sat with her chin in her hands, making no pretence about it. At last she nodded as though she had made up her mind.

'I am glad you came,' she said at last. 'I needed someone very badly to talk to this afternoon. And you are used to that, aren't you?'

'I don't quite understand.'

'I meant people tell you things. You knew what I meant! Why pretend?'

'Well—perhaps—'

She swept on, regardless of anything he had been going to say.

'One could say anything to you. That is because you are half a woman. You know what we feel—what we think—the queer, queer things we do.'

Her voice died away. Tea was brought by a large, smiling Spanish girl. It was good tea—China—Mr Satterthwaite sipped it appreciatively.

'You live here?' he inquired conversationally.

'Yes.'

'But not altogether. The house is usually shut up, is it not? At least so I have been told.'

'I am here a good deal, more than anyone knows. I only use these rooms.'

'You have had the house long?'

'It has belonged to me for twenty-two years—and I lived here for a year before that.'

Mr Satterthwaite said rather inanely (or so he felt): 'That is a very long time.'

'The year? Or the twenty-two years?'

His interest stirred, Mr Satterthwaite said gravely: 'That depends.'

She nodded.

'Yes, it depends. They are two separate periods. They have nothing to do with each other. Which is long? Which is short? Even now I cannot say.'

She was silent for a minute, brooding. Then she said with a little smile:

'It is such a long time since I have talked with anyone—such a long time! I do not apologize. You came to my shutter. You wished to look through my window. And that is what you are always doing, is it not? Pushing aside the shutter and looking through the window into the truth of people's lives. If they will let you. And often if they will not let you! It would be difficult to hide anything from you. You would guess—and guess right.'

Mr Satterthwaite had an odd impulse to be perfectly sincere.

'I am sixty-nine,' he said. 'Everything I know of life I know at second hand. Sometimes that is very bitter to me. And yet, because of it, I know a good deal.'

She nodded thoughtfully.

'I know. Life is very strange. I cannot imagine what it must be like to be that—always a looker-on.'

Her tone was wondering. Mr Satterthwaite smiled.

'No, you would not know. Your place is in the centre of the stage. You will always be the Prima Donna.'

'What a curious thing to say.'

'But I am right. Things have happened to you—will always happen to you. Sometimes, I think, there have been tragic things. Is that so?'

Her eyes narrowed. She looked across at him.

'If you are here long, somebody will tell you of the English swimmer who was drowned at the foot of this cliff. They will tell you how young and strong he was, how handsome, and they will tell you that his young wife looked down from the top of the cliff and saw him drowning.'

'Yes, I have already heard that story.'

'That man was my husband. This was his villa. He brought me out here with him when I was eighteen, and a year later he died—driven by the surf on the black rocks, cut and bruised and mutilated, battered to death.'

Mr Satterthwaite gave a shocked exclamation. She leant forward, her burning eyes focused on his face.

'You spoke of tragedy. Can you imagine a greater tragedy than that? For a young wife, only a year married, to stand helpless while the man she loved fought for his life—and lost it—horribly.'

'Terrible,' said Mr Satterthwaite. He spoke with real emotion. 'Terrible. I agree with you. Nothing in life could be so dreadful.'

Suddenly she laughed. Her head went back.

'You are wrong,' she said. 'There is something more terrible. And that is for a young wife to stand there and hope and long for her husband to drown . . .'

'But good God,' cried Mr Satterthwaite, 'you don't mean——?'

'Yes, I do. That's what it was really. I knelt there—knelt down on the cliff and prayed. The Spanish servants thought I was praying for his life to be saved. I wasn't. I was praying that I might wish him to be spared. I was saying one thing over and over again, "God, help me not to wish him dead. God, help me not to wish him dead." But it wasn't any good. All the time I hoped—hoped—and my hope came true.'

She was silent for a minute or two and then she said very gently in quite a different voice:

'That is a terrible thing, isn't it? It's the sort of thing one can't forget. I was terribly happy when I knew he was really dead and couldn't come back to torture me any more.'

'My child,' said Mr Satterthwaite, shocked.

'I know. I was too young to have that happen to me. Those things should happen to one when one is older—when one is more prepared for—for beastliness. Nobody knew, you know, what he was really like. I thought he was wonderful when I first met him and was so happy and proud when he asked me to marry him. But things went wrong almost at once. He was angry with me—nothing I could do pleased him—and yet I tried so hard. And then he began to like hurting me. And above all to terrify me. That's what he enjoyed most. He thought out all sorts of things . . . dreadful things. I won't tell you. I suppose, really, he must have been a little mad. I was alone here, in his power, and cruelty began to be his hobby.' Her eyes widened and darkened. 'The worst was my baby. I was going to have a baby. Because of some of the things he did to me—it was born dead. My little baby. I nearly died, too—but I didn't. I wish I had.'

Mr Satterthwaite made an inarticulate sound.

'And then I was delivered—in the way I've told you. Some girls who were staying at the hotel dared him. That's how it happened. All the Spaniards told him it was madness to risk the sea just there. But he was very vain—he wanted to show off. And I—I saw him drown—and was glad. God oughtn't to let such things happen.'

Mr Satterthwaite stretched out his little dry hand and took hers. She squeezed it hard as a child might have done. The maturity had fallen away from her face. He saw her without difficulty as she had been at nineteen.

'At first it seemed too good to be true. The house was mine and I could live in it. And no one could hurt me any more! I was an orphan, you know, I had no near relations, no one to care what became of me. That simplified things. I lived on here—in this villa—and it seemed like Heaven. Yes, like Heaven. I've never been so happy since, and never shall again. Just to wake up and know that everything was all right—no pain, no terror, no wondering what he was going to do to me next. Yes, it was Heaven.'

She paused a long time, and Mr Satterthwaite said at last:

'And then?'

'I suppose human beings aren't ever satisfied. At first, just being free was enough. But after a while I began to get—well, lonely, I suppose. I began to think about my baby that died. If only I had had my baby! I wanted it as a baby, and also as a plaything. I wanted dreadfully something or someone to play with. It sounds silly and childish, but there it was.'

'I understand,' said Mr Satterthwaite gravely.

'It's difficult to explain the next bit. It just—well, happened, you see. There was a young Englishman staying at the hotel. He strayed in the garden by mistake. I was wearing Spanish dress and he took me for a Spanish girl. I thought it would be rather fun to pretend I was one, so I played up. His Spanish was very bad but he could just manage a little. I told him the villa belonged to an English lady who was away. I said she had taught me a little English and I pretended to speak broken English. It was such fun—such fun—even now I can remember what fun it was. He began to make love to me. We agreed to pretend that the villa was our home, that we were just married and coming to live there. I suggested that we should try one of the shutters—the one you tried this evening. It was open and inside the room was dusty and uncared for. We crept in. It was exciting and wonderful. We pretended it was our own house.'

She broke off suddenly, looked appealingly at Mr Satterthwaite.

'It all seemed lovely—like a fairy tale. And the lovely thing about it, to me, was that it wasn't true. It wasn't real.'

Mr Satterthwaite nodded. He saw her, perhaps more clearly than she saw herself—that frightened, lonely child entranced with her make-believe that was so safe because it wasn't real.

'He was, I suppose, a very ordinary young man. Out for adventure, but quite sweet about it. We went on pretending.'

She stopped, looked at Mr Satterthwaite and said again:

'You understand? We went on pretending . . .'

She went on again in a minute.

'He came up again the next morning to the villa. I saw him from my bedroom through the shutter. Of course he didn't dream I was inside. He still thought I was a little Spanish peasant girl. He stood there looking about him. He'd asked me to meet him. I'd said I would but I never meant to.

'He just stood there looking worried. I think he was worried about me. It was nice of him to be worried about me. He *was* nice . . .'

She paused again.

'The next day he left. I've never seen him again.

'My baby was born nine months later. I was wonderfully happy all the time. To be able to have a baby so peacefully, with no one to hurt you or make you miserable. I wished I'd remembered to ask my English boy his Christian name. I would have called the baby after him. It seemed unkind not to. It seemed rather unfair. He'd given me the thing I wanted most in the world, and he would never even know about it! But of course I told myself that he wouldn't look at it that way—that to know would probably only worry and annoy him. I had been just a passing amusement for him, that was all.'

'And the baby?' asked Mr Satterthwaite.

'He was splendid. I called him John. Splendid. I wish you could see him now. He's twenty. He's going to be a mining engineer. He's been the best and dearest son in the world to me. I told him his father had died before he was born.'

Mr Satterthwaite stared at her. A curious story. And somehow, a story that was not completely told. There was, he felt sure, something else.

'Twenty years is a long time,' he said thoughtfully. 'You've never contemplated marrying again?'

She shook her head. A slow, burning blush spread over her tanned cheeks.

'The child was enough for you—always?'

She looked at him. Her eyes were softer than he had yet seen them.

'Such queer things happen!' she murmured. 'Such queer things . . . You wouldn't believe them—no, I'm wrong, *you* might, perhaps. I didn't love John's father, not at the time. I don't think I even knew what love was. I assumed, as a matter of course, that the child would be like me. But he wasn't. He mightn't have been my child at all. He was like his father—he was like no one but his father. I learnt to know that man— through his child. Through the child, I learnt to love him. I love him now. I always shall love him. You may say that it's imagination, that I've built up an ideal, but it isn't so. I love the man, the real, human man. I'd know him if I saw him tomorrow—even though it's over twenty years since we met. Loving him has made me into a woman. I love him as a woman loves a man. For twenty years I've lived loving him. I shall die loving him.'

She stopped abruptly—then challenged her listener.

'Do you think I'm mad—to say these strange things?'

'Oh! my dear,' said Mr Satterthwaite. He took her hand again.

'You do understand?'

'I think I do. But there's something more, isn't there? Something that you haven't yet told me?'

Her brow clouded over.

'Yes, there's something. It was clever of you to guess. I knew at once you weren't the sort one can hide things from. But I don't want to tell you—and the reason I don't want to tell you is because it's best for you not to know.'

He looked at her. Her eyes met his bravely and defiantly.

He said to himself: 'This is the test. All the clues are in my hand. I ought to be able to know. If I reason rightly I shall know.'

There was a pause, then he said slowly:

'Something's gone wrong.' He saw her eyelids give the faintest quiver and knew himself to be on the right track.

'Something's gone wrong—suddenly—after all these years.' He felt himself groping—groping—in the dark recesses of her mind where she was trying to hide her secret from him.

'The boy—it's got to do with him. You wouldn't mind about anything else.'

He heard the very faint gasp she gave and knew he had probed correctly. A cruel business but necessary. It was her will against his. She had got a dominant, ruthless will, but he too had a will hidden beneath his meek manners. And he had behind him the Heaven-sent assurance of a man who is doing his proper job. He felt a passing contemptuous pity for men whose business it was to track down such crudities as crime. This detective business of the mind, this assembling of clues, this delving for the truth, this wild joy as one drew nearer to the goal . . . Her very passion to keep the truth from him helped her. He felt her stiffen defiantly as he drew nearer and nearer.

'It is better for me not to know, you say. Better for *me*? But you are not a very considerate woman. You would not shrink from putting a stranger to a little temporary inconvenience. It is more than that, then? If you tell me you make me an accomplice before the fact. That sounds like crime. Fantastic! I could not associate crime with you. Or only one sort of crime. A crime against yourself.'

Her lids drooped in spite of herself, veiled her eyes. He leaned forward and caught her wrist.

'It *is* that, then! You are thinking of taking your life.'

She gave a low cry.

'How did you know? How did you know?'

'But why? You are not tired of life. I never saw a woman less tired of it—more radiantly alive.'

She got up, went to the window, pushing back a strand of her dark hair as she did so.

'Since you have guessed so much I might as well tell you the truth. I should not have let you in this evening. I might have known that you would see too much. You are that kind of man. You were right about the cause. It's the boy. He knows nothing. But last time he was home, he spoke tragically of a friend of his, and I discovered something. If he finds out that he is illegitimate it will break his heart. He is proud—horribly proud!

There is a girl. Oh! I won't go into details. But he is coming very soon—and he wants to know all about his father—he wants details. The girl's parents, naturally, want to know. When he discovers the truth, he will break with her, exile himself, ruin his life. Oh! I know the things you would say. He is young, foolish, wrong-headed to take it like that! All true, perhaps. But does it matter what people ought to be? They are what they are. *It will break his heart* . . . But if, before he comes, there has been an accident, everything will be swallowed up in grief for me. He will look through my papers, find nothing, and be annoyed that I told him so little. But he will not suspect the truth. It is the best way. One must pay for happiness, and I have had so much—oh! so much happiness. And in reality the price will be easy, too. A little courage—to take the leap—perhaps a moment or so of anguish.'

'But, my dear child—'

'Don't argue with me.' She flared round on him. 'I won't listen to conventional arguments. My life is my own. Up to now, it has been needed—for John. But he needs it no longer. He wants a mate—a companion—he will turn to her all the more willingly because I am no longer there. My life is useless, but my death will be of use. And I have the right to do what I like with my own life.'

'Are you sure?'

The sternness of his tone surprised her. She stammered slightly.

'If it is no good to anyone—and I am the best judge of that—'

He interrupted her again.

'Not necessarily.'

'What do you mean?'

'Listen. I will put a case to you. A man comes to a certain place—to commit suicide, shall we say? But by chance he finds another man there, so he fails in his purpose and goes away—to live. The second man has saved the first man's life, not by being necessary to him or prominent in his life, but just by the mere physical fact of having been in a certain place at a certain moment. You take your life today and perhaps, some five, six, seven years hence, someone will go to death or disaster simply for lack of your presence in a given spot or place. It may be a runaway horse coming down a street that swerved aside at sight of you and so fails to trample a child that is playing in the gutter. That child may live to grow up and be a great musician, or discover a cure for cancer. Or it may be less melodramatic than that. He may just grow up to ordinary everyday happiness . . .'

She stared at him.

'You are a strange man. These things you say—I have never thought of them . . .'

'You say your life is your own,' went on Mr Satterthwaite. 'But can you dare to ignore the chance that you are taking part in a gigantic drama under the orders of a divine Producer? Your cue may not come till the end of the play—it may be totally unimportant, a mere walking-on part, but upon it may hang the issues of the play if you do not give the cue to another player. The whole edifice may crumple. You as you, may not matter to anyone in the world, but you as a person in a particular place may matter unimaginably.'

She sat down, still staring.

'What do you want me to do?' she said simply.

It was Mr Satterthwaite's moment of triumph. He issued orders.

'I want you at least to promise me one thing—to do nothing rash for twenty-four hours.'

She was silent for a moment or two and then she said: 'I promise.'

'There is one other thing—a favour.'

'Yes?'

'Leave the shutter of the room I came in by unfastened, and keep vigil there tonight.'

She looked at him curiously, but nodded assent.

'And now,' said Mr Satterthwaite, slightly conscious of anticlimax, 'I really must be going. God bless you, my dear.'

He made a rather embarrassed exit. The stalwart Spanish girl met him in the passage and opened a side door for him, staring curiously at him the while.

It was just growing dark as he reached the hotel. There was a solitary figure sitting on the terrace. Mr Satterthwaite made straight for it. He was excited and his heart was beating quite fast. He felt that tremendous issues lay in his hands. One false move—

But he tried to conceal his agitation and to speak naturally and casually to Anthony Cosden.

'A warm evening,' he observed. 'I quite lost count of time sitting up there on the cliff.'

'Have you been up there all this time?'

Mr Satterthwaite nodded. The swing door into the hotel opened to let someone through, and a beam of light fell suddenly on the other's face, illuminating its look of dull suffering, of uncomprehending dumb endurance.

Mr Satterthwaite thought to himself: 'It's worse for him than it would be for me. Imagination, conjecture, speculation—they can do a lot for you. You can, as it were, ring the changes upon pain. The uncomprehending blind suffering of an animal—that's terrible . . .'

Cosden spoke suddenly in a harsh voice.

'I'm going for a stroll after dinner. You—you understand? The third time's lucky. For God's sake don't interfere. I know your interference will be well-meaning and all that—but take it from me, it's useless.'

Mr Satterthwaite drew himself up.

'I never interfere,' he said, thereby giving the lie to the whole purpose and object of his existence.

'I know what you think—' went on Cosden, but he was interrupted.

'You must excuse me, but there I beg to differ from you,' said Mr Satterthwaite. 'Nobody knows what another person is thinking. They may imagine they do, but they are nearly always wrong.'

'Well, perhaps that's so.' Cosden was doubtful, slightly taken aback.

'Thought is yours only,' said his companion. 'Nobody can alter or influence the use you mean to make of it. Let us talk of a less painful subject. That old villa, for instance. It has a curious charm, withdrawn, sheltered from the world, shielding heaven knows what mystery. It tempted me to do a doubtful action. I tried one of the shutters.'

'You did?' Cosden turned his head sharply. 'But it was fastened, of course?'

'No,' said Mr Satterthwaite. 'It was open.' He added gently: 'The third shutter from the end.'

'Why,' Cosden burst out, 'that was the one—'

He broke off suddenly, but Mr Satterthwaite had seen the light that had sprung up in his eyes. He rose—satisfied.

Some slight tinge of anxiety still remained with him. Using his favourite metaphor of a drama, he hoped that he had spoken his few lines correctly. For they were very important lines.

But thinking it over, his artistic judgment was satisfied. On his way up to the cliff, Cosden would try that shutter. It was not in human nature to resist. A memory of twenty odd years ago had brought him to this spot, the same memory would take him to the shutter. And afterwards?

'I shall know in the morning,' said Mr Satterthwaite, and proceeded to change methodically for his evening meal.

It was somewhere round ten o'clock that Mr Satterthwaite set foot once more in the garden of La Paz. Manuel bade him a smiling 'Good morning,' and handed him a single rosebud which Mr Satterthwaite put carefully into his buttonhole. Then he went on to the house. He stood there for some minutes looking up at the peaceful white walls, the trailing orange creeper, and the faded green shutters. So silent, so peaceful. Had the whole thing been a dream?

But at that moment one of the windows opened and the lady who occupied Mr Satterthwaite's thoughts came out. She came straight to him with a buoyant swaying walk, like someone carried on a great wave of exultation. Her eyes were shining, her colour high. She looked like a figure of joy on a frieze. There was no hesitation about her, no doubts or tremors. Straight to Mr Satterthwaite she came, put her hands on his shoulders and kissed him—not once but many times. Large, dark, red roses, very velvety—that is how he thought of it afterwards. Sunshine, summer, birds singing—that was the atmosphere into which he felt himself caught up. Warmth, joy and tremendous vigour.

'I'm so happy,' she said. 'You darling! How did you know? How *could* you know? You're like the good magician in the fairy tales.'

She paused, a sort of breathlessness of happiness upon her.

'We're going over today—to the Consul—to get married. When John comes, his father will be there. We'll tell him there was some misunderstanding in the past. Oh! he won't ask questions. Oh! I'm so happy—so happy—so happy.'

Happiness did indeed surge from her like a tide. It lapped round Mr Satterthwaite in a warm exhilarating flood.

'It's so wonderful to Anthony to find he has a son. I never dreamt he'd mind or care.' She looked confidently into Mr Satterthwaite's eyes. 'Isn't it strange how things come right and end all beautifully?'

He had his clearest vision of her yet. A child—still a child—with her love of make-believe—her fairy tales that ended beautifully with two people 'living happily ever afterwards'.

He said gently:

'If you bring this man of yours happiness in these last

months, you will indeed have done a very beautiful thing.'

Her eyes opened wide—surprised.

'Oh!' she said. 'You don't think I'd let him die, do you? After all these years—when he's come to me. I've known lots of people whom doctors have given up and who are alive today. Die? Of course he's not going to die!'

He looked at her—her strength, her beauty, her vitality—her indomitable courage and will. He, too, had known doctors to be mistaken . . . The personal factor—you never knew how much and how little it counted.

She said again, with scorn and amusement in her voice:

'You don't think I'd let him die, do you?'

'No,' said Mr Satterthwaite at last very gently. 'Somehow, my dear, I don't think you will . . .'

Then at last he walked down the cypress path to the bench overlooking the sea and found there the person he was expecting to see. Mr Quin rose and greeted him—the same as ever, dark, saturnine, smiling and sad.

'You expected me?' he asked.

And Mr Satterthwaite answered: 'Yes, I expected you.'

They sat together on the bench.

'I have an idea that you have been playing Providence once more, to judge by your expression,' said Mr Quin presently.

Mr Satterthwaite looked at him reproachfully.

'As if you didn't know all about it.'

'You always accuse me of omniscience,' said Mr Quin, smiling.

'If you know nothing, why were you here the night before last—waiting?' countered Mr Satterthwaite.

'Oh, that—?'

'Yes, that.'

'I had a—commission to perform.'

'For whom?'

'You have sometimes fancifully named me an advocate for the dead.'

'The dead?' said Mr Satterthwaite, a little puzzled. 'I don't understand.'

Mr Quin pointed a long, lean finger down at the blue depths below.

'A man was drowned down there twenty-two years ago.'

'I know—but I don't see—'

'Supposing that, after all, that man loved his young wife. Love can make devils of men as well as angels. She had a girlish adoration for him, but he could never touch the womanhood in her—and that drove him mad. He tortured her because he loved her. Such things happen. You know that as well as I do.'

'Yes,' admitted Mr Satterthwaite, 'I have seen such things—but rarely—very rarely . . .'

'And you have also seen, more commonly, that there is such a thing as remorse—the desire to make amends—at all costs to make amends.'

'Yes, but death came too soon . . .'

'Death!' There was contempt in Mr Quin's voice. 'You believe in a life after death, do you not? And who are you to say that the same wishes, the same desires, may not operate in that other life? If the desire is strong enough—a messenger may be found.'

His voice tailed away.

Mr Satterthwaite got up, trembling a little.

'I must get back to the hotel,' he said. 'If you are going that way.'

But Mr Quin shook his head.

'No,' he said. 'I shall go back the way I came.'

When Mr Satterthwaite looked back over his shoulder, he saw his friend walking towards the edge of the cliff.

The Girdle of Hyppolita

One thing leads to another, as Hercule Poirot is fond of saying without much originality.

He adds that this was never more clearly evidenced than in the case of the stolen Rubens.

He was never much interested in the Rubens. For one thing Rubens is not a painter he admires, and then the circumstances of the theft were quite ordinary. He took it up to oblige Alexander Simpson who was by way of being a friend of his and for a certain private reason of his own not unconnected with the classics!

After the theft, Alexander Simpson sent for Poirot and poured out all his woes. The Rubens was a recent discovery, a hitherto unknown masterpiece, but there was no doubt of its authenticity. It had been placed on display at Simpson's Galleries and it had been stolen in broad daylight. It was at the time when the unemployed were pursuing their tactics of lying down on street crossings and penetrating into the Ritz. A small body of them had entered Simpson's Galleries and lain down with the slogan displayed of 'Art is a Luxury. Feed the Hungry.' The police had been sent for, everyone had crowded round in eager curiosity, and it was not till the demonstrators had been forcibly removed by the arm of the law that it was noticed that the new Rubens had been neatly cut out of its frame and removed also!

'It was quite a small picture, you see,' explained Mr Simpson. 'A man could put it under his arm and walk out while everyone was looking at those miserable idiots of unemployed.'

The men in question, it was discovered, had been paid for their innocent part in the robbery. They were to demonstrate at Simpson's Galleries. But they had known nothing of the reason until afterwards.

Hercule Poirot thought that it was an amusing trick but did not see what he could do about it. The police, he pointed out, could be trusted to deal with a straightforward robbery.

Alexander Simpson said:

'Listen to me, Poirot. I know who stole the picture and where it is going.'

According to the owner of Simpson's Galleries it had been stolen by a gang of international crooks on behalf of a certain millionaire who was not above acquiring works of art at a surprisingly low price—and no questions asked! The Rubens, said Simpson, would be smuggled over to France where it would pass into the millionaire's possession. The English and French police were on the alert, nevertheless Simpson was of the opinion that they would fail. 'And once it has passed into this dirty dog's possession, it's going to be more difficult. Rich men have to be treated with respect. That's where *you* come in. The situation's going to be delicate. You're the man for that.'

Finally, without enthusiasm, Hercule Poirot was induced to accept the task. He agreed to depart for France immediately. He was not very interested in his quest, but because of it, he was introduced to the case of the Missing Schoolgirl which interested him very much indeed.

He first heard of it from Chief Inspector Japp who dropped in to see him just as Poirot was expressing approval of his valet's packing.

'Ha,' said Japp. 'Going to France, aren't you?'

Poirot said:

'*Mon cher,* you are incredibly well informed at Scotland Yard.'

Japp chuckled. He said:

'We have our spies! Simpson's got you on to this Rubens business. Doesn't trust us, it seems! Well, that's neither here nor there, but what I want you to do is something quite different. As you're going to Paris anyway, I thought you might as well kill two birds with one stone. Detective Inspector Hearn's over there co-operating with the Frenchies—you know Hearn? Good chap—but perhaps not very imaginative. I'd like your opinion on the business.'

'What is this matter of which you speak?'

'Child's disappeared. It'll be in the papers this evening. Looks as though she's been kidnapped. Daughter of a Canon down at Cranchester. King, her name is, Winnie King.'

He proceeded with the story.

Winnie had been on her way to Paris, to join that select and high-class establishment for English and American girls—Miss Pope's. Winnie had come up from Cranchester by the early train—had been seen across London by a member of Elder Sisters Ltd who undertook such work as seeing girls from one station to another, had been delivered at Victoria to Miss Burshaw, Miss Pope's second-in-command, and had then, in company with eighteen other girls, left Victoria by the boat train. Nineteen girls had crossed the channel, had passed through the customs at Calais, had got into the Paris train, had lunched in the restaurant car. But when, on the outskirts of Paris, Miss Burshaw had counted heads, it was discovered that only *eighteen* girls could be found!

'Aha,' Poirot nodded. 'Did the train stop anywhere?'

'It stopped at Amiens, but at that time the girls were in the restaurant car and they all say positively that Winnie was with them then. They lost her, so to speak, on the return journey to their compartments. That is to say, she did not enter her own compartment with the other five girls who were in it. They did not suspect anything was wrong, merely thought she was in one of the two other reserved carriages.'

Poirot nodded.

'So she was last seen—when exactly?'

'About ten minutes after the train left Amiens.' Japp coughed modestly. 'She was last seen—er—entering the Toilette.'

Poirot murmured:

'Very natural.' He went on: 'There is nothing else?'

'Yes, one thing.' Japp's face was grim. 'Her hat was found by the side of the line—at a spot approximately fourteen miles from Amiens.'

'But no body?'

'No body.'

Poirot asked:

'What do you yourself think?'

'Difficult to know *what* to think! As there's no sign of her body—she can't have fallen off the train.'

'Did the train stop at all after leaving Amiens?'

'No. It slowed up once—for a signal, but it didn't stop, and I doubt if it slowed up enough for anyone to have jumped off without injury. You're thinking that the kid got a panic and tried to run away? It was her first term and she might have been homesick, that's true enough, but all the same she was fifteen and a half—a sensible age, and she'd been in quite good spirits all the journey, chattering away and all that.'

Poirot asked:

'Was the train searched?'

'Oh yes, they went right through it before it arrived at the Nord station. The girl wasn't on the train, that's quite certain.'

Japp added in an exasperated manner:

'She just disappeared—into thin air! It doesn't make sense, M. Poirot. It's crazy!'

'What kind of a girl was she?'

'Ordinary, normal type as far as I can make out.'

'I mean—what did she look like?'

'I've got a snap of her here. She's not exactly a budding beauty.'

He proffered the snapshot to Poirot who studied it in silence.

It represented a lanky girl with her hair in two limp plaits. It was not a posed photograph, the subject had clearly been caught unawares. She was in the act of eating an apple, her lips were parted, showing slightly protruding teeth confined by a dentist's plate. She wore spectacles.

Japp said:

'Plain-looking kid—but then they *are* plain at that age! Was at my dentist's yesterday. Saw a picture in the *Sketch* of Marcia Gaunt, this season's beauty. *I* remember her at fifteen when I was down at the Castle over their burglary business. Spotty, awkward, teeth sticking out, hair all lank and anyhow. They grow into beauties overnight—I don't know how they do it! It's like a miracle.'

Poirot smiled.

'Women,' he said, 'are a miraculous sex! What about the child's family? Have they anything helpful to say?'

Japp shook his head.

'Nothing that's any help. Mother's an invalid. Poor old Canon King is absolutely bowled over. He swears that the girl was frightfully keen to go to Paris—had been looking forward to it. Wanted to study painting and music—that sort of thing. Miss Pope's girls go in for Art with a capital A. As you probably know, Miss Pope's is a very well-known establishment. Lots of society girls go there. She's strict—quite a dragon—and very expensive—and extremely particular whom she takes.'

Poirot sighed.

'I know the type. And Miss Burshaw who took the girls over from England?'

'Not exactly frantic with brains. Terrified that Miss Pope will say it's her fault.'

Poirot said thoughtfully:

'There is no young man in the case?'

Japp gesticulated towards the snapshot.

'Does she look like it?'

'No, she does not. But notwithstanding her appearance, she may have a romantic heart. Fifteen is not so young.'

'Well,' said Japp. 'If a romantic heart spirited her off that train, I'll take to reading lady novelists.'

He looked hopefully at Poirot.

'Nothing strikes you—eh?'

Poirot shook his head slowly. He said:

'They did not, by any chance, find her shoes also by the side of the line?'

'Shoes? No. Why shoes?'

Poirot murmured:

'Just an idea...'

II

Hercule Poirot was just going down to his taxi when the telephone rang. He took off the receiver.

'Yes?'

Japp's voice spoke.

'Glad I've just caught you. It's all off, old man. Found a message at the Yard when I got back. The girl's turned up. At the side of the main road fifteen miles from Amiens. She's dazed and they can't get any coherent story from her, doctor says she's been doped—However, she's all right. Nothing wrong with her.'

Poirot said slowly:

'So you have, then, no need of my services?'

'Afraid not! In fact—sorrrry you have been trrr-roubled.'

Japp laughed at his witticism and rang off.

Hercule Poirot did not laugh. He put back the receiver slowly. His face was worried.

III

Detective Inspector Hearn looked at Poirot curiously.

He said:

'I'd no idea you'd be so interested, sir.'

Poirot said:

'You had word from Chief Inspector Japp that I might consult with you over this matter?'

Hearn nodded.

'He said you were coming over on some business, and that you'd give us a hand with this puzzle. But I didn't expect you now it's all cleared up. I thought you'd be busy on your own job.'

Hercule Poirot said:

'My own business can wait. It is this affair here that interests me. You called it a puzzle, and you say it is now ended. But the puzzle is still there, it seems.'

'Well, sir, we've got the child back. And she's not hurt. That's the main thing.'

'But it does not solve the problem of *how* you got her back, does it? What does she herself say? A doctor saw her, did he not? What did he say?'

'Said she'd been doped. She was still hazy with it. Apparently, she can't remember anything much after starting off from Cranchester. All later events seem to have been wiped out. Doctor thinks she might just possibly have had slight concussion. There's a bruise on the back of her head. Says that would account for a complete blackout of memory.'

Poirot said:

'Which is very convenient for—someone!'

Inspector Hearn said in a doubtful voice:

'You don't think she is shamming, sir?'

'Do you?'

'No, I'm sure she isn't. She's a nice kid—a bit young for her age.'

'No, she is not shamming.' Poirot shook his head. 'But I would like to know *how she got off that train.* I want to know who is responsible—and *why?*'

'As to why, I should say it was an attempt at kidnapping, sir. They meant to hold her to ransom.'

'But they didn't!'

'Lost their nerve with the hue and cry—and planted her by the road quick.'

Poirot inquired sceptically:

'And what ransom were they likely to get from a Canon of Cranchester Cathedral? English Church dignitaries are not millionaires.'

Detective Inspector Hearn said cheerfully:

'Made a botch of the whole thing, sir, in my opinion.'

'Ah, that's your opinion.'

Hearn said, his face flushing slightly:

'What's yours, sir?'

'I want to know *how* she was spirited off that train.'

The policeman's face clouded over.

'That's a real mystery, that is. One minute she was there, sitting in the dining-car, chatting to the other girls. Five minutes later she's vanished—hey presto—like a conjuring trick.'

'Precisely, like a conjuring trick! Who else was there in the coach of the train where Miss Pope's reserved compartments were?'

Inspector Hearn nodded.

'That's a good point, sir. That's important. It's particularly important because it was the last coach on the train and as soon as all the people were back from the restaurant car, the doors between the coaches were locked—actually so as to prevent people crowding along to the restaurant car and demanding tea before they'd had time to clear up lunch and get ready. Winnie King came back to the coach with the others—the school had three reserved compartments there.'

'And in the other compartments of the coach?'

Hearn pulled out his notebook.

'Miss Jordan and Miss Butters—two middle-aged spinsters going to Switzerland. Nothing wrong with them, highly respectable, well known in Hampshire where they come from. Two French commercial travellers, one from Lyons, one from Paris. Both respectable middle-aged men. A young man, James Elliot, and his wife—flashy piece of goods *she* was. He's got a bad reputation, suspected by the police of being mixed up in some questionable transactions—but has never touched kidnapping. Anyway, his compartment was searched and there was nothing in his hand luggage to show that he was mixed up in this. Don't see how he *could* have been. Only other person was an American lady, Mrs Van Suyder, travelling to Paris. Nothing known about her. Looks O.K. That's the lot.'

Hercule Poirot said:

'And it is quite definite that the train did not stop after it left Amiens?'

'Absolutely. It slowed down once, but not enough to let anyone jump off—not without damaging themselves pretty severely and risking being killed.'

Hercule Poirot murmured:

'That is what makes the problem so peculiarly interesting. The schoolgirl vanishes into thin air *just outside Amiens*. She reappears from thin air *just outside Amiens*. Where has she been in the meantime?'

Inspector Hearn shook his head.

'It sounds mad, put like that. Oh! by the way, they told me you were asking something about shoes—the girl's shoes. She had her shoes on all right when she was found, but there *was* a pair of shoes on the line, a signalman found them. Took 'em home with him as they seemed in good condition. Stout black walking shoes.'

'Ah,' said Poirot. He looked gratified.

Inspector Hearn said curiously:

'I don't get the meaning of the shoes, sir? Do they mean anything?'

'They confirm a theory,' said Hercule Poirot. 'A theory of how the conjuring trick was done.'

IV

Miss Pope's establishment was, like many other establishments of the same kind, situated in Neuilly. Hercule Poirot, staring up at its respectable façade, was suddenly submerged by a flow of girls emerging from its portals.

He counted twenty-five of them, all dressed alike in dark blue coats and skirts with uncomfortable-looking British hats of dark blue velour on their heads, round which was tied the distinctive purple and gold of Miss Pope's choice. They were of ages varying from fourteen to eighteen, thick and slim, fair and dark, awkward and graceful. At the end, walking with one of the younger girls, was a grey-haired, fussy looking woman whom Poirot judged to be Miss Burshaw.

Poirot stood looking after them a minute, then he rang the bell and asked for Miss Pope.

Miss Lavinia Pope was a very different person from her second-in-command, Miss Burshaw. Miss Pope had personality. Miss Pope was awe inspiring. Even should Miss Pope unbend graciously to parents, she would still retain that obvious superiority to the rest of the world which is such a powerful asset to a schoolmistress.

Her grey hair was dressed with distinction, her costume was severe but chic. She was competent and omniscient.

The room in which she received Poirot was the room of a woman of culture. It had graceful furniture, flowers, some framed, signed photographs of those of Miss Pope's pupils who were of note in the world—many of them in their presentation gowns and feathers. On the walls hung reproductions of the world's artistic masterpieces and some good watercolour sketches. The whole place was clean and polished to the last degree. No speck of dust, one felt, would have the temerity to deposit itself in such a shrine.

Miss Pope received Poirot with the competence of one whose judgement seldom fails.

'M. Hercule Poirot? I know your name, of course. I suppose you have come about this very unfortunate affair of Winnie King. A most distressing incident.'

Miss Pope did not look distressed. She took disaster as it should be taken, dealing with it competently and thereby reducing it almost to insignificance.

'Such a thing,' said Miss Pope, 'has never occurred before.'

'And never will again!' her manner seemed to say.

Hercule Poirot said:

'It was the girl's first term, here, was it not?'

'It was.'

'You had a preliminary interview with Winnie—and with her parents?'

'Not recently. Two years ago, I was staying near Cranchester—with the Bishop, as a matter of fact—'

Miss Pope's manner said:

('Mark this, please. I am the kind of person who stays with Bishops!')

'While I was there I made the acquaintance of Canon and Mrs King. Mrs King, alas, is an invalid. I met Winnie then. A very well brought up girl, with a decided taste for art. I told Mrs King that I should be happy to receive her here in a year or two—when her general studies were completed. We specialize here, M. Poirot, in Art and Music. The girls are taken to the Opera, to the Comédie Française, they attend lectures at the Louvre. The very best masters come here to instruct them in music, singing, and painting. The broader culture, that is our aim.'

Miss Pope remembered suddenly that Poirot was not a parent and added abruptly:

'What can I do for you, M. Poirot?'

'I would be glad to know what is the present position regarding Winnie?'

'Canon King has come over to Amiens and is taking Winnie back with him. The wisest thing to do after the shock the child has sustained.'

She went on:

'We do not take delicate girls here. We have no special facilities for looking after invalids. I told the Canon that in my opinion he would do well to take the child home with him.'

Hercule Poirot asked bluntly:

'What in your opinion actually occurred, Miss Pope?'

'I have not the slightest idea, M. Poirot. The whole thing, as reported to me, sounds quite incredible. I really cannot see that the member of my staff who was in charge of the girls was in any way to blame—except that she might, perhaps, have discovered the girl's absence sooner.'

Poirot said:

'You have received a visit, perhaps, from the police?'

A faint shiver passed over Miss Pope's aristocratic form. She said glacially:

'A Monsieur Lefarge of the Préfecture called to see me, to see if I could throw any light upon the situation. Naturally I was unable to do so. He then demanded to inspect Winnie's trunk which had, of course, arrived here with those of the other girls. I told him that that had already been called for by another member of the police. Their departments, I fancy, must overlap. I got a telephone call, shortly afterwards, insisting that I had not turned over all Winnie's possessions to them. I was extremely short with them over that. One must not submit to being bullied by officialdom.'

Poirot drew a long breath. He said:

'You have a spirited nature. I admire you for it, Mademoiselle. I presume that Winnie's trunk had been unpacked on arrival?'

Miss Pope looked a little put out of countenance.

'Routine,' she said. 'We live strictly by routine. The girls'trunks are unpacked on arrival and their things put away in the way I expect them to be kept. Winnie's things were unpacked with those of the other girls. Naturally, they were afterwards repacked, so that her trunk was handed over exactly as it had arrived.'

Poirot said: *'Exactly?'*

He strolled over to the wall.

'Surely this is a picture of the famous Cranchester Bridge with the Cathedral showing in the distance.'

'You are quite right, M. Poirot. Winnie had evidently painted that to bring to me as a surprise. It was in her trunk with a wrapper round it and *"For Miss Pope from Winnie"* written on it. Very charming of the child.'

'Ah!' said Poirot. 'And what do you think of it—as a painting?'

He himself had seen many pictures of Cranchester Bridge. It was a subject that could always be found represented at the Academy each year—sometimes as an oil painting—sometimes in the water-colour room. He had seen it painted well, painted in a mediocre fashion, painted boringly. But he had never seen it quite as crudely represented as in the present example.

Miss Pope was smiling indulgently.

She said:

'One must not discourage one's girls, M. Poirot. Winnie will be stimulated to do better work, of course.'

Poirot said thoughtfully:

'It would have been more natural, would it not, for her to do a water-colour?'

'Yes. I did not know she was attempting to paint in oils.'

'Ah,' said Hercule Poirot. 'You will permit me, Mademoiselle?'

He unhooked the picture and took it to the window. He examined it, then, looking up, he said:

'I am going to ask you, Mademoiselle, to give me this picture.'

'Well, really, M. Poirot—'

'You cannot pretend that you are very attached to it. The painting is abominable.'

'Oh, it has no *artistic* merit, I agree. But it is a pupil's work and—'

'I assure you, Mademoiselle, that it is a most unsuitable picture to have hanging upon your wall.'

'I don't know why you should say *that,* M. Poirot.'

'I will prove it to you in a moment.'

He took a bottle, a sponge and some rags from his pocket. He said:

'First I am going to tell you a little story, Mademoiselle. It has a resemblance to the story of the Ugly Duckling that turned into a Swan.'

He was working busily as he talked. The odour of turpentine filled the room.

'You do not perhaps go much to theatrical revues?'

'No, indeed, they seem to me so trivial...'

'Trivial, yes, but sometimes instructive. I have seen a clever revue artist change her personality in the most miraculous way. In one sketch she is a cabaret star, exquisite and glamorous. Ten minutes later, she is an undersized, anæmic child with adenoids, dressed in a gym tunic—ten minutes later still, she is a ragged gypsy telling fortunes by a caravan.'

'Very possible, no doubt, but I do not see—'

'But I am showing you how the conjuring trick was worked on the train. Winnie, the schoolgirl, with her fair plaits, her spectacles, her disfiguring dental plate—goes into the *Toilette*. She emerges a quarter of an hour later as—to use the words of Detective Inspector Hearn—"a flashy piece of goods". Sheer silk stockings, high heeled shoes—a mink coat to cover a school uniform, a daring little piece of velvet called a hat perched on her curls—and a face—oh yes, a face. Rouge, powder, lipstick, mascara! What is the real face of that quick change *artiste* really like? Probably only the good God knows! But you, Mademoiselle, you yourself, you have often seen how the awkward schoolgirl changes almost miraculously into the attractive and well-groomed débutante.'

Miss Pope gasped.

'Do you mean that Winnie King disguised herself as—'

'Not Winnie King—no. Winnie was kidnapped *on the way across London*. Our quick change *artiste* took her place. Miss Burshaw had never seen Winnie King—how was she to know that the schoolgirl with the lank plaits and the brace on her teeth was not Winnie King at all? So far, so good, but the impostor could not afford actually to arrive *here,* since *you* were acquainted with the *real* Winnie. So hey presto, Winnie disappears in the *Toilette* and emerges as wife to a man called Jim Elliot whose passport includes a wife! The fair plaits, the spectacles, the lisle thread stockings, the dental plate—all that can go into a small space. But the thick unglamorous shoes and the hat—that very unyielding British hat—have to be disposed of elsewhere—they go out of the window. Later, the real Winnie is brought across the channel—no one is looking for a sick, half-doped child being brought from *England* to *France*—and is quietly deposited from a car by the side of the main road. If she has been doped all along with scopolamine, she will remember very little of what has occurred.'

Miss Pope was staring at Poirot. She demanded:

'But *why*? What would be the *reason* of such a senseless masquerade?'

Poirot replied gravely:

'Winnie's luggage! These people wanted to smuggle something from England into France—something that every Customs man was on the look-out for—in fact, stolen goods. But what place is safer than a schoolgirl's trunk? You are well-known, Miss Pope, your establishment is justly famous. At the Gare du Nord the trunks of Mesdemoiselles the little Pensionnaires are passed *en bloc*. It is the well-known English school of Miss Pope! And then, after the kidnapping, what more natural than to send and collect the child's luggage—ostensibly from the Préfecture?'

Hercule Poirot smiled.

'But fortunately, there was the school routine of unpacking trunks on arrival—and a present for you from Winnie—*but not the same present that Winnie packed at Cranchester.*'

He came towards her.

'You have given this picture to me. Observe now,

you must admit that it is not suitable for your select school!'

He held out the canvas.

As though by magic Cranchester Bridge had disappeared. Instead was a classical scene in rich, dim colourings.

Poirot said softly:

'*The Girdle of Hyppolita*. Hyppolita gives her girdle to Hercules—painted by Rubens. A great work of art—*mais tout de même* not quite suitable for your drawing-room.'

Miss Pope blushed slightly.

Hyppolita's hand was on her girdle—she was wearing nothing else... Hercules had a lion skin thrown lightly over one shoulder. The flesh of Rubens is rich, voluptuous flesh.

Miss Pope said, regaining her poise:

'A fine work of art... All the same—as you say—after all, one must consider the susceptibilities of parents. Some of them are inclined to be *narrow*... if you know what I mean.'

V

It was just as Poirot was leaving the house that the onslaught took place. He was surrounded, hemmed-in, overwhelmed by a crowd of girls, thick, thin, dark and fair.

'Mon Dieu!' he murmured. 'Here indeed is the attack by the Amazons!'

A tall fair girl was crying out:

'A rumour has gone round—'

They surged closer. Hercule Poirot was surrounded. He disappeared in a wave of young, vigorous femininity.

Twenty-five voices arose, pitched in various keys but all uttering the same momentous phrase.

'*M. Poirot, will you write your name in my autograph book . . . ?*'

The Last Séance

Raoul Daubreuil crossed the Seine humming a little tune to himself. He was a good-looking young Frenchman of about thirty-two, with a fresh-coloured face and a little black moustache. By profession he was an engineer. In due course he reached the Cardonet and turned in at the door of No. 17. The concierge looked out from her lair and gave him a grudging 'Good morning,' to which he replied cheerfully. Then he mounted the stairs to the apartment on the third floor. As he stood there waiting for his ring at the bell to be answered he hummed once more his little tune. Raoul Daubreuil was feeling particularly cheerful this morning. The door was opened by an elderly Frenchwoman whose wrinkled face broke into smiles when she saw who the visitor was.

'Good morning, Monsieur.'

'Good morning, Elise,' said Raoul.

He passed into the vestibule, pulling off his gloves as he did so.

'Madame expects me, does she not?' he asked over his shoulder.

'Ah, yes, indeed, Monsieur.'

Elise shut the front door and turned towards him.

'If Monsieur will pass into the little *salon* Madame will be with him in a few minutes. At the moment she reposes herself.'

Raoul looked up sharply.

'Is she not well?'

'Well!'

Elise gave a snort. She passed in front of Raoul and opened the door of the little *salon* for him. He went in and she followed him.

'Well!' she continued. 'How could she be well, poor lamb? *Séances, séances,* and always *séances!* It is not right— not natural, not what the good God intended for us. For me, I say straight out, it is trafficking with the devil.'

Raoul patted her on the shoulder reassuringly.

'There, there, Elise,' he said soothingly, 'do not excite yourself, and do not be too ready to see the devil in everything you do not understand.'

Elise shook her head doubtingly.

'Ah, well,' she grumbled under her breath, 'Monsieur may say what he pleases, I don't like it. Look at Madame, every day she gets whiter and thinner, and the headaches!'

She held up her hands.

'Ah, no, it is not good, all this spirit business. Spirits indeed! All the good spirits are in Paradise, and the others are in Purgatory.'

'Your view of the life after death is refreshingly simple, Elise,' said Raoul as he dropped into the chair.

The old woman drew herself up.

'I am a good Catholic, Monsieur.'

She crossed herself, went towards the door, then paused, her hand on the handle.

'Afterwards when you are married, Monsieur,' she said pleadingly, 'it will not continue—all this?'

Raoul smiled at her affectionately.

'You are a good faithful creature, Elise,' he said, 'and devoted to your mistress. Have no fear, once she is my wife, all this "spirit business" as you call it, will cease. For Madame Daubreuil there will be no more *séances.*'

Elise's face broke into smiles.

'Is it true what you say?' she asked eagerly.

The other nodded gravely.

'Yes,' he said, speaking almost more to himself than to her. 'Yes, all this must end. Simone has a wonderful gift and she has used it freely, but now she has done her part. As you have justly observed, Elise, day by day she gets whiter and thinner. The life of a medium is a particularly trying and arduous one, involving a terrible nervous strain. All the same, Elise, your mistress is the most wonderful medium in Paris—more, in France. People from all over the world come to her because they know that with her there is no trickery, no deceit.'

Elise gave a snort of contempt.

'Deceit! Ah, no, indeed. Madame could not deceive a new-born babe if she tried.'

'She is an angel,' said the young Frenchman with fervour. 'And I—I shall do everything a man can to make her happy. You believe that?'

Elise drew herself up, and spoke with a certain simple dignity.

'I have served Madame for many years, Monsieur. With all respect I may say that I love her. If I did not believe that you adored her as she deserves to be adored—*eh bien,* Monsieur! I should be willing to tear you limb from limb.'

Raoul laughed.

'Bravo, Elise! you are a faithful friend, and you must approve of me now that I have told you Madame is going to give up the spirits.'

He expected the old woman to receive this pleasantry with a laugh, but somewhat to his surprise she remained grave.

'Supposing, Monsieur,' she said hesitatingly, 'the spirits will not give *her* up?'

Raoul stared at her.

'Eh! What do you mean?'

'I said,' repeated Elise, 'supposing the spirits will not give *her* up?'

'I thought you didn't believe in the spirits, Elise?'

'No more I do,' said Elise stubbornly. 'It is foolish to believe in them. All the same—'

'Well?'

'It is difficult for me to explain, Monsieur. You see, me, I always thought that these mediums, as they call themselves, were just clever cheats who imposed on the poor souls who had lost their dear ones. But Madame is not like that. Madame is good. Madame is honest and—'

She lowered her voice and spoke in a tone of awe.

'Things happen. It is not trickery, things happen, and that is why I am afraid. For I am sure of this, Monsieur, it is not right. It is against nature and le bon Dieu, and *somebody will have to pay.'*

Raoul got up from his chair and came and patted her on the shoulder.

'Calm yourself, my good Elise,' he said, smiling. 'See, I will give you some good news. Today is the last of these *séances*; after today there will be no more.'

'There *is* one today then?' asked the old woman suspiciously.

'The last, Elise, the last.'

Elise shook her head disconsolately.

'Madame is not fit—' she began.

But her words were interrupted, the door opened and a tall, fair woman came in. She was slender and graceful, with the face of a Botticelli Madonna. Raoul's face lighted up, and Elise withdrew quickly and discreetly.

'Simone!'

He took both her long, white hands in his and kissed each in turn. She murmured his name very softly.

'Raoul, my dear one.'

Again he kissed her hands and then looked intently into her face.

'Simone, how pale you are! Elise told me you were resting; you are not ill, my well-beloved?'

'No, not ill—' she hesitated.

He led her over to the sofa and sat down on it beside her.

'But tell me then.'

The medium smiled faintly.

'You will think me foolish,' she murmured.

'I? Think you foolish? Never.'

Simone withdrew her hand from his grasp. She sat perfectly still for a moment or two gazing down at the carpet. Then she spoke in a low, hurried voice.

'I am afraid, Raoul.'

He waited for a minute or two expecting her to go on, but as she did not he said encouragingly:

'Yes, afraid of what?'

'Just afraid—that is all.'

'But—'

He looked at her in perplexity, and she answered the look quickly.

'Yes, it is absurd, isn't it, and yet I feel just that. Afraid, nothing more. I don't know what of, or why, but all the time I am possessed with the idea that something terrible—terrible, is going to happen to me . . .'

She stared out in front of her. Raoul put an arm gently round her.

'My dearest,' he said, 'come, you must not give way. I know what it is, the strain, Simone, the strain of a medium's life. All you need is rest—rest and quiet.'

She looked at him gratefully.

'Yes, Raoul, you are right. That is what I need, rest and quiet.'

She closed her eyes and leant back a little against his arm.

'And happiness,' murmured Raoul in her ear.

His arm drew her closer. Simone, her eyes still closed, drew a deep breath.

'Yes,' she murmured, 'yes. When your arms are round me I feel safe. I forget my life—the terrible life—of a medium. You know much, Raoul, but even you do not know all it means.'

He felt her body grow rigid in his embrace. Her eyes opened again, staring in front of her.

'One sits in the cabinet in the darkness, waiting, and the darkness is terrible, Raoul, for it is the darkness of emptiness, of nothingness. Deliberately one gives oneself up to be lost in it. After that one knows nothing, one feels nothing, but at last there comes the slow, painful return, the awakening out of sleep, but so tired—so terribly tired.'

'I know,' murmured Raoul, 'I know.'

'So tired,' murmured Simone again.

Her whole body seemed to droop as she repeated the words.

'But you are wonderful, Simone.'

He took her hands in his, trying to rouse her to share his enthusiasm.

'You are unique—the greatest medium the world has ever known.'

She shook her head, smiling a little at that.

'Yes, yes,' Raoul insisted.

He drew two letters from his pocket.

'See here, from Professor Roche of the *Salpêtrière,* and this one from Dr Genir at Nancy, both imploring that you will continue to sit for them occasionally.'

'Ah, no!'

Simone sprang suddenly to her feet.

'I will not, I will not. It is to be all finished—all done with. You promised me, Raoul.'

Raoul stared at her in astonishment as she stood wavering, facing him almost like a creature at bay. He got up and took her hand.

'Yes, yes,' he said. 'Certainly it is finished, that is understood. But I am so proud of you, Simone, that is why I mentioned those letters.'

She threw him a swift sideways glance of suspicion.

'It is not that you will ever want me to sit again?'

'No, no,' said Raoul, 'unless perhaps you yourself would care to, just occasionally for these old friends—'

But she interrupted him, speaking excitedly.

'No, no, never again. There is danger. I tell you. I can feel it, great danger.'

She clasped her hands on her forehead a minute, then walked across to the window.

'Promise me never again,' she said in a quieter voice over her shoulder.

Raoul followed her and put his arms round her shoulders.

'My dear one,' he said tenderly, 'I promise you after today you shall never sit again.'

He felt the sudden start she gave.

'Today,' she murmured. 'Ah, yes—I had forgotten Madame Exe.'

Raoul looked at his watch.

'She is due any minute now; but perhaps, Simone, if you do not feel well—'

Simone hardly seemed to be listening to him; she was following out her own train of thought.

'She is—a strange woman, Raoul, a very strange woman. Do you know I—I have almost a horror of her.'

'Simone!'

There was reproach in his voice, and she was quick to feel it.

'Yes, yes, I know, you are like all Frenchmen, Raoul. To you a mother is sacred and it is unkind of me to feel like that about her when she grieves so for her lost child. But—I cannot explain it, she is so big and black, and her hands—have you ever noticed her hands, Raoul? Great big strong hands, as strong as a man's. Ah!'

She gave a little shiver and closed her eyes. Raoul withdrew his arm and spoke almost coldly.

'I really cannot understand you, Simone. Surely you, a woman, should have nothing but sympathy for another woman, a mother bereft of her only child.'

Simone made a gesture of impatience.

'Ah, it is you who do not understand, my friend! One cannot help these things. The first moment I saw her I felt—'

She flung her hands out.

'Fear! You remember, it was a long time before I would consent to sit for her? I felt sure in some way she would bring me misfortune.'

Raoul shrugged his shoulders.

'Whereas, in actual fact, she brought you the exact opposite,' he said drily. 'All the sittings have been attended with marked success. The spirit of the little Amelie was able to control you at once, and the materializations have really been striking. Professor Roche ought really to have been present at the last one.'

'Materializations,' said Simone in a low voice. 'Tell me, Raoul (you know that I know nothing of what takes place while I am in the trance), are the materializations really so wonderful?'

He nodded enthusiastically.

'At the first few sittings the figure of the child was visible in a kind of nebulous haze,' he explained, 'but at the last *séance*—'

'Yes?'

He spoke very softly.

'Simone, the child that stood there was an actual living child of flesh and blood. I even touched her—but seeing that the touch was acutely painful to you, I would not permit Madame Exe to do the same. I was afraid that her self-control might break down, and that some harm to you might result.'

Simone turned away again towards the window.

'I was terribly exhausted when I woke,' she murmured. 'Raoul, are you sure—are you really sure that all this is *right*? You know what dear old Elise thinks, that I am trafficking with the devil?'

She laughed rather uncertainly.

'You know what I believe,' said Raoul gravely. 'In the handling of the unknown there must always be danger, but the cause is a noble one, for it is the cause of Science. All over the world there have been martyrs to Science, pioneers who have paid the price so that others may follow safely in their footsteps. For ten years now you have worked for Science at the cost of a terrific nervous strain. Now your part is done, from today onward you are free to be happy.'

She smiled at him affectionately, her calm restored. Then she glanced quickly up at the clock.

'Madame Exe is late,' she murmured. 'She may not come.'

'I think she will,' said Raoul. 'Your clock is a little fast, Simone.'

Simone moved about the room, rearranging an ornament here and there.

'I wonder who she is, this Madame Exe?' she observed. 'Where she comes from, who her people are? It is strange that we know nothing about her.'

Raoul shrugged his shoulders.

'Most people remain incognito if possible when they

come to a medium,' he observed. 'It is an elementary precaution.'

'I suppose so,' agreed Simone listlessly.

A little china vase she was holding slipped from her fingers and broke to pieces on the tiles of the fireplace. She turned sharply on Raoul.

'You see,' she murmured, 'I am not myself. Raoul, would you think me very—very cowardly if I told Madame Exe I could not sit today?'

His look of pained astonishment made her redden.

'You promised, Simone—' he began gently.

She backed against the wall.

'I won't do it, Raoul. I won't do it.'

And again that glance of his, tenderly reproachful, made her wince.

'It is not of the money I am thinking, Simone, though you must realize that the money this woman has offered you for the last sitting is enormous—simply enormous.'

She interrupted him defiantly.

'There are things that matter more than money.'

'Certainly there are,' he agreed warmly. 'That is just what I am saying. Consider—this woman is a mother, a mother who has lost her only child. If you are not really ill, if it is only a whim on your part—you can deny a rich woman a caprice, can you deny a mother one last sight of her child?'

The medium flung her hands out despairingly in front of her.

'Oh, you torture me,' she murmured. 'All the same you are right. I will do as you wish, but I know now what I am afraid of—it is the word "mother".'

'Simone!'

'There are certain primitive elementary forces, Raoul. Most of them have been destroyed by civilization, but motherhood stands where it stood at the beginning. Animals—human beings, they are all the same. A mother's love for her child is like nothing else in the world. It knows no law, no pity, it dares all things and crushes down remorselessly all that stands in its path.'

She stopped, panting a little, then turned to him with a quick, disarming smile.

'I am foolish today, Raoul. I know it.'

He took her hand in his.

'Lie down for a minute or two,' he urged. 'Rest till she comes.'

'Very well.' She smiled at him and left the room.

Raoul remained for a minute or two lost in thought, then he strode to the door, opened it, and crossed the little hall. He went into a room the other side of it, a sitting room very much like the one he had left, but at one end was an alcove with a big armchair set in it. Heavy black velvet curtains were arranged so as to pull across the alcove. Elise was busy arranging the room. Close to the alcove she had set two chairs and a small round table. On the table was a tambourine, a horn, and some paper and pencils.

'The last time,' murmured Elise with grim satisfaction. 'Ah, Monsieur, I wish it were over and done with.'

The sharp ting of an electric bell sounded.

'There she is, that great gendarme of a woman,' continued the old servant. 'Why can't she go and pray decently for her little one's soul in a church, and burn a candle to Our Blessed Lady? Does not the good God know what is best for us?'

'Answer the bell, Elise,' said Raoul peremptorily.

She threw him a look, but obeyed. In a minute or two she returned ushering in the visitor.

'I will tell my mistress you are here, Madame.'

Raoul came forward to shake hands with Madame Exe. Simone's words floated back to his memory.

'So big and so black.'

She *was* a big woman, and the heavy black of French mourning seemed almost exaggerated in her case. Her voice when she spoke was very deep.

'I fear I am a little late, Monsieur.'

'A few moments only,' said Raoul, smiling. 'Madame Simone is lying down. I am sorry to say she is far from well, very nervous and overwrought.'

Her hand, which she was just withdrawing, closed on his suddenly like a vice.

'But she will sit?' she demanded sharply.

'Oh, yes, Madame.'

Madame Exe gave a sigh of relief, and sank into a chair, loosening one of the heavy black veils that floated round her.

'Ah, Monsieur!' she murmured, 'you cannot imagine, you cannot conceive the wonder and the joy of these *séances* to me! My little one! My Amelie! To see her, to hear her, even—perhaps—yes, perhaps to be even able to—stretch out my hand and touch her.'

Raoul spoke quickly and peremptorily.

'Madame Exe—how can I explain?—on no account must you do anything except under my express directions, otherwise there is the gravest danger.'

'Danger to me?'

'No, Madame,' said Raoul, 'to the medium. You must

understand that the phenomena that occur are explained by Science in a certain way. I will put the matter very simply, using no technical terms. A spirit, to manifest itself, has to use the actual physical substance of the medium. You have seen the vapour of fluid issuing from the lips of the medium. This finally condenses and is built up into the physical semblance of the spirit's dead body. But this ectoplasm we believe to be the actual substance of the medium. We hope to prove this some day by careful weighing and testing—but the great difficulty is the danger and pain which attends the medium on any handling of the phenomena. Were anyone to seize hold of the materialization roughly the death of the medium might result.'

Madame Exe had listened to him with close attention.

'That is very interesting, Monsieur. Tell me, shall not a time come when the materialization shall advance so far that it shall be capable of detachment from its parent, the medium?'

'That is a fantastic speculation, Madame.'

She persisted.

'But, on the facts, not impossible?'

'Quite impossible today.'

'But perhaps in the future?'

He was saved from answering, for at that moment Simone entered. She looked languid and pale, but had evidently regained entire control of herself. She came forward and shook hands with Madame Exe, though Raoul noticed the faint shiver that passed through her as she did so.

'I regret, Madame, to hear that you are indisposed,' said Madame Exe.

'It is nothing,' said Simone rather brusquely. 'Shall we begin?'

She went to the alcove and sat down in the armchair. Suddenly Raoul in his turn felt a wave of fear pass over him.

'You are not strong enough,' he exclaimed. 'We had better cancel the *séance*. Madame Exe will understand.'

'Monsieur!'

Madame Exe rose indignantly.

'Yes, yes, it is better not, I am sure of it.'

'Madame Simone promised me one last sitting.'

'That is so,' agreed Simone quietly, 'and I am prepared to carry out my promise.'

'I hold you to it, Madame,' said the other woman.

'I do not break my word,' said Simone coldly. 'Do not fear, Raoul,' she added gently, 'after all, it is for the last time—the last time, thank God.'

At a sign from her Raoul drew the heavy black curtains across the alcove. He also pulled the curtains of the window so that the room was in semi-obscurity. He indicated one of the chairs to Madame Exe and prepared himself to take the other. Madame Exe, however, hesitated.

'You will pardon me, Monsieur, but—you understand I believe absolutely in your integrity and in that of Madame Simone. All the same, so that my testimony may be the more valuable, I took the liberty of bringing this with me.'

From her handbag she drew a length of fine cord.

'Madame!' cried Raoul. 'This is an insult!'

'A precaution.'

'I repeat it is an insult.'

'I don't understand your objection, Monsieur,' said Madame Exe coldly. 'If there is no trickery you have nothing to fear.'

Raoul laughed scornfully.

'I can assure you that I have nothing to fear, Madame. Bind me hand and foot if you will.'

His speech did not produce the effect he hoped for, for Madame Exe merely murmured unemotionally:

'Thank you, Monsieur,' and advanced upon him with her roll of cord.

Suddenly Simone from behind the curtain gave a cry.

'No, no, Raoul, don't let her do it.'

Madame Exe laughed derisively.

'Madame is afraid,' she observed sarcastically.

'Yes, I am afraid.'

'Remember what you are saying, Simone,' cried Raoul. 'Madame Exe is apparently under the impression that we are charlatans.'

'I must make sure,' said Madame Exe grimly.

She went methodically about her task, binding Raoul securely to his chair.

'I must congratulate you on your knots, Madame,' he observed ironically when she had finished. 'Are you satisfied now?'

Madame Exe did not reply. She walked round the room examining the panelling of the walls closely. Then she locked the door leading into the hall, and, removing the key, returned to her chair.

'Now,' she said in an indescribable voice, 'I am ready.'

The minutes passed. From behind the curtain the sound of Simone's breathing became heavier and more stertorous. Then it died away altogether, to be succeeded by a series of moans. Then again there was silence for a little while, broken by the sudden clattering of the tambourine. The horn was caught up from the table and dashed to the ground. Ironic laughter was heard. The curtains of the alcove seemed to have been pulled back a little, the medium's figure was just visible through the opening, her head fallen forward on her breast. Suddenly Madame Exe drew in her breath sharply. A ribbon-like stream of mist was issuing from the medium's mouth. It condensed and began gradually to assume a shape, the shape of a little child.

'Amelie! My little Amelie!'

The hoarse whisper came from Madame Exe. The hazy figure condensed still further. Raoul stared almost incredulously. Never had there been a more successful materialization. Now, surely it was a real child, a real flesh and blood child standing there.

'*Maman!*'

The soft childish voice spoke.

'My child!' cried Madame Exe. 'My child!'

She half-rose from her seat.

'Be careful, Madame,' cried Raoul warningly.

The materialization came hesitatingly through the curtains. It was a child. She stood there, her arms held out.

'*Maman!*'

'Ah!' cried Madame Exe.

Again she half-rose from her seat.

'Madame,' cried Raoul, alarmed, 'the medium—'

'I must touch her,' cried Madame Exe hoarsely.

She moved a step forward.

'For God's sake, Madame, control yourself,' cried Raoul. He was really alarmed now.

'Sit down at once.'

'My little one, I must touch her.'

'Madame, I command you, sit down!'

He was writhing desperately in his bonds, but Madame Exe had done her work well; he was helpless. A terrible sense of impending disaster swept over him.

'In the name of God, Madame, sit down!' he shouted. 'Remember the medium.'

Madame Exe paid no attention to him. She was like a woman transformed. Ecstasy and delight showed plainly in her face. Her outstretched hand touched the little figure that stood in the opening of the curtains. A terrible moan came from the medium.

'My God!' cried Raoul. 'My God! This is terrible. The medium—'

Madame Exe turned on him with a harsh laugh.

'What do I care for your medium?' she cried. 'I want my child.'

'You are mad!'

'My child, I tell you. Mine! My own! My own flesh and blood! My little one come back to me from the dead, alive and breathing.'

Raoul opened his lips, but no words would come. She was terrible, this woman! Remorseless, savage, absorbed by her own passion. The baby lips parted, and for the third time the same word echoed:

'Maman!'

'Come then, my little one,' cried Madame Exe.

With a sharp gesture she caught up the child in her arms. From behind the curtains came a long-drawn scream of utter anguish.

'Simone!' cried Raoul. 'Simone!'

He was aware vaguely of Madame Exe rushing past him, of the unlocking of the door, of the retreating footsteps down the stairs.

From behind the curtains there still sounded the terrible high long-drawn scream—such a scream as Raoul had never heard. It died away in a horrible kind of gurgle. Then there came the thud of a body falling . . .

Raoul was working like a maniac to free himself from his bonds. In his frenzy he accomplished the impossible, snapping the rope by sheer strength. As he struggled to his feet, Elise rushed in crying, 'Madame!'

'Simone!' cried Raoul.

Together they rushed forward and pulled the curtain.

Raoul staggered back.

'My God!' he murmured. 'Red—all red . . .'

Elise's voice came beside him harsh and shaking.

'So Madame is dead. It is ended. But tell me, Monsieur, what has happened. *Why is Madame all shrunken away—why is she half her usual size? What has been happening here?*'

'I do not know,' said Raoul.

His voice rose to a scream.

'I do not know. I do not know. But I think—I am going mad . . . Simone! Simone!'

The Oracle at Delphi

Mrs Willard J. Peters did not really care for Greece. And of Delphi she had, in her secret heart, no opinion at all.

Mrs Peters' spiritual homes were Paris, London and the Riviera. She was a woman who enjoyed hotel life, but her idea of a hotel bedroom was a soft-pile carpet, a luxurious bed, a profusion of different arrangements of electric light, including a shaded bedside lamp, plenty of hot and cold water and a telephone beside the bed, by means of which you could order tea, meals, mineral waters, cocktails and speak to your friends.

In the hotel at Delphi there were none of these things. There was a marvellous view from the windows, the bed was clean and so was the whitewashed room. There was a chair, a wash-stand and a chest of drawers. Baths took place by arrangement and were occasionally disappointing as regarded hot water.

It would, she supposed, be nice to say that you had been to Delphi, and Mrs Peters had tried hard to take an interest in Ancient Greece, but she found it difficult. Their statuary seemed so unfinished; so lacking in heads and arms and legs. Secretly, she much preferred the handsome marble angel complete with wings which was erected on the late Mr Willard Peters' tomb.

But all these secret opinions she kept carefully to herself, for fear her son Willard should despise her. It was for Willard's sake that she was here, in this chilly and uncomfortable room, with a sulky maid and a disgusted chauffeur in the offing.

For Willard (until recently called Junior—a title which he hated) was Mrs Peters' eighteen-year-old son, and she worshipped him to distraction. It was Willard who had this strange passion for bygone art. It was Willard, thin, pale, spectacled and dyspeptic, who had dragged his adoring mother on this tour through Greece.

They had been to Olympia, which Mrs Peters thought a sad mess. She had enjoyed the Parthenon, but she considered Athens a hopeless city. And a visit to Corinth and Mycenae had been agony to both her and the chauffeur.

Delphi, Mrs Peters thought unhappily, was the last straw. Absolutely nothing to do but walk along the road and look at the ruins. Willard spent long hours on his knees deciphering Greek inscriptions, saying, 'Mother, just listen to this! Isn't it splendid?' And then he would read out something that seemed to Mrs Peters the quintessence of dullness.

This morning Willard had started early to see some Byzantine mosaics. Mrs Peters, feeling instinctively that Byzantine mosaics would leave her cold (in the literal as well as the spiritual sense), had excused herself.

'I understand, Mother,' Willard had said. 'You want to be alone just to sit in the theatre or up in the stadium and look down over it all and let it sink in.'

'That's right, pet,' said Mrs Peters.

'I knew this place would get you,' said Willard exultantly, and departed.

Now, with a sigh, Mrs Peters prepared to rise and breakfast.

She came into the dining-room to find it empty save for four people. A mother and daughter, dressed in what seemed to Mrs Peters a most peculiar style (not recognizing the peplum as such), who were discoursing on the art of self-expression in dancing; a plump, middle-aged gentleman who had rescued a suitcase for her when she got off the train and whose name was Thompson; and a newcomer, a middle-aged gentleman with a bald head who had arrived on the preceding evening.

This personage was the last left in the breakfast room, and Mrs Peters soon fell into conversation with him. She was a friendly woman and liked someone to talk to. Mr Thompson had been distinctly discouraging in manner (British reserve, Mrs Peters called it), and the mother and daughter had been very superior and highbrow, though the girl had got on rather well with Willard.

Mrs Peters found the newcomer a very pleasant person. He was informative without being highbrow. He told her several interesting, friendly little details about the Greeks, which made her feel much more as though they were real people and not just tiresome history out of a book.

Mrs Peters told her new friend all about Willard and what a clever boy he was, and how Culture might be said to be his middle name. There was something about this benevolent and bland personage which made him easy to talk to.

What he himself did and what his name was, Mrs Peters did not learn. Beyond the fact that he had been travelling and that he was having a complete rest from business (what business?) he was not communicative about himself.

Altogether, the day passed more quickly than might have been anticipated. The mother and daughter and Mr Thompson continued to be unsociable. They encountered the latter coming out of the museum, and he immediately turned in the opposite direction.

Mrs Peters' new friend looked after him with a little frown.

'Now I wonder who that fellow is!' he said.

Mrs Peters supplied him with the other's name, but could do no more.

'Thompson—Thompson. No, I don't think I've met him before and yet somehow or other his face seems familiar. But I can't place him.'

In the afternoon Mrs Peters enjoyed a quiet nap in a shady spot. The book she took with her to read was not the excellent one on Grecian Art recommended to her by her son but was, on the contrary, entitled *The River Launch Mystery*. It had four murders in it, three abductions, and a large and varied gang of dangerous criminals. Mrs Peters found herself both invigorated and soothed by the perusal of it.

It was four o'clock when she returned to the hotel. Willard, she felt sure, would be back by this time. So far was she from any presentiment of evil that she almost forgot to open a note which the proprietor said had been left for her by a strange man during the afternoon.

It was an extremely dirty note. Idly she ripped it

open. As she read the first few lines, her face blanched and she put out a hand to steady herself. The handwriting was foreign but the language employed was English.

Lady (it began),—This to hand to inform you that your son is being held captive by us in place of great security. No harm shall happen to honoured young gentleman if you obey orders of yours truly. We demand for him ransom of ten thousand English pounds sterling. If you speak of this to hotel proprietor or police or any such person your son will be killed. This is given you to reflect. Tomorrow directions in way of paying money will be given. If not obeyed the honoured young gentleman's ears will be cut off and sent you. And following day if still not obeyed he will be killed. Again this is not idle threat. Let the Kyria reflect again—above all—be silent.
    Demetrius the Black Browed

It were idle to describe the poor lady's state of mind. Preposterous and childishly worded as the demand was, it yet brought home to her a grim atmosphere of peril. Willard, her boy, her pet, her delicate, serious Willard.

She would go at once to the police; she would rouse the neighbourhood. But perhaps, if she did—She shivered.

Then, rousing herself, she went out of her room in search of the hotel proprietor—the sole person in the hotel who could speak English.

'It is getting late,' she said. 'My son has not returned yet.'

The pleasant little man beamed at her. 'True. Monsieur dismissed the mules. He wished to return on foot. He should have been here by now, but doubtless he has lingered on the way.' He smiled happily.

'Tell me,' said Mrs Peters abruptly, 'have you any bad characters in the neighbourhood?'

Bad characters was a term not embraced by the little man's knowledge of English. Mrs Peters made her meaning plainer. She received in reply an assurance that all around Delphi were very good, very quiet people—all well disposed towards foreigners.

Words trembled on her lips, but she forced them back. That sinister threat tied her tongue. It might be the merest bluff. But suppose it wasn't? A friend of hers in America had had a child kidnapped, and on her informing the police, the child had been killed. Such things did happen.

She was nearly frantic. What was she to do? Ten thousand pounds—what was that?—between forty or fifty thousand dollars! What was that to her in comparison with Willard's safety? But how could she obtain such a sum? There were endless difficulties just now as regarded money and the drawing of cash. A letter of credit for a few hundred pounds was all she had with her.

Would the bandits understand this? Would they be reasonable? Would they *wait*?

When her maid came to her, she dismissed the girl fiercely. A bell sounded for dinner, and the poor lady was driven to the dining-room. She ate mechanically. She saw no one. The room might have been empty as far as she was concerned.

With the arrival of fruit, a note was placed before her. She winced, but the handwriting was entirely different from that which she had feared to see—a neat, clerkly English hand. She opened it without much interest, but she found its contents intriguing:

At Delphi you can no longer consult the oracle (so it ran), but you can consult Mr Parker Pyne.

Below that there was a cutting of an advertisement pinned to the paper, and at the bottom of the sheet a passport photograph was attached. It was the photograph of her bald-headed friend of the morning.

Mrs Peters read the printed cutting twice.

Are you happy? If not, consult Mr Parker Pyne.

Happy? Happy? Had anyone ever been so unhappy? It was like an answer to prayer.

Hastily she scribbled on a loose sheet of paper she happened to have in her bag:

Please help me. Will you meet me outside the hotel in ten minutes?

She enclosed it in an envelope and directed the waiter to take it to the gentleman at the table by the window. Ten minutes later, enveloped in a fur coat, for the night was chilly, Mrs Peters went out of the hotel and strolled slowly along the road to the ruins. Mr Parker Pyne was waiting for her.

'It's just the mercy of heaven you're here,' said Mrs Peters breathlessly. 'But how did you guess the terrible trouble I'm in? That's what I want to know.'

'The human countenance, my dear madam,' said Mr Parker Pyne gently. 'I knew at once that *something* had happened, but what it is I am waiting for you to tell me.'

Out it came in a flood. She handed him the letter, which he read by the light of his pocket torch.

'H'm,' he said. 'A remarkable document. A most remarkable document. It has certain points—'

But Mrs Peters was in no mood to listen to a discussion of the finer points of the letter. What was she to do about Willard? Her own dear, delicate Willard.

Mr Parker Pyne was soothing. He painted an attractive picture of Greek bandit life. They would be especially careful of their captive, since he represented a potential gold mine. Gradually he calmed her down.

'But what am I to do?' wailed Mrs Peters.

'Wait until tomorrow,' said Mr Parker Pyne. 'That is, unless you prefer to go straight to the police.'

Mrs Peters interrupted him with a shriek of terror. Her darling Willard would be murdered out of hand!

'You think I'll get Willard back safe and sound?'

'There is no doubt of that,' said Mr Parker Pyne soothingly. 'The only question is whether you can get him back without paying ten thousand pounds.'

'All I want is my boy.'

'Yes, yes,' said Mr Parker Pyne soothingly. 'Who brought the letter, by the way?'

'A man the landlord didn't know. A stranger.'

'Ah! There are possibilities there. The man who brings the letter tomorrow might be followed. What are you telling the people at the hotel about your son's absence?'

'I haven't thought.'

'I wonder, now.' Mr Parker Pyne reflected. 'I think you might quite naturally express alarm and concern at his absence. A search party could be sent out.'

'You don't think these fiends—?' She choked.

'No, no. So long as there is no word of the kidnapping or the ransom, they cannot turn nasty. After all, you can't be expected to take your son's disappearance with no fuss at all.'

'Can I leave it all to you?'

'That is my business,' said Mr Parker Pyne.

They started back towards the hotel again but almost ran into a burly figure.

'Who was that?' asked Mr Parker Pyne sharply.

'I think it was Mr Thompson.'

'Oh!' said Mr Parker Pyne thoughtfully.

'Thompson, was it? Thompson—hm.'

Mrs Peters felt as she went to bed that Mr Parker Pyne's idea about the letter was a good one. Whoever brought it *must* be in touch with the bandits. She felt consoled, and fell asleep much sooner than she could ever have believed possible.

When she was dressing on the following morning she suddenly noticed something lying on the floor by the window. She picked it up—and her heart missed a beat. The same dirty, cheap envelope; the same hated characters. She tore it open.

> *Good-morning lady. Have you made reflections? Your son is well and unharmed—so far. But we must have the money. It may not be easy for you to get this sum, but it has been told us that you have with you a necklace of diamonds. Very fine stones. We will be satisfied with that, instead. Listen, this is what you must do. You, or anyone you choose to send must take this necklace and bring it to*

the Stadium. From there go up to where there is a tree by a big rock. Eyes will watch and see that only one person comes. Then your son will be exchanged for necklace. The time must be tomorrow six o'clock in the morning just after sunrise. If you put police on us afterwards we shoot your son as your car drives to station.

This is our last word, lady. If no necklace tomorrow morning your son's ears sent you. Next day he die.

With salutations, lady,
Demetrius

Mrs Peters hurried to find Mr Parker Pyne. He read the letter attentively.

'Is this true,' he asked, 'about a diamond necklace?'

'Absolutely. A hundred thousand dollars my husband paid for it.'

'Our well-informed thieves,' murmured Mr Parker Pyne.

'What's that you say?'

'I was just considering certain aspects of the affair.'

'My word, Mr Pyne, we haven't got time for aspects. I've got to get my boy back.'

'But you are a woman of spirit, Mrs Peters. Do you enjoy being bullied and cheated out of ten thousand dollars? Do you enjoy giving up your diamonds meekly to a set of ruffians?'

'Well, of course, if you put it like that!' The woman of spirit in Mrs Peters wrestled with the mother. 'How I'd like to get even with them—the cowardly brutes! The very minute I get my boy back, Mr Pyne, I shall set the whole police of the neighbourhood on them, and, if necessary, I shall hire an armoured car to take Willard and myself to the railway station!' Mrs Peters was flushed and vindictive.

'Ye—es,' said Mr Parker Pyne. 'You see, my dear madam, I'm afraid they will be prepared for that move on your part. They know that once Willard is restored to you nothing will keep you from setting the whole neighbourhood on the alert. Which leads one to suppose that they have prepared for that move.'

'Well, what do you want to do?'

Mr Parker Pyne smiled. 'I want to try a little plan of my own.' He looked around the dining-room. It was empty and the doors at both ends were closed. 'Mrs Peters, there is a man I know in Athens—a jeweller. He specializes in good artificial diamonds—first-class stuff.' His voice dropped to a whisper. 'I'll get him by telephone. He can get here this afternoon, bringing a good selection of stones with him.'

'You mean?'

'He'll extract the real diamonds and replace them with paste replicas.'

'Why, if that isn't the cutest thing I've ever heard of!' Mrs Peters gazed at him with admiration.

'Sh! Not so loud. Will you do something for me?'

'Surely.'

'See that nobody comes within earshot of the telephone.'

Mrs Peters nodded.

The telephone was in the manager's office. He vacated it obligingly, after having helped Mr Parker Pyne to obtain the number. When he emerged, he found Mrs Peters outside.

'I'm just waiting for Mr Parker Pyne,' she said. 'We're going for a walk.'

'Oh, yes, madam.'

Mr Thompson was also in the hall. He came towards them and engaged the manager in conversation.

Were there any villas to be let in Delphi? No? But surely there was one above the hotel?

'That belongs to a Greek gentleman, monsieur. He does not let it.'

'And are there no other villas?'

'There is one belonging to an American lady. That is the other side of the village. It is shut up now. And there is one belonging to an English gentleman, an artist—that is on the cliff edge looking down to Itéa.'

Mrs Peters broke in. Nature had given her a loud voice and she purposely made it louder. 'Why,' she said, 'I'd just adore to have a villa here! So unspoilt and natural. I'm simply crazy about the place, aren't you, Mr Thompson? But of course you must be if you want a villa. Is it your first visit here? You don't say so.'

She ran on determinedly till Mr Parker Pyne emerged from the office. He gave her just the faintest smile of approval.

Mr Thompson walked slowly down the steps and out into the road where he joined the highbrow mother and daughter, who seemed to be feeling the wind cold on their exposed arms.

All went well. The jeweller arrived just before dinner with a car full of other tourists. Mrs Peters took her necklace to his room. He grunted approval. Then he spoke in French.

'Madame peut être tranquille. Je réussirai.' He extracted some tools from his little bag and began work.

At eleven o'clock Mr Parker Pyne tapped on Mrs Peters' door. 'Here you are!'

He handed her a little chamois bag. She glanced inside.

'My diamonds!'

'Hush! Here is the necklace with the paste replacing the diamonds. Pretty good, don't you think?'

'Simply wonderful.'

'Aristopoulous is a clever fellow.'

'You don't think they'll suspect?'

'How should they? They know you have the necklace with you. You hand it over. How can they suspect the trick?'

'Well, I think it's wonderful,' Mrs Peters reiterated, handing the necklace back to him. 'Will you take it to them? Or is that asking too much of you?'

'Certainly I will take it. Just give me the letter, so that I have the directions clear. Thank you. Now, good-night and *bon courage*. Your boy will be with you tomorrow for breakfast.'

'Oh, if only that's true!'

'Now, don't worry. Leave everything in my hands.'

Mrs Peters did not spend a good night. When she slept, she had terrible dreams. Dreams where armed bandits in armoured cars fired off a fusillade at Willard, who was running down the mountain in his pyjamas.

She was thankful to wake. At last came the first glimmer of dawn. Mrs Peters got up and dressed. She sat—waiting.

At seven o'clock there came a tap on the door. Her throat was so dry she could hardly speak.

'Come in,' she said.

The door opened and Mr Thompson entered. She stared at him. Words failed her. She had a sinister presentiment of disaster. And yet his voice when he spoke was completely natural and matter-of-fact. It was a rich, bland voice.

'Good-morning, Mrs Peters,' he said.

'How dare you, sir! How dare you—'

'You must excuse my unconventional visit at so early an hour,' said Mr Thompson. 'But you see, I have a matter of business to transact.'

Mrs Peter leaned forward with accusing eyes. 'So it was you who kidnapped my boy! It wasn't bandits at all!'

'It certainly wasn't bandits. Most unconvincingly done, that part of it, I thought. Inartistic, to say the least of it.'

Mrs Peters was a woman of a single idea. 'Where's my boy?' she demanded, with the eyes of an angry tigress.

'As a matter of fact,' said Mr Thompson, 'he's just outside the door.'

'Willard!'

The door was flung open. Willard, sallow and spectacled and distinctly unshaven, was clasped to his mother's heart. Mr Thompson stood looking benignly on.

'All the same,' said Mrs Peters, suddenly recovering herself and turning on him, 'I'll have the law on you for this. Yes, I will.'

'You've got it all wrong, Mother,' said Willard. 'This gentleman rescued me.'

'Where were you?'

'In a house on the cliff point. Just a mile from here.'

'And allow me, Mrs Peters,' said Mr Thompson, 'to restore your property.'

He handed her a small packet loosely wrapped in tissue paper. The paper fell away and revealed the diamond necklace.

'You need not treasure that other little bag of stones, Mrs Peters,' said Mr Thompson, smiling. 'The real stones are still in the necklace. The chamois bag contains some excellent imitation stones. As your friend said, Aristopoulous is quite a genius.'

'I just don't understand a word of all this,' said Mrs Peters faintly.

'You must look at the case from my point of view,' said Mr Thompson. 'My attention was caught by the use of a certain name. I took the liberty of following you and your fat friend out of doors and I listened—I admit it frankly—to your exceedingly interesting conversation. I found it remarkably suggestive, so much so that I took the manager into my confidence. He took a note of the number to which your plausible friend telephoned and he also arranged that a waiter should listen to your conversation in the dining-room this morning.

'The whole scheme worked very clearly. You were being made the victim of a couple of clever jewel thieves. They know all about your diamond necklace; they follow you here; they kidnap your son, and write the rather comic "bandit" letter, and they arrange that you shall confide in the chief instigator of the plot.

'After that, all is simple. The good gentleman hands you a bag of imitation diamonds and—clears out with his pal. This morning, when your son did not appear, you would be frantic. The absence of your friend would lead you to believe that he had been kidnapped too. I gather that they had arranged for someone to go to the villa tomorrow. That person would have discovered your son, and by the time you and he had put your heads together you might have got an inkling of the plot. But by that time the villains would have got an excellent start.'

'And now?'

'Oh, now they are safely under lock and key. I arranged for that.'

'The villain,' said Mrs Peters, wrathfully remembering her own trustful confidences. 'The oily, plausible villain.'

'Not at all a nice fellow,' agreed Mr Thompson.

'It beats me how you got on to it,' said Willard admiringly. 'Pretty smart of you.'

The other shook his head deprecatingly. 'No, no,' he said. 'When you are travelling incognito and hear your own name being taken in vain—'

Mrs Peters stared at him. 'Who are you?' she demanded abruptly.

'I *am Mr Parker Pyne,*' explained that gentleman.

The World's End

Mr Satterthwaite had come to Corsica because of the Duchess. It was out of his beat. On the Riviera he was sure of his comforts, and to be comfortable meant a lot to Mr Satterthwaite. But though he liked his comfort, he also liked a Duchess. In his way, a harmless, gentlemanly, old-fashioned way, Mr Satterthwaite was a snob. He liked the best people. And the Duchess of Leith was a very authentic Duchess. There were no Chicago pork butchers in her ancestry. She was the daughter of a Duke as well as the wife of one.

For the rest, she was rather a shabby-looking old lady, a good deal given to black bead trimmings on her clothes. She had quantities of diamonds in old-fashioned settings, and she wore them as her mother before her had worn them: pinned all over her indiscriminately. Someone had suggested once that the Duchess stood in the middle of the room whilst her maid flung brooches at her haphazard. She subscribed generously to charities, and looked well after her tenants and dependants, but was extremely mean over small sums. She cadged lifts from her friends, and did her shopping in bargain basements.

The Duchess was seized with a whim for Corsica. Cannes bored her and she had a bitter argument with the hotel proprietor over the price of her rooms.

'And you shall go with me, Satterthwaite,' she said firmly. 'We needn't be afraid of scandal at our time of life.'

Mr Satterthwaite was delicately flattered. No one had ever mentioned scandal in connection with him before. He was far too insignificant. Scandal—and a Duchess—delicious!

'Picturesque you know,' said the Duchess. 'Brigands—all that sort of thing. And extremely cheap, so I've heard. Manuel was positively impudent this morning. These hotel proprietors need putting in their place. They can't expect to get the best people if they go on like this. I told him so plainly.'

'I believe,' said Mr Satterthwaite, 'that one can fly over quite comfortably. From Antibes.'

'They probably charge you a pretty penny for it,' said the Duchess sharply. 'Find out, will you?'

'Certainly, Duchess.'

Mr Satterthwaite was still in a flutter of gratification despite the fact that his role was clearly to be that of a glorified courier.

When she learned the price of a passage by Avion, the Duchess turned it down promptly.

'They needn't think I'm going to pay a ridiculous sum like that to go in one of their nasty dangerous things.'

So they went by boat, and Mr Satterthwaite endured ten hours of acute discomfort. To begin with, as the boat sailed at seven, he took it for granted that there would be dinner on board. But there was no dinner.

The boat was small and the sea was rough. Mr Satterthwaite was decanted at Ajaccio in the early hours of the morning more dead than alive.

The Duchess, on the contrary, was perfectly fresh. She never minded discomfort if she could feel she was saving money. She waxed enthusiastic over the scene on the quay, with the palm trees and the rising sun. The whole population seemed to have turned out to watch the arrival of the boat, and the launching of the gangway was attended with excited cries and directions.

'*On dirait*,' said a stout Frenchman who stood beside them, '*que jamais avant on n'a fait cette manoeuvre là!*'

'That maid of mine has been sick all night,' said the Duchess. 'The girl's a perfect fool.'

Mr Satterthwaite smiled in a pallid fashion.

'A waste of good food, I call it,' continued the Duchess robustly.

'Did she get any food?' asked Mr Satterthwaite enviously.

'I happened to bring some biscuits and a stick of chocolate on board with me,' said the Duchess. 'When I found there was no dinner to be got, I gave the lot to her. The lower classes always make such a fuss about going without their meals.'

With a cry of triumph the launching of the gangway was accomplished. A Musical Comedy chorus of brigands rushed aboard and wrested hand-luggage from the passengers by main force.

'Come on, Satterthwaite,' said the Duchess. 'I want a hot bath and some coffee.'

So did Mr Satterthwaite. He was not wholly successful, however. They were received at the hotel by a bowing manager and were shown to their rooms. The Duchess's had a bathroom attached. Mr Satterthwaite, however, was directed to a bath that appeared to be situated in somebody else's bedroom. To expect the water to be hot at that hour in the morning was, perhaps, unreasonable. Later he drank intensely black coffee, served in a pot without a lid. The shutters and the window of his room had been flung open, and the crisp morning air came in fragrantly. A day of dazzling blue and green.

The waiter waved his hand with a flourish to call attention to the view.

'Ajaccio,' he said solemnly. '*Le plus beau port du monde!*'

And he departed abruptly.

Looking out over the deep blue of the bay, with the snowy mountains beyond, Mr Satterthwaite was almost inclined to agree with him. He finished his coffee, and lying down on the bed, fell fast asleep.

At *déjeuner* the Duchess was in great spirits.

'This is just what will be good for you, Satterthwaite,' she said. 'Get you out of all those dusty little old-maidish ways of yours.' She swept a *lorgnette* round the room. 'Upon my word, there's Naomi Carlton Smith.'

She indicated a girl sitting by herself at a table in the window. A round-shouldered girl, who slouched as she sat. Her dress appeared to be made of some kind of brown sacking. She had black hair, untidily bobbed.

'An artist?' asked Mr Satterthwaite.

He was always good at placing people.

'Quite right,' said the Duchess. 'Calls herself one anyway. I knew she was mooching around in some queer quarter of the globe. Poor as a church mouse, proud as Lucifer, and a bee in her bonnet like all the Carlton Smiths. Her mother was my first cousin.'

'She's one of the Knowlton lot then?'

The Duchess nodded.

'Been her own worst enemy,' she volunteered. 'Clever girl too. Mixed herself up with a most undesirable young man. One of that Chelsea crowd. Wrote plays or poems or something unhealthy. Nobody took 'em, of course. Then he stole somebody's jewels and got caught out. I forget what they gave him. Five years, I think. But you must remember? It was last winter.'

'Last winter I was in Egypt,' explained Mr Satterthwaite. 'I had 'flu very badly the end of January, and the doctors insisted on Egypt afterwards. I missed a lot.'

His voice rang with a note of real regret.

'That girl seems to me to be moping,' said the Duchess, raising her *lorgnette* once more. 'I can't allow that.'

On her way out, she stopped by Miss Carlton Smith's table and tapped the girl on the shoulder.

'Well, Naomi, you don't seem to remember me?'

Naomi rose rather unwillingly to her feet.

'Yes, I do, Duchess. I saw you come in. I thought it was quite likely you mightn't recognize me.'

She drawled the words lazily, with a complete indifference of manner.

'When you've finished your lunch, come and talk to me on the terrace,' ordered the Duchess.

'Very well.'

Naomi yawned.

'Shocking manners,' said the Duchess, to Mr Satterthwaite, as she resumed her progress. 'All the Carlton Smiths have.'

They had their coffee outside in the sunshine. They had been there about six minutes when Naomi Carlton Smith lounged out from the hotel and joined them. She let herself fall slackly on to a chair with her legs stretched out ungracefully in front of her.

An odd face, with its jutting chin and deep-set grey eyes. A clever, unhappy face—a face that only just missed being beautiful.

'Well, Naomi,' said the Duchess briskly. 'And what are you doing with yourself?'

'Oh, I dunno. Just marking time.'

'Been painting?'

'A bit.'

'Show me your things.'

Naomi grinned. She was not cowed by the autocrat. She was amused. She went into the hotel and came out again with a portfolio.

'You won't like 'em, Duchess,' she said warningly. 'Say what you like. You won't hurt my feelings.'

Mr Satterthwaite moved his chair a little nearer. He was interested. In another minute he was more interested still. The Duchess was frankly unsympathetic.

'I can't even see which way the things ought to be,' she complained. 'Good gracious, child, there was never a sky that colour—or a sea either.'

'That's the way I see 'em,' said Naomi placidly.

'Ugh!' said the Duchess, inspecting another. 'This gives me the creeps.'

'It's meant to,' said Naomi. 'You're paying me a compliment without knowing it.'

It was a queer vorticist study of prickly pear—just recognizable as such. Grey-green with splodges of violent colour where the fruit glittered like jewels. A swirling mass of evil, fleshy—festering. Mr Satterthwaite shuddered and turned his head aside.

He found Naomi looking at him and nodding her head in comprehension.

'I know,' she said. 'But it *is* beastly.'

The Duchess cleared her throat.

'It seems quite easy to be an artist nowadays,' she observed witheringly. 'There's no attempt to copy things. You just shovel on some paint—I don't know what with, not a brush, I'm sure—'

'Palette knife,' interposed Naomi, smiling broadly once more.

'A good deal at a time,' continued the Duchess. 'In lumps. And there you are! Everyone says: "How clever." Well, I've no patience with that sort of thing. Give me—'

'A nice picture of a dog or a horse, by Edwin Landseer.'

'And why not?' demanded the Duchess. 'What's wrong with Landseer?'

'Nothing,' said Naomi. 'He's all right. And you're all right. The tops of things are always nice and shiny and smooth. I respect you, Duchess, you've got force. You've met life fair and square and you've come out on top. But the people who are underneath see the under side of things. And that's interesting in a way.'

The Duchess stared at her.

'I haven't the faintest idea what you're talking about,' she declared.

Mr Satterthwaite was still examining the sketches. He realized, as the Duchess could not, the perfection of technique behind them. He was startled and delighted. He looked up at the girl.

'Will you sell me one of these, Miss Carlton Smith?' he asked.

'You can have any one you like for five guineas,' said the girl indifferently.

Mr Satterthwaite hesitated a minute or two and then he selected a study of prickly pear and aloe. In the foreground was a vivid blur of yellow mimosa, the scarlet of the aloe flower danced in and out of the picture, and inexorable, mathematically underlying the whole, was the oblong pattern of the prickly pear and the sword motif of the aloe.

He made a little bow to the girl.

'I am very happy to have secured this, and I think I have made a bargain. Some day, Miss Carlton Smith, I shall be able to sell this sketch at a very good profit—if I want to!'

The girl leant forward to see which one he had taken. He saw a new look come into her eyes. For the first time she was really aware of his existence, and there was respect in the quick glance she gave him.

'You have chosen the best,' she said. 'I—I am glad.'

'Well, I suppose you know what you're doing,' said the Duchess. 'And I daresay you're right. I've heard that you are quite a connoisseur. But you can't tell me that all this new stuff is art, because it isn't. Still, we needn't go into that. Now I'm only going to be here a few days and I want to see something of the island. You've got a car, I suppose, Naomi?'

The girl nodded.

'Excellent,' said the Duchess. 'We'll make a trip somewhere tomorrow.'

'It's only a two-seater.'

'Nonsense, there's a dickey, I suppose, that will do for Mr Satterthwaite?'

A shuddering sigh went through Mr Satterthwaite. He had observed the Corsican roads that morning. Naomi was regarding him thoughtfully.

'I'm afraid my car would be no good to you,' she said. 'It's a terribly battered old bus. I bought it second-hand for a mere song. It will just get me up the hills—with coaxing. But I can't take passengers. There's quite a good garage, though, in the town. You can hire a car there.'

'Hire a car?' said the Duchess, scandalized. 'What an idea. Who's that nice-looking man, rather yellow, who drove up in a four-seater just before lunch?'

'I expect you mean Mr Tomlinson. He's a retired Indian judge.'

'That accounts for the yellowness,' said the Duchess. 'I was afraid it might be jaundice. He seems quite a decent sort of man. I shall talk to him.'

That evening, on coming down to dinner, Mr Satterthwaite found the Duchess resplendent in black velvet and diamonds, talking earnestly to the owner of the four-seater car. She beckoned authoritatively.

'Come here, Mr Satterthwaite, Mr Tomlinson is telling me the most interesting things, and what do you think?—he is actually going to take us on an expedition tomorrow in his car.'

Mr Satterthwaite regarded her with admiration.

'We must go in to dinner,' said the Duchess. 'Do come and sit at our table, Mr Tomlinson, and then you can go on with what you were telling me.'

'Quite a decent sort of man,' the Duchess pronounced later.

'With quite a decent sort of car,' retorted Mr Satterthwaite.

'Naughty,' said the Duchess, and gave him a resounding blow on the knuckles with the dingy black fan she always carried. Mr Satterthwaite winced with pain.

'Naomi is coming too,' said the Duchess. 'In her car. That girl wants taking out of herself. She's very selfish. Not exactly self-centred, but totally indifferent to everyone and everything. Don't you agree?'

'I don't think that's possible,' said Mr Satterthwaite, slowly. 'I mean, everyone's interest must go *somewhere*. There are, of course, the people who revolve round themselves—but I agree with you, she's not one of that kind. She's totally uninterested in herself. And yet she's got a strong character—there must be *something*. I thought at first it was her art—but it isn't. I've never met anyone so detached from life. That's dangerous.'

'Dangerous? What do you mean?'

'Well, you see—it must mean an obsession of some kind, and obsessions are always dangerous.'

'Satterthwaite,' said the Duchess, 'don't be a fool. And listen to me. About tomorrow—'

Mr Satterthwaite listened. It was very much his role in life.

They started early the following morning, taking their lunch with them. Naomi, who had been six months in the island, was to be the pioneer. Mr Satterthwaite went over to her as she sat waiting to start.

'You are sure that—I can't come with you?' he said wistfully.

She shook her head.

'You'll be much more comfortable in the back of the

other car. Nicely padded seats and all that. This is a regular old rattle trap. You'd leap in the air going over the bumps.'

'And then, of course, the hills.'

Naomi laughed.

'Oh, I only said that to rescue you from the dickey. The Duchess could perfectly well afford to have hired a car. She's the meanest woman in England. All the same, the old thing is rather a sport, and I can't help liking her.'

'Then I could come with you after all?' said Mr Satterthwaite eagerly.

She looked at him curiously.

'Why are you so anxious to come with me?'

'Can you ask?' Mr Satterthwaite made his funny old-fashioned bow.

She smiled, but shook her head.

'That isn't the reason,' she said thoughtfully. 'It's odd . . . But you can't come with me—not today.'

'Another day, perhaps,' suggested Mr Satterthwaite politely.

'Oh, another day!' she laughed suddenly, a very queer laugh, Mr Satterthwaite thought. 'Another day! Well, we'll see.'

They started. They drove through the town, and then round the long curve of the bay, winding inland to cross a river and then back to the coast with its hundreds of little sandy coves. And then they began to climb. In and out, round nerve-shattering curves, upwards, ever upwards on the tortuous winding road. The blue bay was far below them, and on the other side of it Ajaccio sparkled in the sun, white, like a fairy city.

In and out, in and out, with a precipice first one side of them, then the other. Mr Satterthwaite felt slightly giddy, he also felt slightly sick. The road was not very wide. And still they climbed.

It was cold now. The wind came to them straight off the snow peaks. Mr Satterthwaite turned up his coat collar and buttoned it tightly under his chin.

It was very cold. Across the water, Ajaccio was still bathed in sunlight, but up here thick grey clouds came drifting across the face of the sun. Mr Satterthwaite ceased to admire the view. He yearned for a steam-heated hotel and a comfortable armchair.

Ahead of them Naomi's little two-seater drove steadily forward. Up, still up. They were on top of the world now. On either side of them were lower hills, hills sloping down to valleys. They looked straight across to the snow peaks. And the wind came tearing over them, sharp, like a knife. Suddenly Naomi's car stopped, and she looked back.

'We've arrived,' she said. 'At the World's End. And I don't think it's an awfully good day for it.'

They all got out. They had arrived in a tiny village, with half a dozen stone cottages. An imposing name was printed in letters a foot high.

'Coti Chiaveeri.'

Naomi shrugged her shoulders.

'That's its official name, but I prefer to call it the World's End.'

She walked on a few steps, and Mr Satterthwaite joined her. They were beyond the houses now. The road stopped. As Naomi had said, this was the end, the back of beyond, the beginning of nowhere. Behind them the white ribbon of the road, in front of them—nothing. Only far, far below, the sea . . .

Mr Satterthwaite drew a deep breath.

'It's an extraordinary place. One feels that anything might happen here, that one might meet—anyone—'

He stopped, for just in front of them a man was sitting on a boulder, his face turned to the sea. They had not seen him till this moment, and his appearance had the suddenness of a conjuring trick. He might have sprung from the surrounding landscape.

'I wonder—' began Mr Satterthwaite.

But at that minute the stranger turned, and Mr Satterthwaite saw his face.

'Why, Mr Quin! How extraordinary. Miss Carlton Smith, I want to introduce my friend Mr Quin to you. He's the most unusual fellow. You are, you know. You always turn up in the nick of time—'

He stopped, with the feeling that he had said something awkwardly significant, and yet for the life of him he could not think what it was.

Naomi had shaken hands with Mr Quin in her usual abrupt style.

'We're here for a picnic,' she said. 'And it seems to me we shall be pretty well frozen to the bone.'

Mr Satterthwaite shivered.

'Perhaps,' he said uncertainly, 'we shall find a sheltered spot?'

'Which this isn't,' agreed Naomi. 'Still, it's worth seeing, isn't it?'

'Yes, indeed.' Mr Satterthwaite turned to Mr Quin. 'Miss Carlton Smith calls this place the World's End. Rather a good name, eh?'

Mr Quin nodded his head slowly several times.

'Yes—a very suggestive name. I suppose one only comes once in one's life to a place like that—a place where one can't go on any longer.'

'What do you mean?' asked Naomi sharply.

He turned to her.

'Well, usually, there's a choice, isn't there? To the right or to the left. Forward or back. Here—there's the road behind you and in front of you—nothing.'

Naomi stared at him. Suddenly she shivered and began to retrace her steps towards the others. The two men fell in beside her. Mr Quin continued to talk, but his tone was now easily conversational.

'Is the small car yours, Miss Carlton Smith?'

'Yes.'

'You drive yourself? One needs, I think, a good deal of nerve to do that round here. The turns are rather appalling. A moment of inattention, a brake that failed to hold, and—over the edge—down—down—down. It would be—very easily done.'

They had now joined the others. Mr Satterthwaite introduced his friend. He felt a tug at his arm. It was Naomi. She drew him apart from the others.

'Who is he?' she demanded fiercely.

Mr Satterthwaite gazed at her in astonishment.

'Well, I hardly know. I mean, I have known him for some years now—we have run across each other from time to time, but in the sense of knowing actually—'

He stopped. These were futilities that he was uttering, and the girl by his side was not listening. She was standing with her head bent down, her hands clenched by her sides.

'He knows things,' she said. 'He knows things . . . How does he know?'

Mr Satterthwaite had no answer. He could only look at her dumbly, unable to comprehend the storm that shook her.

'I'm afraid,' she muttered.

'Afraid of Mr Quin?'

'I'm afraid of his eyes. He sees things . . .'

Something cold and wet fell on Mr Satterthwaite's cheek. He looked up.

'Why, it's snowing,' he exclaimed, in great surprise.

'A nice day to have chosen for a picnic,' said Naomi.

She had regained control of herself with an effort.

What was to be done? A babel of suggestions broke out. The snow came down thick and fast. Mr Quin made a suggestion and everyone welcomed it. There was a little stone Cassecroute at the end of the row of houses. There was a stampede towards it.

'You have your provisions,' said Mr Quin, 'and they will probably be able to make you some coffee.'

It was a tiny place, rather dark, for the one little window did little towards lighting it, but from one end came a grateful glow of warmth. An old Corsican woman was just throwing a handful of branches on the fire. It blazed up, and by its light the newcomers realized that others were before them.

Three people were sitting at the end of a bare wooden table. There was something unreal about the scene to Mr Satterthwaite's eye, there was something even more unreal about the people.

The woman who sat at the end of the table looked like a duchess—that is, she looked more like a popular conception of a duchess. She was the ideal stage *grande dame*. Her aristocratic head was held high, her exquisitely dressed hair was of a snowy white. She was dressed in grey—soft draperies that fell about her in artistic folds. One long white hand supported her chin, the other was holding a roll spread with *pâté de foie gras*. On her right was a man with a very white face, very black hair, and horn-rimmed spectacles. He was marvellously and beautifully dressed. At the moment his head was thrown back, and his left arm was thrown out as though he were about to declaim something.

On the left of the white-haired lady was a jolly-looking little man with a bald head. After the first glance, nobody looked at him.

There was just a moment of uncertainty, and then the Duchess (the authentic Duchess) took charge.

'Isn't this storm too dreadful?' she said pleasantly, coming forward, and smiling a purposeful and efficient smile that she had found very useful when serving on Welfare and other committees. 'I suppose you've been caught in it just like we have? But Corsica is a marvellous place. I only arrived this morning.'

The man with the black hair got up, and the Duchess with a gracious smile slipped into his seat.

The white-haired lady spoke.

'We have been here a week,' she said.

Mr Satterthwaite started. Could anyone who had once heard that voice ever forget it? It echoed round the stone room, charged with emotion—with exquisite melancholy. It seemed to him that she had said something wonderful, memorable, full of meaning. She had spoken from her heart.

He spoke in a hurried aside to Mr Tomlinson.

'The man in spectacles is Mr Vyse—the producer, you know.'

The retired Indian judge was looking at Mr Vyse with a good deal of dislike.

'What does he produce?' he asked. 'Children?'

'Oh, dear me, no,' said Mr Satterthwaite, shocked by the mere mention of anything so crude in connection with Mr Vyse. 'Plays.'

'I think,' said Naomi, 'I'll go out again. It's too hot in here.'

Her voice, strong and harsh, made Mr Satterthwaite jump. She made almost blindly, as it seemed, for the door, brushing Mr Tomlinson aside. But in the doorway itself she came face to face with Mr Quin, and he barred her way.

'Go back and sit down,' he said.

His voice was authoritative. To Mr Satterthwaite's surprise the girl hesitated a minute and then obeyed. She sat down at the foot of the table as far from the others as possible.

Mr Satterthwaite bustled forward and button-holed the producer.

'You may not remember me,' he began, 'my name is Satterthwaite.'

'Of course!' A long bony hand shot out and enveloped the other's in a painful grip. 'My dear man. Fancy meeting you here. You know Miss Nunn, of course?'

Mr Satterthwaite jumped. No wonder that voice had been familiar. Thousands, all over England, had thrilled to those wonderful emotion-laden tones. Rosina Nunn! England's greatest emotional actress. Mr Satterthwaite too had lain under her spell. No one like her for interpreting a part—for bringing out the finer shades of meaning. He had thought of her always as an intellectual actress, one who comprehended and got inside the soul of her part.

He might be excused for not recognizing her. Rosina Nunn was volatile in her tastes. For twenty-five years of her life she had been a blonde. After a tour in the States she had returned with the locks of the raven, and she had taken up tragedy in earnest. This 'French Marquise' effect was her latest whim.

'Oh, by the way, Mr Judd—Miss Nunn's husband,' said Vyse, carelessly introducing the man with the bald head.

Rosina Nunn had had several husbands, Mr Satterthwaite knew. Mr Judd was evidently the latest.

Mr Judd was busily unwrapping packages from a hamper at his side. He addressed his wife.

'Some more *pâté,* dearest? That last wasn't as thick as you like it.'

Rosina Nunn surrendered her roll to him, as she murmured simply:

'Henry thinks of the most enchanting meals. I always leave the commissariat to him.'

'Feed the brute,' said Mr Judd, and laughed. He patted his wife on the shoulder.

'Treats her just as though she were a dog,' murmured the melancholy voice of Mr Vyse in Mr Satterthwaite's ear. 'Cuts up her food for her. Odd creatures, women.'

Mr Satterthwaite and Mr Quin between them unpacked lunch. Hard-boiled eggs, cold ham and Gruyère cheese were distributed round the table. The

Duchess and Miss Nunn appeared to be deep in murmured confidences. Fragments came along in the actress's deep contralto.

'The bread must be lightly toasted, you understand? Then just a *very* thin layer of marmalade. Rolled up and put in the oven for one minute—not more. Simply delicious.'

'That woman lives for food,' murmured Mr Vyse. 'Simply lives for it. She can't think of anything else. I remember in *Riders to the Sea*—you know "and it's the fine quiet time I'll be having." I could *not* get the effect I wanted. At last I told her to think of peppermint creams— she's very fond of peppermint creams. I got the effect at once—a sort of far-away look that went to your very soul.'

Mr Satterthwaite was silent. He was remembering.

Mr Tomlinson opposite cleared his throat preparatory to entering into conversation.

'You produce plays, I hear, eh? I'm fond of a good play myself. *Jim the Penman,* now, that was a play.'

'My God,' said Mr Vyse, and shivered down all the long length of him.

'A tiny clove of garlic,' said Miss Nunn to the Duchess. 'You tell your cook. It's wonderful.'

She sighed happily and turned to her husband.

'Henry,' she said plaintively, 'I've never even *seen* the caviare.'

'You're as near as nothing to sitting on it,' returned Mr Judd cheerfully. 'You put it behind you on the chair.'

Rosina Nunn retrieved it hurriedly, and beamed round the table.

'Henry is too wonderful. I'm so terribly absent-minded. I never know where I've put anything.'

'Like the day you packed your pearls in your sponge bag,' said Henry jocosely. 'And then left it behind at the hotel. My word, I did a bit of wiring and phoning that day.'

'They were insured,' said Miss Nunn dreamily. 'Not like my opal.'

A spasm of exquisite heartrending grief flitted across her face.

Several times, when in the company of Mr Quin, Mr Satterthwaite had had the feeling of taking part in a play. The illusion was with him very strongly now. This was a dream. Everyone had his part. The words 'my opal' were his own cue. He leant forward.

'Your opal, Miss Nunn?'

'Have you got the butter, Henry? Thank you. Yes, my opal. It was stolen, you know. And I never got it back.'

'Do tell us,' said Mr Satterthwaite.

'Well—I was born in October—so it was lucky for me to wear opals, and because of that I wanted a real beauty. I waited a long time for it. They said it was one of the most perfect ones known. Not very large—about the size of a two-shilling piece—but oh! the colour and the fire.'

She sighed. Mr Satterthwaite observed that the Duchess was fidgeting and seemed uncomfortable, but nothing could stop Miss Nunn now. She went on, and the exquisite inflections of her voice made the story sound like some mournful saga of old.

'It was stolen by a young man called Alec Gerard. He wrote plays.'

'Very good plays,' put in Mr Vyse professionally. 'Why, I once kept one of his plays for six months.'

'Did you produce it?' asked Mr Tomlinson.

'Oh, *no*,' said Mr Vyse, shocked at the idea. 'But do you know, at one time I actually thought of doing so?'

'It had a wonderful part in it for me,' said Miss Nunn. *'Rachel's Children*, it was called—though there wasn't anyone called Rachel in the play. He came to talk to me about it—at the theatre. I liked him. He was a nice-looking—and very shy, poor boy. I remember'—a beautiful far-away look stole over her face—'he bought me some peppermint creams. The opal was lying on the dressing-table. He'd been out in Australia, and he knew something about opals. He took it over to the light to look at it. I suppose he must have slipped it into his pocket then. I missed it as soon as he'd gone. There *was* a to-do. You remember?'

She turned to Mr Vyse.

'Oh, I remember,' said Mr Vyse with a groan.

'They found the empty case in his rooms,' continued the actress. 'He'd been terribly hard up, but the very next day he was able to pay large sums into his bank. He pretended to account for it by saying that a friend of his had put some money on a horse for him, but he couldn't produce the friend. He said he must have put the case in his pocket by mistake. I think that was a terribly weak thing to say, don't you? He might have thought of something better than that . . . I had to go and give evidence. There were pictures of me in all the papers. My press agent said it was very good publicity—but I'd much rather have had my opal back.'

She shook her head sadly.

'Have some preserved pineapple?' said Mr Judd.

Miss Nunn brightened up.

'Where is it?'

'I gave it to you just now.'

Miss Nunn looked behind her and in front of her, eyed her grey silk pochette, and then slowly drew up a large purple silk bag that was reposing on the ground beside her. She began to turn the contents out slowly on the table, much to Mr Satterthwaite's interest.

There was a powder puff, a lip-stick, a small jewel case, a skein of wool, another powder puff, two handkerchiefs, a box of chocolate creams, an enamelled paper knife, a mirror, a little dark brown wooden box, five letters, a walnut, a small square of mauve crêpe de chine, a piece of ribbon and the end of a *croissant*. Last of all came the preserved pineapple.

'Eureka,' murmured Mr Satterthwaite softly.

'I beg your pardon?'

'Nothing,' said Mr Satterthwaite hastily. 'What a charming paper knife.'

'Yes, isn't it? Somebody gave it to me. I can't remember who.'

'That's an Indian box,' remarked Mr Tomlinson. 'Ingenious little things, aren't they?'

'Somebody gave me that too,' said Miss Nunn. 'I've had it a long time. It used always to stand on my dressing-table at the theatre. I don't think it's very pretty, though, do you?'

The box was of plain dark brown wood. It pushed open from the side. On the top of it were two plain flaps of wood that could be turned round and round.

'Not pretty, perhaps,' said Mr Tomlinson with a chuckle. 'But I'll bet you've never seen one like it.'

Mr Satterthwaite leaned forward. He had an excited feeling.

'Why did you say it was ingenious?' he demanded.

'Well, isn't it?'

The judge appealed to Miss Nunn. She looked at him blankly.

'I suppose I mustn't show them the trick of it—eh?'

Miss Nunn still looked blank.

'What trick?' asked Mr Judd.

'God bless my soul, don't you know?'

He looked round the inquiring faces.

'Fancy that now. May I take the box a minute? Thank you.'

He pushed it open.

'Now then, can anyone give me something to put in it—not too big. Here's a small piece of Gruyère cheese. That will do capitally. I place it inside, shut the box.'

He fumbled for a minute or two with his hands.

'Now see—'

He opened the box again. It was empty.

'Well, I never,' said Mr Judd. 'How do you do it?'

'It's quite simple. Turn the box upside down, and move the left hand flap half-way round, then shut the right hand flap. Now to bring our piece of cheese back again we must reverse that. The right hand flap half-way round, and the left one closed, still keeping the box upside down. And now—Hey Presto!'

The box slid open. A gasp went round the table. The cheese was there—but so was something else. A round thing that blinked forth every colour of the rainbow.

'*My opal!*'

It was a clarion note. Rosina Nunn stood upright, her hands clasped to her breast.

'My opal! How did it get there?'

Henry Judd cleared his throat.

'I—er—I rather think, Rosy, my girl, you must have put it there yourself.'

Someone got up from the table and blundered out into the air. It was Naomi Carlton Smith. Mr Quin followed her.

'But when? Do you mean—?'

Mr Satterthwaite watched her while the truth dawned on her. It took over two minutes before she got it.

'You mean last year—at the theatre.'

'You know,' said Henry apologetically. 'You *do* fiddle with things, Rosy. Look at you with the caviare today.'

Miss Nunn was painfully following out her mental processes.

'I just slipped it in without thinking, and then I suppose I turned the box about and did the thing by accident, but then—but then—' At last it came. 'But then Alec Gerard didn't steal it after all. Oh!'—a full-throated cry, poignant, moving—'How dreadful!'

'Well,' said Mr Vyse, 'that can be put right now.'

'Yes, but he's been in prison a year.' And then she startled them. She turned sharp on the Duchess. 'Who is that girl—that girl who has just gone out?'

'Miss Carlton Smith,' said the Duchess, 'was engaged to Mr Gerard. She—took the thing very hard.'

Mr Satterthwaite stole softly away. The snow had stopped. Naomi was sitting on the stone wall. She had a sketch book in her hand, some coloured crayons were scattered around. Mr Quin was standing beside her.

She held out the sketch book to Mr Satterthwaite. It was a very rough affair—but it had genius. A kaleidoscopic whirl of snowflakes with a figure in the centre.

'Very good,' said Mr Satterthwaite.

Mr Quin looked up at the sky.

'The storm is over,' he said. 'The roads will be slippery, but I do not think there will be any accident—now.'

'There will be no accident,' said Naomi. Her voice was charged with some meaning that Mr Satterthwaite did not understand. She turned and smiled at him—a sudden dazzling smile. 'Mr Satterthwaite can drive back with me if he likes.'

He knew then to what length desperation had driven her.

'Well,' said Mr Quin, 'I must bid you goodbye.'

He moved away.

'Where is he going?' said Mr Satterthwaite, staring after him.

'Back where he came from, I suppose,' said Naomi in an odd voice.

'But—but there isn't anything there,' said Mr Satterthwaite, for Mr Quin was making for that spot on the edge of the cliff where they had first seen him. 'You know you said yourself it was the World's End.'

He handed back the sketch book.

'It's very good,' he said. 'A very good likeness. But why—er—why did you put him in Fancy Dress?'

Her eyes met his for a brief second.

'I see him like that,' said Naomi Carlton Smith.

The Chocolate Box

It was a wild night. Outside, the wind howled malevolently, and the rain beat against the windows in great gusts.

Poirot and I sat facing the hearth, our legs stretched out to the cheerful blaze. Between us was a small table. On my side of it stood some carefully brewed hot toddy; on Poirot's was a cup of thick, rich chocolate which I would not have drunk for a hundred pounds! Poirot sipped the thick brown mess in the pink china cup, and sighed with contentment.

'*Quelle belle vie!*' he murmured.

'Yes, it's a good old world,' I agreed. 'Here am I with a job, and a good job too! And here are you, famous—'

'Oh, *mon ami!*' protested Poirot.

'But you are. And rightly so! When I think back on your long line of successes, I am positively amazed. I don't believe you know what failure is!'

'He would be a droll kind of original who could say that!'

'No, but seriously, *have* you ever failed?'

'Innumerable times, my friend. What would you? *La bonne chance*, it cannot always be on your side. I have been called in too late. Very often another, working towards the same goal, has arrived there first. Twice have I been stricken down with illness just as I was on the point of success. One must take the downs with the ups, my friend.'

'I didn't quite mean that,' I said. 'I meant, had you ever been completely down and out over a case through your own fault?'

'Ah, I comprehend! You ask if I have ever made the complete prize ass of myself, as you say over here? Once, my friend—' A slow, reflective smile hovered over his face. 'Yes, once I made a fool of myself.'

He sat up suddenly in his chair.

'See here, my friend, you have, I know, kept a record of my little successes. You shall add one more story to the collection, the story of a failure!'

He leaned forward and placed a log on the fire. Then, after carefully wiping his hands on a little duster that hung on a nail by the fireplace, he leaned back and commenced his story.

That of which I tell you (said M. Poirot) took place in Belgium many years ago. It was at the time of the terrible struggle in France between church and state. M. Paul Déroulard was a French deputy of note. It was an open secret that the portfolio of a Minister awaited him. He was among the bitterest of the anti-Catholic party, and it was certain that on his accession to power, he would have to face violent enmity. He was in many ways a peculiar man. Though he neither drank nor smoked, he was nevertheless not so scrupulous in other ways. You comprehend, Hastings, *c'était des femmes—toujours des femmes!*

He had married some years earlier a young lady from Brussels who had brought him a substantial dot. Undoubtedly the money was useful to him in his career, as his family was not rich, though on the other hand he was entitled to call himself M. le Baron if he chose. There were no children of the marriage, and his wife died after two years—the result of a fall downstairs. Among the property which she bequeathed to him was a house on the Avenue Louise in Brussels.

It was in this house that his sudden death took place, the event coinciding with the resignation of the Minister whose portfolio he was to inherit. All the papers printed long notices of his career. His death, which had taken place quite suddenly in the evening after dinner, was attributed to heart-failure.

At that time, *mon ami,* I was, as you know, a member of the Belgian detective force. The death of M. Paul Déroulard was not particularly interesting to me. I am, as you also know, *bon catholique,* and his demise seemed to me fortunate.

It was some three days afterwards, when my vacation had just begun, that I received a visitor at my own apartments—a lady, heavily veiled, but evidently quite young; and I perceived at once that she was a *jeune fille tout à fait comme il faut.*

'You are Monsieur Hercule Poirot?' she asked in a low sweet voice.

I bowed.

'Of the detective service?'

Again I bowed. 'Be seated, I pray of you, mademoiselle,' I said.

She accepted a chair and drew aside her veil. Her face

was charming, though marred with tears, and haunted as though with some poignant anxiety.

'Monsieur,' she said, 'I understand that you are now taking a vacation. Therefore you will be free to take up a private case. You understand that I do not wish to call in the police.'

I shook my head. 'I fear what you ask is impossible, mademoiselle. Even though on vacation, I am still of the police.'

She leaned forward. *'Ecoutez, monsieur.* All that I ask of you is to investigate. The result of your investigations you are at perfect liberty to report to the police. If what I believe to be true *is* true, we shall need all the machinery of the law.'

That placed a somewhat different complexion on the matter, and I placed myself at her service without more ado.

A slight colour rose in her cheeks. 'I thank you, monsieur. It is the death of M. Paul Déroulard that I ask you to investigate.'

'Comment?' I exclaimed, surprised.

'Monsieur, I have nothing to go upon—nothing but my woman's instinct, but I am convinced—*convinced,* I tell you—that M. Déroulard did not die a natural death!'

'But surely the doctors—'

'Doctors may be mistaken. He was so robust, so strong. Ah, Monsieur Poirot, I beseech of you to help me—'

The poor child was almost beside herself. She would have knelt to me. I soothed her as best I could.

'I will help you, mademoiselle. I feel almost sure that your fears are unfounded, but we will see. First, I will ask you to describe to me the inmates of the house.'

'There are the domestics, of course, Jeannette, Félice, and Denise the cook. She has been there many years; the others are simple country girls. Also there is François, but he too is an old servant. Then there is Monsieur Déroulard's mother who lived with him, and myself. My name is Virginie Mesnard. I am a poor cousin of the late Madame Déroulard, M. Paul's wife, and I have been a member of their ménage for over three years. I have now described to you the household. There were also two guests staying in the house.'

'And they were?'

'M. de Saint Alard, a neighbour of M. Déroulard's in France. Also an English friend, Mr John Wilson.'

'Are they still with you?'

'Mr Wilson, yes, but M. de Saint Alard departed yesterday.'

'And what is your plan, Mademoiselle Mesnard?'

'If you will present yourself at the house in half an hour's time, I will have arranged some story to account for your presence. I had better represent you to be connected with journalism in some way. I shall say you have come from Paris, and that you have brought a card of introduction from M. de Saint Alard. Madame Déroulard is very feeble in health, and will pay little attention to details.'

On mademoiselle's ingenious pretext I was admitted to the house, and after a brief interview with the dead deputy's mother, who was a wonderfully imposing and aristocratic figure though obviously in failing health, I was made free of the premises.

I wonder, my friend (continued Poirot), whether you can possibly figure to yourself the difficulties of my task?

Here was a man whose death had taken place three days previously. If there *had* been foul play, only one possibility was admittable—*poison!* And I had no chance of seeing the body, and there was no possibility of examining, or analysing, any medium in which the poison could have been administered. There were no clues, false or otherwise, to consider. Had the man been poisoned? Had he died a natural death? I, Hercule Poirot, with nothing to help me, had to decide.

First, I interviewed the domestics, and with their aid, I recapitulated the evening. I paid especial notice to the food at dinner, and the method of serving it. The soup had been served by M. Déroulard himself from a tureen. Next a dish of cutlets, then a chicken. Finally, a compote of fruits. And all placed on the table, and served by Monsieur himself. The coffee was brought in a big pot to the dinner-table. Nothing there, *mon ami*—impossible to poison one without poisoning all!

After dinner Madame Déroulard had retired to her own apartments and Mademoiselle Virginie had accompanied her. The three men had adjourned to M. Déroulard's study. Here they had chatted amicably for some time, when suddenly, without any warning, the deputy had fallen heavily to the ground. M. de Saint Alard had rushed out and told François to fetch the doctor immediately. He said it was without doubt an apoplexy, explained the man. But when the doctor arrived, the patient was past help.

Mr John Wilson, to whom I was presented by Mademoiselle Virginie, was what was known in those days as a regular John Bull Englishman, middle-aged and burly.

His account, delivered in very British French, was substantially the same.

'Déroulard went very red in the face, and down he fell.'

There was nothing further to be found out there. Next I went to the scene of the tragedy, the study, and was left alone there at my own request. So far there was nothing to support Mademoiselle Mesnard's theory. I could not but believe that it was a delusion on her part. Evidently she had entertained a romantic passion for the dead man which had not permitted her to take a normal view of the case. Nevertheless, I searched the study with meticulous care. It was just possible that a hypodermic needle might have been introduced into the dead man's chair in such a way as to allow of a fatal injection. The minute puncture it would cause was likely to remain unnoticed. But I could discover no sign to support that theory. I flung myself down in the chair with a gesture of despair.

'*Enfin,* I abandon it!' I said aloud. 'There is not a clue anywhere! Everything is perfectly normal.'

As I said the words, my eyes fell on a large box of chocolates standing on a table near by, and my heart gave a leap. It might not be a clue to M. Déroulard's death, but here at least was something that was *not* normal. I lifted the lid. The box was full, untouched; not a chocolate was missing—but that only made the peculiarity that had caught my eye more striking. For, see you, Hastings, while the box itself was pink, the lid was *blue.* Now, one often sees a blue ribbon on a pink box, and vice versa, but a box of one colour, and a lid of another—no, decidedly—*ça ne se voit jamais!*

I did not as yet see that this little incident was of any use to me, yet I determined to investigate it as being out of the ordinary. I rang the bell for François, and asked him if his late master had been fond of sweets. A faint melancholy smile came to his lips.

'Passionately fond of them, monsieur. He would always have a box of chocolates in the house. He did not drink wine of any kind, you see.'

'Yet this box has not been touched?' I lifted the lid to show him.

'Pardon, monsieur, but that was a new box purchased on the day of his death, the other being nearly finished.'

'Then the other box was finished on the day of his death,' I said slowly.

'Yes, monsieur, I found it empty in the morning and threw it away.'

'Did M. Déroulard eat sweets at all hours of the day?'

'Usually after dinner, monsieur.'

I began to see light.

'François,' I said, 'you can be discreet?'

'If there is need, monsieur.'

'*Bon!* Know, then, that I am of the police. Can you find me that other box?'

'Without doubt, monsieur. It will be in the dustbin.'

He departed, and returned in a few minutes with a dust-covered object. It was the duplicate of the box I held, save for the fact that this time the box was *blue* and the lid was *pink*. I thanked François, recommended him once more to be discreet, and left the house in the Avenue Louise without more ado.

Next I called upon the doctor who had attended M. Déroulard. With him I had a difficult task. He entrenched himself prettily behind a wall of learned phraseology, but I fancied that he was not quite as sure about the case as he would like to be.

'There have been many curious occurrences of the kind,' he observed, when I had managed to disarm him somewhat. 'A sudden fit of anger, a violent emotion—after a heavy dinner, *c'est entendu*—then, with an access of rage, the blood flies to the head, and pst!—there you are!'

'But M. Déroulard had had no violent emotion.'

'No? I made sure that he had been having a stormy altercation with M. de Saint Alard.'

'Why should he?'

'*C'est évident!*' The doctor shrugged his shoulders. 'Was not M. de Saint Alard a Catholic of the most fanatical? Their friendship was being ruined by this question of church and state. Not a day passed without discussions. To M. de Saint Alard, Déroulard appeared almost as Antichrist.'

This was unexpected, and gave me food for thought.

'One more question, Doctor: would it be possible to introduce a fatal dose of poison into a chocolate?'

'It would be possible, I suppose,' said the doctor slowly. 'Pure prussic acid would meet the case if there were no chance of evaporation, and a tiny globule of anything might be swallowed unnoticed—but it does not seem a very likely supposition. A chocolate full of morphine or strychnine—' He made a wry face. 'You comprehend, M. Poirot—one bite would be enough! The unwary one would not stand upon ceremony.'

'Thank you, M. le Docteur.'

I withdrew. Next I made inquiries of the chemists,

especially those in the neighbourhood of the Avenue Louise. It is good to be of the police. I got the information I wanted without any trouble. Only in one case could I hear of any poison having been supplied to the house in question. This was some eye drops of atropine sulphate for Madame Déroulard. Atropine is a potent poison, and for the moment I was elated, but the symptoms of atropine poisoning are closely allied to those of ptomaine, and bear no resemblance to those I was studying. Besides, the prescription was an old one. Madame Déroulard had suffered from cataracts in both eyes for many years.

I was turning away discouraged when the chemist's voice called me back.

'Un moment, M. Poirot. I remember, the girl who brought that prescription, she said something about having to go on to the *English* chemist. You might try there.'

I did. Once more enforcing my official status, I got the information I wanted. On the day before M. Déroulard's death they had made up a prescription for Mr John Wilson. Not that there was any making up about it. They were simply little tablets of trinitrine. I asked if I might see some. He showed me them, and my heart beat faster—for the tiny tablets were of *chocolate*.

'Is it a poison?' I asked.

'No, monsieur.'

'Can you describe to me its effect?'

'It lowers the blood-pressure. It is given for some forms of heart trouble—angina pectoris for instance. It relieves the arterial tension. In arteriosclerosis—'

I interrupted him. *'Ma foi!* This rigmarole says nothing to me. Does it cause the face to flush?'

'Certainly it does.'

'And supposing I ate ten—twenty of your little tablets, what then?'

'I should not advise you to attempt it,' he replied drily.

'And yet you say it is not poison?'

'There are many things not called poison which can kill a man,' he replied as before.

I left the shop elated. At last, things had begun to march!

I now knew that John Wilson had the means for the crime—but what about the motive? He had come to Belgium on business, and had asked M. Déroulard, whom he knew slightly, to put him up. There was apparently no way in which Déroulard's death could benefit him. Moreover, I discovered by inquiries in England that he had suffered for some years from that painful form of heart disease known as angina. Therefore he had a genuine right to have those tablets in his possession. Nevertheless, I was convinced that someone had gone to the chocolate box, opening the full one first by mistake, and had abstracted the contents of the last chocolate, cramming in instead as many little trinitrine tablets as it would hold. The chocolates were large ones. Between twenty or thirty tablets, I felt sure, could have been inserted. But who had done this?

There were two guests in the house. John Wilson had the means. Saint Alard had the motive. Remember, he was a fanatic, and there is no fanatic like a religious fanatic. Could he, by any means, have got hold of John Wilson's trinitrine?

Another little idea came to me. Ah, you smile at my little ideas! Why had Wilson run out of trinitrine? Surely he would bring an adequate supply from England. I called once more at the house in the Avenue Louise. Wilson was out, but I saw the girl who did his room, Félice. I demanded of her immediately whether it was not true that M. Wilson had lost a bottle from his washstand some little time ago. The girl responded eagerly. It was quite true. She, Félice, had been blamed for it. The English gentleman had evidently thought that she had broken it, and did not like to say so. Whereas she had never even touched it. Without doubt it was Jeannette—always nosing round where she had no business to be—

I calmed the flow of words, and took my leave. I knew now all that I wanted to know. It remained for me to prove my case. That, I felt, would not be easy. *I* might be sure that Saint Alard had removed the bottle of trinitrine from John Wilson's washstand, but to convince others, I would have to produce evidence. And I had none to produce!

Never mind. I *knew*—that was the great thing. You remember our difficulty in the Styles case, Hastings? There again, I *knew*—but it took me a long time to find the last link which made my chain of evidence against the murderer complete.

I asked for an interview with Mademoiselle Mesnard. She came at once. I demanded of her the address of M. de Saint Alard. A look of trouble came over her face.

'Why do you want it, monsieur?'

'Mademoiselle, it is necessary.'

She seemed doubtful—troubled.

'He can tell you nothing. He is a man whose thoughts are not in this world. He hardly notices what goes on around him.'

'Possibly, mademoiselle. Nevertheless, he was an old friend of M. Déroulard's. There may be things he can tell me—things of the past—old grudges—old love-affairs.'

The girl flushed and bit her lip. 'As you please—but—but I feel sure now that I have been mistaken. It was good of you to accede to my demand, but I was upset—almost distraught at the time. I see now that there is no mystery to solve. Leave it, I beg of you, monsieur.'

I eyed her closely.

'Mademoiselle,' I said, 'it is sometimes difficult for a dog to find a scent, but once he *has* found it, nothing on earth will make him leave it! That is if he is a good dog! And I, mademoiselle, I, Hercule Poirot, am a very good dog.'

Without a word she turned away. A few minutes later she returned with the address written on a sheet of paper. I left the house. François was waiting for me outside. He looked at me anxiously.

'There is no news, monsieur?'

'None as yet, my friend.'

'Ah! *Pauvre* Monsieur Déroulard!' he sighed. 'I too was of his way of thinking. I do not care for priests. Not that I would say so in the house. The women are all devout—a good thing perhaps. *Madame est très pieuse—et Mademoiselle Virginie aussi.*'

Mademoiselle Virginie? Was she *'très pieuse?'* Thinking of the tear-stained passionate face I had seen that first day, I wondered.

Having obtained the address of M. de Saint Alard, I wasted no time. I arrived in the neighbourhood of his château in the Ardennes but it was some days before I could find a pretext for gaining admission to the house. In the end I did—how do you think—as a plumber, *mon ami!* It was the affair of a moment to arrange a neat little gas leak in his bedroom. I departed for my tools, and took care to return with them at an hour when I knew I should have the field pretty well to myself. What I was searching for, I hardly knew. The one thing needful, I could not believe there was any chance of finding. He would never have run the risk of keeping it.

Still when I found the little cupboard above the washstand locked, I could not resist the temptation of seeing what was inside it. The lock was quite a simple one to pick. The door swung open. It was full of old bottles. I took them up one by one with a trembling hand. Suddenly, I uttered a cry. Figure to yourself, my friend, I held in my hand a little phial with an English chemist's label. On it were the words: *'Trinitrine Tablets. One to be taken when required. Mr John Wilson.'*

I controlled my emotion, closed the cupboard, slipped the bottle into my pocket, and continued to repair the gas leak! One must be methodical. Then I left the château, and took train for my own country as soon as possible. I arrived in Brussels late that night. I was writing out a report for the préfet in the morning, when a note was brought to me. It was from old Madame Déroulard, and it summoned me to the house in the Avenue Louise without delay.

François opened the door to me.

'Madame la Baronne is awaiting you.'

He conducted me to her apartments. She sat in state in a large armchair. There was no sign of Mademoiselle Virginie.

'M. Poirot,' said the old lady, 'I have just learned that you are not what you pretend to be. You are a police officer.'

'That is so, madame.'

'You came here to inquire into the circumstances of my son's death?'

Again I replied: 'That is so, madame.'

'I should be glad if you would tell me what progress you have made.'

I hesitated.

'First I would like to know how you have learned all this, madame.'

'From one who is no longer of this world.'

Her words, and the brooding way she uttered them, sent a chill to my heart. I was incapable of speech.

'Therefore, monsieur, I would beg of you most urgently to tell me exactly what progress you have made in your investigation.'

'Madame, my investigation is finished.'

'My son?'

'Was killed deliberately.'

'You know by whom?'

'Yes, madame.'

'Who, then?'

'M. de Saint Alard.'

The old lady shook her head.

'You are wrong. M. de Saint Alard is incapable of such a crime.'

'The proofs are in my hands.'

'I beg of you once more to tell me all.'

This time I obeyed, going over each step that had led me to the discovery of the truth. She listened attentively. At the end she nodded her head.

'Yes, yes, it is all as you say, all but one thing. It was not M. de Saint Alard who killed my son. It was I, his mother.'

I stared at her. She continued to nod her head gently.

'It is well that I sent for you. It is the providence of the good God that Virginie told me before she departed for the convent, what she had done. Listen, M. Poirot! My son was an evil man. He persecuted the church. He led a life of mortal sin. He dragged down other souls beside his own. But there was worse than that. As I came out of my room in this house one morning, I saw my daughter-in-law standing at the head of the stairs. She was reading a letter. I saw my son steal up behind her. One swift push, and she fell, striking her head on the marble steps. When they picked her up she was dead. My son was a murderer, and only I, his mother, knew it.'

She closed her eyes for a moment. 'You cannot conceive, monsieur, of my agony, my despair. What was I to do? Denounce him to the police? I could not bring myself to do it. It was my duty, but my flesh was weak. Besides, would they believe me? My eyesight had been failing for some time—they would say I was mistaken. I kept silence. But my conscience gave me no peace. By keeping silence I too was a murderer. My son inherited his wife's money. He flourished as the green bay tree. And now he was to have a Minister's portfolio. His persecution of the church would be redoubled. And there was Virginie. She, poor child, beautiful, naturally pious, was fascinated by him. He had a strange and terrible power over women. I saw it coming. I was powerless to prevent it. He had no intention of marrying her.

The time came when she was ready to yield everything to him.

'Then I saw my path clear. He was my son. I had given him life. I was responsible for him. He had killed one woman's body, now he would kill another's soul! I went to Mr Wilson's room, and took the bottle of tablets. He had once said laughingly that there were enough in it to kill a man! I went into the study and opened the big box of chocolates that always stood on the table. I opened a new box by mistake. The other was on the table also. There was just one chocolate left in it. That simplified things. No one ate chocolates except my son and Virginie. I would keep her with me that night. All went as I had planned—'

She paused, closing her eyes a minute then opened them again.

'M. Poirot, I am in your hands. They tell me I have not many days to live. I am willing to answer for my action before the good God. Must I answer for it on earth also?'

I hesitated. 'But the empty bottle, madame,' I said to gain time. 'How came that into M. de Saint Alard's possession?'

'When he came to say goodbye to me, monsieur, I slipped it into his pocket. I did not know how to get rid of it. I am so infirm that I cannot move about much without help, and finding it empty in my rooms might have caused suspicion. You understand, monsieur—' she drew herself up to her full height—'it was with no idea of casting suspicion on M. de Saint Alard! I never dreamed of such a thing. I thought his valet would find an empty bottle and throw it away without question.'

I bowed my head. 'I comprehend, madame,' I said.

'And your decision, monsieur?'

Her voice was firm and unfaltering, her head held as high as ever.

I rose to my feet.

'Madame,' I said, 'I have the honour to wish you good day. I have made my investigations—and failed! The matter is closed.'

He was silent for a moment, then said quietly: 'She died just a week later. Mademoiselle Virginie passed through her novitiate, and duly took the veil. That, my friend, is the story. I must admit that I do not make a fine figure in it.'

'But that was hardly a failure,' I expostulated. 'What else could you have thought under the circumstances?'

'*Ah, sacré, mon ami,*' cried Poirot, becoming suddenly animated. 'Is it that you do not see? But I was thirty-six times an idiot! My grey cells, they functioned not at all. The whole time I had the clue in my hands.'

'What clue?'

'*The chocolate box!* Do you not see? Would anyone in possession of their full eyesight make such a mistake? I knew Madame Déroulard had cataracts—the atropine drops told me that. There was only one person in the household whose eyesight was such that she could not see which lid to replace. It was the chocolate box that started me on the track, and yet up to the end I failed consistently to perceive its real significance!

'Also my psychology was at fault. Had M. de Saint Alard been the criminal, he would never have kept an incriminating bottle. Finding it was a proof of his innocence. I had learned already from Mademoiselle Virginie that he was absent-minded. Altogether it was a miserable affair that I have recounted to you there! Only to you have I told the story. You comprehend, I do not figure well in it! An old lady commits a crime in such a simple and clever fashion that I, Hercule Poirot, am completely deceived. *Sapristi!* It does not bear thinking of! Forget it. Or no—remember it, and if you think at any time that I am growing conceited—it is not likely, but it might arise.'

I concealed a smile.

'*Eh bien,* my friend, you shall say to me, "Chocolate box". Is it agreed?'

'It's a bargain!'

'After all,' said Poirot reflectively, 'it was an experience! I, who have undoubtedly the finest brain in Europe at present, can afford to be magnanimous!'

'Chocolate box,' I murmured gently.

'*Pardon, mon ami?*'

I looked at Poirot's innocent face, as he bent forward inquiringly, and my heart smote me. I had suffered often at his hands, but I, too, though not possessing the finest brain in Europe, could afford to be magnanimous!

'Nothing,' I lied, and lit another pipe, smiling to myself.

BIBLIOGRAPHY

Agatha Christie's short stories typically appeared first in magazines and then in her short story books, which tended to be different collections in the UK and the US. This list attempts to catalogue the first publication of each of the stories included in this collection, and gives alternative story titles when used.

Introduction

Excerpted from *An Autobiography* (1977) © 1975 Agatha Christie Limited.

The Arcadian Deer

© 1940 Agatha Christie Limited. First published in the *Strand Magazine*, January 1940, and then in the USA as 'Vanishing Lady' in *This Week*, 19 May 1940. It was reprinted in *The Labours of Hercules* (US and UK, 1946).

The Case of the City Clerk

© 1932 Agatha Christie Limited. First published in the USA as 'The Clerk Who Wanted Excitement' in *Cosmopolitan*,

August 1932, and then as 'The £10 Adventure' in *Strand Magazine*, November 1932. Reprinted in *Parker Pyne Investigates* (UK, 1934) and *Mr Parker Pyne, Detective* (US, 1946).

The Soul of the Croupier

© 1926 Agatha Christie Limited. First published in the US in *Flynn's Weekly* Vol. 19, No. 5, 13 November 1926, and in the UK as 'The Magic of Mr Quin No. 2: The Soul of the Croupier' in *The Story-Teller*, January 1927. Reprinted in *The Mysterious Mr Quin* (1930).

The Stymphalean Birds

© 1939 Agatha Christie Limited. First published in the USA as 'The Vulture Women' in *This Week*, 17 September 1939, then as 'Birds of Ill Omen' in *The Strand*, April 1940. It was reprinted in *The Labours of Hercules* (US and UK, 1946).

The Companion

© 1930 Agatha Christie Limited. First published as 'The Resurrection of Amy Durrant' in *The Story-Teller*, February 1930, and then in the USA as 'Companions' in *Pictorial Review*, March 1930. The story was reprinted in *The Thirteen Problems* (UK, 1932) and *The Tuesday Club Murders* (US, 1933).

Have You Got Everything You Want?

© 1933 Agatha Christie Limited. First published in the US in *Cosmopolitan*, April 1933, and in the UK as 'On the

Pyne Investigates (UK, 1934) and *Mr Parker Pyne, Detective* (US, 1934).

The World's End

© 1926 Agatha Christie Limited. First published in the UK as 'The World's End' in *The Story-Teller*, February 1927, and in the US in *Flynn's Weekly*, Vol. 19, No. 6, on 20 November 1926. Reprinted in *The Mysterious Mr Quin* (1930).

The Chocolate Box

© 1923 Agatha Christie Limited. First published in the UK as 'The Clue of the Chocolate Box' in *The Sketch*, Number 1582, on 23 May 1923, and in the US in *Blue Book Magazine*, Vol. 40, No. 4, in February 1925. Reprinted in *Poirot Investigates* (US edition, 1925) and *Poirot's Early Cases* (UK, 1974).

Orient Express' in *Nash's Pall Mall* Vol. 91, No. 481, June 1933. Reprinted in *Parker Pyne Investigates* (UK, 1934) and *Mr Parker Pyne, Detective* (US, 1946).

The Man from the Sea

© 1929 Agatha Christie Limited. First published in *Britannia & Eve*, October 1929. Reprinted in *The Mysterious Mr Quin* (1930).

The Girdle of Hyppolita

© 1939 Agatha Christie Limited. First published in the USA as 'The Disappearance of Winnie King' in *This Week*, 10 September 1939, then as 'The Girdle of Hippolyte' in *The Strand*, July 1940. It was reprinted in The Labours of Hercules (US and UK, 1946).

The Last Séance

© 1926 Agatha Christie Limited. First published in the US as 'The Woman Who Stole a Ghost' in the November 1926 issue of *Ghost Stories*, and in the UK as 'The Stolen Ghost' in issue 87 of *The Sovereign Magazine* in March 1927. Reprinted in *The Hound of Death and Other Stories* (UK, 1933) and *Double Sin and Other Stories* (US, 1961).

The Oracle at Delphi

© 1933 Agatha Christie Limited. First published in the UK in *Nash's Pall Mall* Vol. 91, No. 482, July 1933, and in the US in *Cosmopolitan*, April 1933. Reprinted in *Parker*